BLOW

a love story

TRACY EWENS

BLOW

a love story

Book design by Maureen Cutajar
www.gopublished.com

ISBN: (print) 978-1-7323216-3-2
ISBN: (e-book) 978-1-7323216-2-5

This one is yours, Katie McCoach.
For every gentle push, teaching me to trust myself,
and never letting me settle for half-assed.
Thank you.

Romance gets disparaged for the happy endings. But all genres have expectations and all genres require narrative resolution. It's disparaged because it's happy. And if it was important, it would be tragic. Which is bullshit! Look at *Much Ado About Nothing* – everybody is happy!

– NORA ROBERTS

Chapter One

Millie Hart had never seen so many rosy-cheeked men. Her key was under one of them and if she didn't find the little bastard before her phone battery died, she'd be spending the night in a neon-green rental car. The same rental car she'd torn apart moments earlier looking for the Post-it on which her assistant, Karen, wrote the "pertinent cottage access information."

Karen loved Post-its.

Millie did not because they disappeared like socks in a dryer. Not that she shared that or the fact it was no longer 1985 with Karen, but if she'd emailed or a texted even, Millie would have the information on her trusty—her phone battery dropped to 7 percent. In the middle of the night, in the middle of nowhere, her assistant managed a jab.

"Post-its still suck," she whispered as a chill tickled the edge of her sweatshirt and her Converse sank deeper into the soggy green front yard of a cottage to which she had no key.

Realizing thoughts alone didn't move her closer to a warm bed, Millie cataloged the things she knew. The key was under a gnome statue. The gnome held... flowers, maybe? She surveyed all the little men. There must have been close to fifty. Roughly a third were in some state of bloom, so Millie got to work.

Holding a flower and leaning on a rainbow? No *Feeding ducks among the flowers?* Damn.

After lifting every gnome with a flower or near a flower, her hands were dirty, the knees of her jeans were damp, and she still had no key. Not for the first time in her life, Millie felt ridiculous. How was she supposed to write a serious novel if she couldn't even get inside?

Sitting back on her heels, she was struck by the silence. The drive up from San Francisco had been surreal moonlight and curves of jagged coast, like a twisted path rescuing her from the noisy bustle. But now, practically on her hands and knees in some stranger's yard, the hush seemed intimate like she was trespassing. Save the gentle lapping of water somewhere and the tinging of what sounded like boat masts, it was pin-drop quiet.

A breeze strummed the wind chimes along the house awning. Millie sighed, crossed her arms for warmth, and faced the night sky. There were so many stars. Her logical mind knew it was the same sky over her apartment balcony back home, but it sure seemed like Bodega Bay received a bonus pack of constellations. Crisp and clear against the endless black, Millie lifted her hand but snapped it back down and stood.

It was late. She had no access to her rental, and there she was reaching for stars dangling millions of miles away.

"You *are* ridiculous, Mildred Hartfield," she whispered with her father's exacting tone.

A gnome holding flowers behind his back sat a few steps toward the gate. Millie tipped him over. Nothing. She even lifted the paint-chipped one who looked like he might have worn a flower wreath back in his prime.

Were there no female gnomes? Her phone battery dropped another percent.

She should have left the city earlier. The plan was to be on the road by three, which would have given her plenty of time to search for the key in daylight, maybe even stop for groceries instead of rutting around in the dark. But she'd lost track of time researching antique stamps and the best boots for shorter legs. A heated thread on Twitter she stayed out of—but still giggled at some comments—followed by a couple of emails, and before she knew it, she was in the rabbit hole of distractions. Millie had never mastered distraction.

"It's the internet's fault," she whispered, lifting another statue and cursed again when she found nothing but matted grass.

If she hoped to join the ranks of the literary elite, she needed to make and stick to a plan. Outlines, timelines, schedules, and keys. Millie wasn't a planner by nature, she was a show-up-and-see-what-happens kind of person.

Life was short, she knew firsthand, but her work kept those lines between her eyebrows at bay. To her father's eternal disappointment, Millie had "insisted on the sunny side of the street."

Another thing, she reminded herself, that would need to change. No more sun, and that started with her writing. None of the meet-cutes and sarcastic banter that had put her squarely on every best-seller list. No sun-soaked getaways and absolutely no winking.

For the next four months, if one of these stubborn gnomes coughed up the key, Millie would step to the overcast side and silence her romantic heart. It was time to delve into the mind of her alter ego and far more serious novelist, Mildred Hartfield. She was determined to become the queen of the metaphors, seriously messed-up character backstories, and lush descriptions. Truly, she would describe the hell out of everything for hundreds of pages if she could only find a key.

Why couldn't the Millers use a lock box like the rest of the world?

Hoisting the bag she'd left on the cobblestone path to her shoulder, Millie considered if it was possible to fall asleep in such a small rental car. Even if she turned over every little man, with or without flowers, her phone battery would die before she finished.

The front door of the cottage smirked at her from under a yellow awning. A mason jar light, barely doing its job, hung over a doorbell shaped like a rainbow fish. This place looked like it belonged on the board of a Candy Land game and wasn't even close to the "remote and moody retreat" Millie had asked Karen to find.

Candy Land.

She could still hear her mom's laughter. Reminding herself that she always felt more when she was tired, Millie swallowed the memories. In a last-ditch effort before folding herself back into a car for the night, she shined her light toward a gnome placed beneath the most elaborate birdbath she'd ever seen. No flowers, just a pick over his shoulder, but there were daisies on the birdbath, so she checked anyway. No key.

"Damn, damn, damn."

"It's the one by the door," a rough male voice called out from nowhere. "The one holding the beehive."

"The beehive. That's right." Her bag slipped off her shoulder and hung heavy at her elbow as she attempted to shine light in the direction of the voice. That was the exact moment her phone died, plunging her into darkness as the unmistakable slap of a screen door echoed through the distance.

"Thank you," she said, knowing no one was there. Hopefully she hadn't pissed off someone already, not that she'd be borrowing sugar or anything.

It was strange that in all her imaginings leading up to her self-imposed retreat, she'd never imagined people. She'd pictured her writing space, the foggy ambience, the quiet contemplation of her masterpiece, but not neighbors, which was silly. Bodega Bay surely existed on its own with or without her imaginings.

Back at the front door, she found an old chair beneath a matching daisy bird feeder. There were two pinwheels stuck in a pot of flowers and another gnome. The little beehive-holding bastard grinned up at her, some paint flaking from his cherub cheeks. Millie tipped back the statue and on a huge exhale found a silver ring with two keys. She could kiss the man behind the mystery voice, and although he probably looked a lot like the gnomes, she'd kiss him anyway.

Finally letting herself into the cottage, she set her bag down, flipped the switch on the wall, and was again reminded that Karen operated in a vacuum. There was nothing dark or brooding about this cottage. She'd nailed the quiet part, so that was something, but everywhere Millie looked was beach-vacation charming. Rich wood floors, tiny colored tiles in the kitchen, and a rowboat-shaped mug holder near a small sink. Painted-over cabinets with heavy glass inlays and brass fixtures. Even the doorknob still nestled in her hand was a comfortable welcome, as was the tattered rug along with a slipcovered couch and chair.

Everything seemed to have a place and was at least three decades old, but none of it was offensive. Charm, only charm. Even the creaks and groans of the floorboards as she looked around the corner and into the nautical-themed bedroom were friendly. Millie loved it, but love would not help Mildred Hartfield write a literary masterpiece complete with murder, mayhem, and well, lots of alliteration.

Finding a plug for her phone in the bedroom, she returned to the car for the rest of her bags, the litterbox, and Pop-Tart, who had no problem sleeping in a car. Pajamas on, Millie locked the door, careful to hang the keys on the hook at the entry.

"Glass half full," she mumbled, pulling back the covers and scooting Pop-Tart over. She could write a serious novel in a happy space. First thing in the morning, she'd pull the blinds and do what she'd mastered most of her adult life—she'd slip into another world.

At least it was quiet.

~

Well, shit.

Drake Branch was well on his way to becoming a chamomile tea believer. He'd had his doubts when his sister Jules suggested it, but after two mugs, he'd barely been able to count the bolts in the ceiling of his Airstream. He'd fallen off to blissful sleep around ten o'clock. No nightmares, no running to-do lists until the latest in a long line of Miller cottage renters slammed her car door a little after midnight. He'd rolled over hoping the chamomile would take him back under, but he needed to think about more insulation. And he'd forgotten about the gnomes.

Drake had a theory that the Millers hid the key among their army of gnomes as some kind of initiation. Something to get the renters up close and personal with the garden statuary because every single renter, since Bob and Beatrice Miller moved closer to their grandkids and rented out their house, arrived only to wander the yard in frustration. Drake's Airstream was ten stone steps from the Millers' gate. He'd settled there almost three years ago when he and his best friend since forever, Tyler, opened BP Glass Works.

In that time, there had been hundreds of renters, most of whom had the decency to show up before midnight. Drake would admit it was entertaining watching pastel-wearing interlopers hunt around the tiny yard. Hell, he and Tyler had been known to pop open a few beers after work and watch for well over thirty minutes before helping out. There was some animosity between locals and tourists in Bodega Bay. The typical love-hate relationship. Not exactly ill will, save a few who were "knob-noxious" as Bella, his niece, would say, but more a locals-first mantra.

This was their home, their town. The Bay was their collective history and the added stories of generations who'd grown up close. Drake hadn't always appreciated the town that raised him. Truth be told, there were a lot of things he screwed up in his quest to break free, but that was a long time ago.

The Millers' latest renter was no doubt here for a girls' weekend or maybe another bachelorette party. She would park in restricted areas, ask obvious questions like, "So, do you guys actually live here?" and when it got too cold or too rainy, she'd be on her way back to the big city or wherever she'd packed her bags excited for a "getaway."

While Drake knew full well that tourists lined up for his parents' crab cakes and kept his friends in business another year, they were still a pain in the ass. Especially ones who showed up in the middle of the night and scared off his chamomile.

But, by the time Drake finally gave up on the hope of sleep and ducked beneath the hot spray of the shower around five o'clock, all was forgiven and almost forgotten. Hopefully their latest gnome whisperer spent a ton of cash in town and was only around for a week at the most. Resting his hand on the shower wall, he willed away exhaustion and tried to recall his list for the day.

Drake rinsed his hair, turned off the water, and grabbed a towel to dry his face and most of his body. Grinning at the robe that hung unused on the back of his bathroom door, he tossed the towel on the rack and stepped into his sleeping area. His mom had bought him that robe years ago when she'd learned he could no longer wrap a towel around his waist.

"Robes are great," she'd said while his sisters held in their laughter and his dad made some reference to Hugh Hefner.

Despite their mocking, he'd tried it, but it proved more trouble than it was worth. He'd learned to dry what he could reach, and the air took care of the rest. Of all the things he missed most about having two hands, the simplicity of wrapping a towel around his waist continued to make the top ten.

After getting dressed and rubbing sanitizer onto his bicep, he pushed into his prosthesis and checked the time. Mondays and Wednesdays, he picked up Bella from his parents and walked her to school. His parents owned the Crab Shack and were usually up to their asses in work by sunrise. Bayside Elementary wasn't that far, and Jules usually had the boats from either a run or a fishing tour back by eight in time to make the walk herself. Bella started band this year, though, and needed to be at school by seven on Mondays and Wednesdays. So, Mondays and Wednesdays became Drake's favorite mornings.

Stepping into the dawn and enjoying the soft glow of the horizon, he glanced over at the Millers' cottage. All was quiet now. Rental car. He noticed the plate. Damn tourists.

Drake climbed into his truck and drove to his childhood home, tucked behind the Crab Shack on a few acres. They'd extended the restaurant patio recently and paved the parking lot. There were people lined up before they opened most days. He remembered being a kid and waking up late on Saturdays to the rumble of motorcycles and slamming doors as people gathered for his mom and dad's famous crab cakes and chowder.

Bella would have those memories now, he realized as she ran from her room, hands full and still blinking away sleep.

"Cinnamon rolls?" she asked, sitting at the base of the stairs to tie her shoes.

Drake gave a pained expression. "They only had bran muffins."

Her face fell.

"Of course, cinnamon rolls." He crouched down and tickled her. "Get your stuff, and don't forget your horn."

Still giggling and shaking her head at him, she grabbed her stuff and they gave out a round of kisses at the restaurant before heading off to school.

"How's the Iron Man arm?" Bella asked, chomping on her breakfast and holding up his hand. Drake flexed his bicep, firing off the fingers in the prosthesis. Bella smiled. "That's still so cool."

"Ya think?"

She nodded.

Bella was six back when she'd named him Iron Man and unknowingly lightened a very heavy load. Since then, Drake had always made sure to wear his prosthesis around her, and the rest of his family. It was part of the superhero mystique, he'd decided. They approached the front of the school and Drake handed over her trumpet.

"How's band going?"

She took the instrument and shook her head. "The French horns need to get it together or our recital will stink."

"Always the French horns, huh?" He shook his head too. "Did that kid who kept spitting on you cut it out, or do you need me to take care of him?"

She giggled. "Mr. Mandel talked to him." She glanced toward the entrance.

"Okay, well you're five minutes early." He kissed her forehead. "Have a great day, Beauty."

She scowled and whispered, "You can't call me that here."

"Why not? You're beautiful. They all know it."

"Fifth grade is rough. It's not like it was back when you and Mom were little. Before like electricity and stuff."

Drake tickled her. "Aren't you hysterical? Get in there, brat."

She leaned up on her toes and kissed his cheek. "Love you, Iron

Man," she whispered and ran off to join her bandmates who were gathering outside.

Drake's heart thumped true in his chest as he walked back and climbed into his truck. He knew his luck now. Grateful for his niece, his family, his friends. Grateful to be alive.

After swinging by Swept Away Books to help Auntie N with whatever chores she made up for him as an excuse to visit and gossip, Drake made it to his studio by nine. Everyone else had arrived, including the guys in the metal shop next door, so Drake cranked the music and got down to creating glass magic.

Chapter Two

Millie was either having another George Michael dream or someone was blaring Wham. Either way, George was pleading with her to wake him up before she went anywhere. Praying for the dream, she squeezed her eyes tight and tried to conjure a dream where hot-damn George was... brewing coffee for her before leaving to drop off their four adorable children at school. Four? Did she seriously want four children? No, something else. Maybe half-naked George Michael. It had been a while since she'd had a naughty dream.

Realizing she was plotting in her sleep and not dreaming at all, she cracked open one eye. It was morning, evidenced by the beam of sun spread across the ruffled bedspread and bathing one sprawled Pop-Tart in glorious warmth. Pop always found the sun too. Millie scratched her cat's favorite behind-the-ear spot before remembering she hadn't ordered sun. Weren't coastal towns supposed to be overcast and dreary? She lifted up to get a glimpse through the window, only to flop back down. Blue sky. She could have stayed in the city and at least had a gray-sky morning.

Jitterbug. Jitterbug.

"Oh, for crying out loud." She sat up, slapping the covers in a wasted dramatic gesture before pushing her mass of wayward curls out of her eyes.

This level of Wham was not fit for any time of the day let alone — Millie reached for her phone — nine o'clock in the morning. So, not only was she in a Candy Land cottage, but now some idiot devoid of empathy or sympathy, she always mixed those two up, was blaring Wham.

Her half-full glass from last night was dangerously close to empty. Millie rolled over, tangling herself further in the quilt she'd pulled up from the bottom of the bed at some point last night. She shoved her face deeper into the pillow. Rosewater. She sighed. Even the sheets were sweet.

She put another pillow over her head. She didn't want to wake up. Serious writers weren't morning people. That's why, despite her penchant for early to bed and early to rise, she'd stayed up until two and forgot to wash her face and floss her teeth. Running her tongue over her teeth, she dismissed the yuck. Hemingway didn't floss. No way. He drank and smoked. She'd never master either of those, but skipping the floss and sleeping in were two things she could easily put in her toolbox. Except... Wham.

How the hell long is this song anyway?

As if the heavens had heard her cry, the music stopped. Millie smiled and had barely closed her eyes when it started again. Same volume, this time Whitney Houston.

The Eighties, of course. Because if you're going to wake up a woman trying to escape into a world of death and despair, why not pick the era of fluff and neon?

By the time Whitney had bellowed that she wanted to dance with somebody, Millie had her hair contained with the elastic she'd left on the bedside table and had slipped her bare feet into the Converse she'd kicked off before falling asleep.

After stopping to notice again how lovely her little cottage was in the morning light, she remembered to focus. She would put these people in their place and return for coffee and her first few brilliant pages.

She swung open the front door, which was heavier than it had seemed the night before, and the music grew even louder. Great insulation for a tiny house, she thought. Weaving her way through the collection of gnomes whose smirks seemed less sinister in daylight, she followed the direction of the noise. Wet grass tickled her bare ankles before she found the pavers leading her toward a giant Airstream and some sort of metal-and-wood warehouse.

She glanced toward the bay when she reached the last paver. Gorgeous and calm blue hugged by overgrown green on either side, it reminded her of puzzle pieces nestled seamlessly together. Morning glinted off the surface of the water, and she wondered if it was cold. She'd never swum in the ocean before. Not that she was going to now, but there was no denying the gray outstretched dock was doing a great job inviting her in.

The music switched to some hair band she probably knew but couldn't place, snapping Millie back to what wasn't working.

Who the hell plays music so loud? Maybe there's a dance studio nearby .She probably looked crazy, eyes wild like she was searching for a leak or a lost pet. *Do people still dance to eighties music?* And if there was something fun like a dance studio near the quiet, remote place she'd specifically asked Karen for, Millie was going to shove a Post-it right up her—Millie slipped but managed to grab the side of the Airstream to stop from falling on her ass.

Karen Karma strikes again.

Straightening, she realized the dance party was coming from the warehouse behind the Airstream. She stepped cautiously toward the music.

"She's a lovely person, but I specifically asked for remote and quiet," Millie whined to herself.

Making her way through a small empty parking lot, she realized the music had stopped again. Standing in front of a corrugated metal-and-wood building that should not have been striking but was put together in a way that made people spend more money on whatever they were selling, Millie read the sign above the door—BP Glass Works. She was almost intrigued before Bon Jovi blared to life with "Shot through the heart!" She actually liked this song, but not today, and not at this insane volume.

Hand to her own frantic heart, she grabbed hold of the multicolored glass knob and slid open the door.

~

It was dark save a few blips of light streaming in from high windows. Millie blinked several times as her eyes acclimated and took in the massive open space. What appeared to be an inferno of fire barely tucked behind metal doors sat center space on the far wall. It reminded her of a cartoon character she couldn't place. Next to it was another smaller glow also encased in steel. There were benches and metal counters. Endless shelves and what seemed like giant rods sticking out of buckets like bouquets without the flowers. She had set her books in dozens of spaces. In fact, her first *New York Times* best seller centered around a motorcycle shop. She'd been to some cool places in her life and her mind, but she still had no point of reference for a space like this. It was cool and raging at the same time. Clearly purposeful and industrial-size intimidating, but also appealing in its function and surprisingly welcoming.

Peering around the front counter, she saw no one. When she turned around, she found the front wall covered in framed pictures, newspaper clippings, and splashes of color pinned to boards near the door. A small hallway off to the right led to darkness. A half-full coffee pot and an open box of doughnuts sat on a metal ledge near the door she'd walked through determined to give her obnoxious neighbors a piece of her mind. Now, despite the blare of eighties noise, she was turning in a circle, once again distracted and enraptured by the unexpected.

At the glorious pause between songs, someone laughed, and Millie spun around to find a man handing one of those metal rods to a young woman and taking one for himself. They were mid-conversation. Small miracle they could hear one another over the music. She was going to say something, announce her arrival, but Howard Jones or maybe it was Tears for Fears jumped through the overhead speakers this time and there was no point. They wouldn't hear her anyway.

She could have walked beyond the counter, but it seemed almost dangerous so early in the morning. They both appeared to be in long pants and long-sleeved T-shirts from what she could make out in the dim light. Feeling a bit less like a badass now, she stood watching them work and hoping someone would notice they were not alone before the music got any worse.

The woman's hair was long and dark, Millie noticed once they turned on an overhead light that illuminated the work area. Her hair was pulled back under a backward baseball cap. They both had on what resembled athletic sunglasses, but with clear lenses. The woman put her pipe into the largest fire and when she pulled it back out, there was a glowing amber blob on the end. She blew into a small tube at one end and began spinning the pipe about waist high. The man returned from the fire with the same glow. They both moved to the smaller fire. Barely noticing the music now, she was caught up in a silent film tableau, both people moving in an unfamiliar dance. Millie loved new things. There were so many questions swirling in her mind.

Are those pipes heavy? How do they keep the blob from falling off the end?

Somewhere, she knew she'd stomped over to put an end to the noise, but she couldn't fight the fascination.

The young woman laughed at something the man said as she lifted the tubing to her mouth again and noticed they had company. Before Millie had a chance to wave, the woman tapped the man and he glanced over, the metal pipe still twirling at his waist. The woman picked up a remote from the bench and the space fell into blissful silence, save what sounded like screeching metal from some place next door.

"Can I help you?" the man said as he walked with casual confidence through the patch of shadow separating their workspace from where Millie stood. The pipe was still turning, the glass at the end now larger than it had seemed before.

"I'm renting the house a little way over," Millie said louder than she intended before clearing her throat. "I can't hear myself think with the—" She was suddenly aware that she sounded bitchy, so she started again. "I'm sorry to disturb, but I was hoping—"

The man came into full view and Millie's previous outrage took a seat. He was older than she thought. Maybe her age or even thirty-fiveish. Cargo pants rumpled from either an already-productive morning or because they'd been pulled from a laundry basket. His arms, still turning were covered in a long-sleeved black T-shirt. Boots, probably steel-tipped. Her mind gathered every inch of him like a character sketch. The glasses were eye protection, she could see that now. His hair, unkempt and sticking out like feathers from beneath a bandanna that held it off his face, was dark. Not black, but deep brown.

He still hadn't said a word past his suspicious greeting, but neither had she, so her mind continued a few seconds more. Tall, built like an athlete, but rough like... something else. She was supposed to be angry, not working on a character nowhere near suited for her current work in progress. She was prepared to write him off as a standard good-looking, if not rumpled and unfriendly guy, and then her eyes found his left arm. The sleeve of his T-shirt was pulled to the elbow and the rest of his arm was black and silver, a bit like a sleek sports car. The pipe he was still turning was clamped onto the end of what she could now see was a prosthesis. Halting her curiosity, she met his eyes. They were brown, with little—*Stop it and say something!*

Millie cleared her throat. "I can see that you're working, but I can't hear or sleep or work. Your music is too loud so—"

He turned his back to her and stepped away to hand the pipe to the young woman.

Brushing his hands on his pants, he returned, threaded his eyewear through the neck of his T-shirt, and leaned back on the counter. In her initial awe, Millie hadn't noticed the green-blue glass bowl she now realized was sitting on the counter. Waiting for his response, her gaze took in the shelves climbing one side of the wall closer to where they were working. More glass in endless colors.

Still, without a word, his eyes seemingly amused, he folded his arms across his chest and propped the tip of one boot across the other. Was this some sort of small-town intimidation stance? She wanted to tell him she'd made a lot of money writing alphas. He could stand down.

The young woman stepped closer to most likely eavesdrop now that the music was gone and they could all hear.

Um, you're welcome, Millie wanted to say, but didn't. Instead she cleared her throat yet again, this time with her initial annoyance back in full force. "Look, I'm sorry to disturb, but I'm renting next door and while I realize it's nine o'clock—"

"Nine-thirty," he said, eyes flicking to the clock Millie knew was above the coffee pot.

"Right, whatever. The point is"—she shifted her weight—"the music is too loud. That's the easiest way to put it. Simple is always best," she said almost to herself before leveling a decent bit of her own intimidation. "Could you please turn it down?"

Still spinning the metal pipe, the young woman grinned, her arms flexing in a rhythm that must keep the glass moving or from falling off? She looked like she might say something but instead turned back toward the fire, both arms working like the axle of a car. Millie had done research on cars and car maintenance a few years ago when she wrote a hero who was a mechanic. She knew more about axles than she'd ever thought possible. People didn't realize the work that went into creating realistic dialogue or even convincing character movement. All of it had to be grounded in reality or readers would know. Not that her characters were real. She knew the difference between the men spun with her imagination and the one standing in front of her. Mostly.

Besides, that hero was also an ex-con and a spy and a way bigger badass than the guy currently giving her the silent once-over, but she kept that to herself too.

"That's the point," he finally said, squinting as he pushed off the counter and walked straight into the sunlight streaming from the windows above where she stood. Millie added lovely creases at the edges of his eyes and that his top lip had a heavy bow to her list of observations before she realized he wasn't going to say anything else.

"Sorry?" she asked, in response to his dramatic pause. Yeah, if she were writing this guy, he'd definitely have more dialogue.

"The music. It is loud inspiration. Our ambience so to speak."

"I see." Her eyes went wide at the idea of eighties music being anyone's ambience. "Well, I can appreciate being inspired, but I'm living next door and it's... not exactly inspiring me." Millie looked down and realized she was still in her pajamas. Paired with her Converse, it was not a look that demanded anyone to take her seriously.

She'd been so disoriented by the late arrival and George Michael that she'd skipped a few crucial morning tasks that were obvious under the scrupulous gaze of arrogant Thor or maybe Iron Man. Despite her original gusto, Millie now felt slightly foolish.

"Are those cats playing poker?" he asked.

Okay, a lot foolish.

Chapter Three

The Millers had rented their cottage to some colorful people over the years, most recently the old guy who dove naked into the bay every morning after yelling, "I'm coming for you, Mother Nature," at the top of his lungs. Lou had only stayed over a long weekend and turned out to be a cool guy despite sharing more of his ass than Drake cared to remember. But a woman barging into his studio in her pajamas was a new one even for the Millers. So were the most gorgeous eyes Drake had ever seen.

He tried not to stare. He was always prepared for another entitled tourist, but the hot mess currently demanding he lower their eighties playlist threw him for a second. It seemed like an unfair gift that her eyes were that big and that color. It was a blue that had to be seen and he'd never be able to describe it after she left, which he hoped was happening soon because they had seven orders to finish by the end of the day. Long list, he kept reminding himself amid the spark of interest. Ocean blue was too soft and steel blue wasn't nearly as interesting. Her eyes were beyond his vocabulary. Add to them her riotous red hair struggling to stay put and this woman was proving difficult to dismiss, tourist or not.

"Yes, they are cats." She looked down at herself. "Playing poker." She pushed away a mass of curls that had escaped and fallen into her face. "Mildred Hartfield," she said, extending her hand amid a glare of obvious annoyance.

Cute. No question, but he still had a list to get to.

"Drake." He shook her hand, not at all surprised by the strength despite her size. "Mildred Hartfield. Kind of an old lady name, isn't it?"

She rolled her shoulders back. Clearly defensive, and Drake found he was anticipating her next move.

"I've never thought of it that way, but I am named after my great-grandmother, so I suppose it is. Have you ever heard of people in glass houses, *Drake*? Not exactly a common name."

"Sir Francis Drake was a pirate. I'm good." He returned to his stance leaning on the counter. He was screwing with her because, well, it was tradition to screw with the tourists. And who was he, gorgeous eyes or not, to mess with tradition.

"Your mother named you after Sir Francis Drake? Are you British?"

"Nope."

"Interesting."

"Is it?"

She nodded. "I keep a pretty extensive list of names broken down by year and region. I don't have Drake. I'll be sure to add it," she said to herself but out loud.

He really needed to stop staring.

She has a list of names? What the hell, is she a spy?

Hazel had finished up the last of the highball glasses and was now at Drake's shoulder. No doubt she'd been listening the entire time waiting for her opportunity to join the conversation. Hazel was turning twenty next week. She'd been his apprentice for a year and a summer. The third daughter of Esteban, their master glassmaker, Hazel would be off to college in a few months if she ever finished her applications. The whole town had watched her and her sisters grow up. Drake would miss her almost as much as her own father, but he supposed everyone deserved a chance to run away from home.

"Well, Mildred, as I'm sure you saw from the sign outside, if you bothered to notice, this is a glass studio and the music is an important part of our, of my, process. So, maybe you could head into town during our work hours? They're posted right next to the door."

She didn't budge or respond, so Drake pushed a little more, confident she'd be storming back to her three- or four-day rental and cursing the locals in no time.

"I'm sure you are very excited to get started on your seaside getaway with your"—he paused for effect—"fiancé? Maybe a married guy you're dating? Don't worry, we locals are real discreet."

Mildred appeared downright stoic now, so Drake called in reinforcements.

"Not an affair. Okay. Hazel, what other types of renters have the Millers blessed us with?"

"Other than Lou?"

He nodded, holding back a smirk.

"How about the guy who painted all the naked women right out there on the patio in frickin' daylight like it was totally normal."

Hazel had set the glasses in the cooler, and Drake decided he'd stay an hour later to make up the time they were spending messing around.

"That was an interesting weekend," he said, attention back on Mildred.

"Oh, and the wine ladies." Hazel washed her hands and returned to his side.

"At least three bottles a day," he said.

Mildred's eyes widened as she looked between them.

"Wasn't there something about her fiancé not showing up for the wedding and the girls wanting a—?"

"Wild and crazy weekend," Hazel confirmed in her best drunk-tourist voice.

Their latest victim, who was supposed to be intimidated and mocked by this point, leaned against the wall, arms crossed, her gaze fixed on him. After a minute, Drake realized she was mimicking him and unfolded his arms.

"Are we done playing torture the tourist?" she asked. "By the way, those are all great stories and Hazel, your name is gorgeous." She extended her hand.

"Thank you." Hazel flushed before shaking her hand and whispering, "She's nice," when she returned to his side.

Drake's brow furrowed. "Are you adding her name to your list too?"

"It's already on my list." Mildred smiled, and cute gave way to stunning. The new renter was attractive and a surprisingly formidable opponent, but game time was over.

As he moved toward the door to reinforce the locals-first policy and send her on her way, Tyler slid the door open and stopped short.

"Oh, sorry. I didn't know you had company," he said.

"What?" Drake looked at Mildred and back to Tyler.

Hazel laughed and went back to work. Just as well. She was zero help.

"This is not... she's not company."

"Sure looks like company." Tyler noticed the pajamas.

"Yeah, well looks can be deceiving."

Mildred tightened her arms across her chest at either being reminded that she was wearing her PJs in public, or because she was ready to stage a sit-in. Drake sure as hell hoped it was the PJs.

Tyler, always the gentleman, extended his hand, and she stepped forward. "I'm Millie, actually Mildred, I'm Mildred."

Tyler nodded. "Good to meet you, Mildred. Family name?"

"I'm renting the cottage right over—Yes, it is a family name. Why do you ask?"

Drake raised a brow and wondered if his friend would have better luck outwitting their new neighbor.

"No reason. It's a classic." He grinned. Again, no help.

"Charmer." Drake put his hand on Tyler's shoulder. "Mildred, or maybe now it's Millie, is renting the Millers' place." He tightened his grip and waited for Tyler to pick up the screw-with-the-tourist baton.

"Great," he said, shrugging off Drake's grip, setting his stuff down on the counter, and pouring some coffee. "Welcome. Hope we're not making too much noise."

Hello? Am I the only one who still knows how to play this game?

Seemingly reminded why she'd stormed over in the first place, Mildred straightened in her poker-cat pajamas, poised to reregister her complaint. "Well, that's the thing. The noise, the music is—"

"Loud." Tyler stirred in some sugar. "I know, it's been that way ever since Drake let Chase move—"

"We play the music loud because... we like it loud. Period." Drake stepped between the two of them.

"What are you doing?" he growled softly at Tyler, who seemed confused like they always shared their life and hang-ups with complete strangers. Drake glared until Tyler finally came to his senses and stepped back.

"Right. We do like loud music." Tyler laughed. "How long are you here for, Mildred?"

She turned from looking around the studio again. It was like she couldn't control her curiosity. Perfect, an outspoken and nosy neighbor. When was she leaving? Three days? A week tops?

"I'm here for four months and nine days," she said.

"Wow." Tyler looked at Drake, who couldn't hide his surprise. "That's a long time."

Drake nodded and knew he was staring again. Blue-green maybe? *Son of a bitch. Focus, man. Four months. Did you hear that?*

"It is a long time," Mildred said. "So, about the music." She crossed her arms.

Drake raised a brow.

She shook her head like that might magically get rid of him and his eighties playlist too. "Look, I don't want to take up any more of your time, but I'm trying—I'm serious about the music. I'm renting the cottage so I can work on a project. A serious project."

"Sounds serious." Drake couldn't resist.

Tyler laughed again. "I like this one." He picked up his stuff. "Mildred, I'm glad you'll be sticking around. Don't mind him. He's screwing with you. It's what we do." He balanced his coffee cup and a doughnut on a stack of folders and started toward the back.

"But the music has to stay." He looked at Drake and back at Mildred. "Sorry," he added, wincing a little. "But he needs it." Tyler nodded acknowledgment that was all he would say and made to leave.

"I like your bag," Mildred said as randomly as the rest of her appearance so far.

Tyler turned. "Right? Etsy. Portland Leather."

"Lovely. It looks handmade." She stepped toward him and smoothed her hand over the leather.

For someone with such a serious complaint and a serious project, Mildred Hartfield was crazy observant and seemingly unable to control her bursts of friendliness.

Drake cleared his throat. They both looked at him and resumed talking. He was suddenly like a kid whose mom ran into someone she knew at the grocery store. With a shrug, he poured himself another cup of coffee and waited.

"Thank you," Mildred said as Tyler walked away.

Christ, how could her name be Mildred? That brought images of old ladies with their stockings rolled down to their ankles. The thought made him smile.

"Your work is lovely," she said, touching the edge of a large bowl they kept on the front counter.

"Thank you."

Holding her gaze for what felt longer than necessary, Drake wondered if this was some sort of trick. If, like a siren, Mildred complimented and stared at men until she got her way because despite his very real need for loud music, he was tempted to say he'd keep it down.

"I'm sorry." She broke eye contact and took her hand from the bowl. "I understand creative space and I'm only renting, so I'll figure something out." She moved toward the door.

"Okay." Well, shit, that was a one-eighty and now he felt bad. Sliding the door open, he tried to focus on his small victory and not that Mildred smelled like candy as she passed through to the door. *Who the hell smelled like candy, especially in the morning?*

"So, these are your hours," she said on a sigh as he walked out. "Great. Any idea if this person likes loud parties at night?" She pointed to his Airstream. "Because that might run me out of town. Not that you and your friends in there would be all that disappointed."

"I don't party. Not anymore, so you should be good."

"Wait." She tapped the side of his home on wheels, which should have pissed him off but didn't. "You... live here?"

"I do."

"Huh. So, you helped me with the gnomes."

"I did."

"Thank you." She touched his left forearm and while Drake's instinct was to compensate for his hardware around people he didn't know, it was like it didn't even register with her. He knew she'd noticed his prosthesis, the woman appeared to notice everything, but hadn't changed the way she dealt with him. Her touch was a genuine extension of gratitude and not in that fake I-have-friends-with-missing-parts way. Drake was surprised again.

"I would have been out there forever." She glanced back toward the cottage.

Somehow, what had ruined a perfectly good night's sleep wasn't such a big deal anymore. There she went again being friendly.

"You would have figured it out. Eventually."

"Well, it was nice meet—" She caught herself midsentence. Probably remembering she was about to begin a four-month dance party. "*Interesting*. It was interesting meeting you."

Yeah, the frustration was back.

"Likewise." *What in the hell?* He'd never said likewise in his entire life. "I'll let you get back to that serious work."

She nodded. "And I'll let you get back to disturbing the peace."

"Aw, and here I thought we had a truce."

Seemingly tired of their game or put out that she lost, Mildred walked away.

"You could try headphones," he called out. His sisters were right: sometimes he was a real ass.

"I don't like having things in my ears."

"Weird. Me neither."

She spun at the gate to the Millers' cottage like she was ready to get back in the ring but must have changed her mind. She nodded and went inside.

Drake walked back toward his studio and realized he was smiling. He had to give it to the Millers, they kept things interesting.

Chapter Four

Millie woke early the next morning with renewed purpose. She'd pieced her first novel together by sending emails to herself from her crappy insurance adjuster job. Her second book, the one that finally got her an agent, was written entirely after nine at night because she lived below a family of four who all played piano in an apartment with the thinnest walls ever made. And even now that she'd reached a certain comfort level in her writing career, she barely eked out the first draft of her latest release in the relentless throes of the flu from hell.

Writers made magic, and sometimes in the most difficult of situations, so Millie knew about being resourceful. The great Nora Roberts wrote it best in her book *Vision in White*—"Some things in life are out of your control. You can make it a party or a tragedy."

Millie preferred parties. So, she was awake, showered, and ready to work by six o'clock. She'd meant what she said about hating headphones. She never could stand having things in her ears and only broke out the over-the-ear headphones for long-distance flights. She loved music, but not when she was writing. It was too many words when she was trying to find her own. But, if her neighbor wanted to play music that could be heard in Seattle, so be it. She'd work around him.

Sir Francis Drake and his taste in playlists were "of no consequence," as her father was fond of saying. Ooh, she was already sounding like a literary snob.

After feeding Pop-Tart, she stood in the kitchen grinding coffee. She would need an entire pot because the plan was to put her butt in the chair until the outline she'd started weeks ago finally made sense. Millie didn't normally outline, but nothing about this new project was normal. She'd read some outlining books, even watched a webinar on plotting, and now it was time to put what she'd learned to work. Structure and steps were exactly what she needed to ensure she didn't get lost in her complicated plot line.

It wasn't complicated yet, but it would be. She had a lot of ideas that needed to find their way to paper. Today. Millie parted the blinds of the kitchen window as the coffee pot gurgled that life-affirming aroma around the cottage. Not a cloud in the early morning water-colored sky. Craning her neck for a glimpse of the sun as it rose up around the weathered wood of the docks, she decided she'd be fine in Bodega Bay. More than fine. She closed her eyes as the sun crept near the edges of her window. There were worse things than loud neighbors, and she was crazy fortunate to have four months of solitude to work on her new manuscript. There, glass half full, she thought. After another deep breath, she opened her eyes

She was centered and even appreciating the sun. Ready to enjoy her coffee and knock out the best outline ever. And then her eyes found Drake in a single handstand at the end of the middle dock. In shorts and a form-fitting T-shirt, he looked like a whole lot of beautiful yoga-bending consequence.

Millie managed to pour a cup of coffee, knowing somewhere in the temporary lust-fog of her mind that she was gawking, but she couldn't look away. The man was defying gravity. The sunlight loved him, wrapped around the angles of his body like some preplanned special effect. From bunched shoulders to long legs, Drake was practically floating on one wrist.

Her goal of being productive still above a whisper, Millie sipped her coffee and managed to pop bread into the toaster before returning to the window. He was still upside down.

"How in the hell?" she said, grabbing the butter from the fridge as Pop-Tart wove through her legs. She tugged at the small kitchen window and opened it a few inches. No music. No noise at all. He was out there all alone with nothing but the silent dawn. How did a person even practice something like that? Maybe he started with a coach or ropes? Something. A guy didn't simply head out to a dock and prop himself up on one arm.

Silencing her questions, she allowed herself total appreciation for the smug man she'd wanted to smack less than twenty-four hours ago. The entire weight of his quite lovely body, since she was admitting things, resting on nothing more than one arm while his sports car arm lay flat along his other side like a weapon at rest.

"Sweet Jesus." Millie set her cup down on the counter like she might applaud.

A moment later he tilted out of the handstand and landed firmly on the dock. She moved back from the window.

Was it possible to sense strange women leering from cottage windows?

She was such an only child sometimes. The guy clearly had a morning yoga practice.

"He couldn't care less about us, right Pop?" she said, scooping up her favorite ball of fur and closing the window. "We have things to do today. We do not have time for hot guys doing the impossible. Do we?" She nuzzled Pop's silver and white face.

"All right, time to get to work." Millie set Pop-Tart down and opened her laptop.

Returning to the kitchen for her coffee and toast, she parted the blinds one more time, telling herself she was checking on him to gauge how much quiet time she had left. She'd always been excellent at telling herself stories.

Drake had pulled on a sweatshirt and now stood looking out over the water. He seemed utterly comfortable with himself despite what many would consider a disadvantage. Millie tried to stop her mind from writing his story, but he was so writable it was annoying.

After a quick glance at Pop, who was now sprawled out over her laptop resigned that nothing was getting done for a least the span of a quick nap, Millie grabbed her toast and returned to her spying spot. She couldn't take her eyes off him as he walked down the dock toward his studio, smooth as the water on the early windless bay. Millie was suddenly aware of her own breath and the sun again now having fully arrived to start the day.

Her lips curved into a lazy smile that came from somewhere deep and private in her chest. Drake may be her loud and unwelcoming neighbor, but he was something else altogether when no one was watching. Releasing the blinds for what she promised herself and her untouched outline would be the last time, she crunched into a piece of toast. She sat at her makeshift desk and ran her fingers along the trackpad. Her screen came to life as Pop yawned, his one little eye sewn closed in a perpetual wink, looking super cute at the moment.

Millie was a writer. There was no need to box that in to any particular genre. She had a masters in creative writing. Granted, she'd gone to Berkeley because her father had gone there and she'd pursued a graduate degree because he only had his bachelors, but none of that mattered now.

Jade was right, her daddy issues had brought her to this cottage, maybe cornered her into this specific project, but she was here now. A thirty-three-year-old accomplished writer with over a dozen novels under her belt. She knew how to write a good story. And she had the "teeth" as so many literary journals put it, for great writing. So, there was no reason to doubt that her next novel wouldn't be a smashing success. That her as-yet-unwritten masterpiece would sit high on the prestigious shelves of even her father's bookstore.

Psyched and ready to go, Millie managed four words before her phone vibrated.

"Abandoned agent, how can I help you," Jade said before Millie got out a greeting.

"You called me."

"Did I?"

"Jade."

"Oh, fine. I just miss you."

"It's been three days."

"I know, but you're not only my client, you're my best friend and I feel so lost navigating The Tinder without you. Swipe left, swipe right. It's too much. I need you to come home."

Millie laughed. "It's Tinder, The Tinder sounds like something medieval."

Jade snorted.

"I thought you were starting with Bumble so you could make the choices."

"I am. Well, I'm not making any choices because they're all creepy as hell. Have these guys ever heard of a decent headshot? Here's a tip, gentlemen: women are not inclined to swipe anything when you're posing with some other woman in a bikini. Oh, sorry. Hold."

Her agent and best friend's muffled voice mixed with someone else as Millie put her phone on speaker and set it on the table. When Jade said, "Hold," it could be as simple as answering a question or as complicated as a temperamental author on another line. Millie usually gave her five minutes and then hung up. Jade called back when she was free. She was a senior agent for Pickman-Brown and usually crazy busy. Now that she was two years on the other side of a nasty divorce, she'd decided to start dating. She announced this the same night Millie mentioned her new project. They often went through things on the same schedule, which made for an interesting friendship. In fact, they'd both announced their "big news" at their standing weeknight dinner. Millie couldn't cook and Jade still couldn't stand cooking for one, so they ate out most nights.

"Sorry." Jade came back on the line. "Where were we?"

"You were telling me about Tinder, which I hope you mean Bumble. We read that Bumble was better for newbies, remember?"

"I do, and it is. I meant Bumble. Not that it matters because I have no idea what I'm doing and I know you're going through a professional renaissance, but I am shelving my stupid dating idea until you get back."

"You're shelving it for four months?"

"Why not? I've gone this long without a date and even longer without sex. What's a few more months? Oops... What is it, Celia?" Jade said, interrupted again. "No, no. Right, and please, close my door."

"Sorry again. You know the new reality star who is all over the tabloids right now? I will not name names because these walls have ears, but we talked about this right before you left."

Millie tried to connect back to their real world of gossip. "The wannabe singer or the guy right out of rehab?"

"Singer. Yeah, she just wrote a book."

"Really? About what?"

"No idea, but she is now prestigious Pickman-Brown's newest client."

"That is news. I'm sure she'll bring in a bundle. Is she your client?"

"Mils, the woman flashed her tit on *Sesame Street*. I don't care if she's written *War and Peace*, I will quit my job first."

Millie laughed again. That was twice in twenty minutes. She missed Jade too.

"So, do you see what I'm dealing with here?"

"I do. And I will be back in the city for dinner in a couple of weeks. You and your crazy life will be fine until then."

Jade sighed. "I know. I'm being a crap friend. Ignore me. How's the cottage?"

"It's... adorable."

"Well, you're adorable, so that's a good fit. Not exactly what you were looking for, I take it?"

"No."

"But you're not calling Karen because you're afraid of her?"

"I'm sure she did her best and maybe this was the only one available for such a long rental."

"Yeah, you're afraid of your own assistant."

"Afraid is a strong word. I will admit to being slightly intimidated."

Jade groaned. "Okay, so you're in an adorable cottage. How's the outline coming?"

"I'm still getting settled."

"Ooh, any good restaurants or local bars? I'm feeling a meet-cute in the wind. Out-of-town author casually bumps into burly fishing man with an enormous—"

"Okay. Can we be done now? Because I'm trying to focus on this book. No meet-cute. No first kiss. No HEA."

"Jesus, can't we at least have an HEA?" she pleaded amid the familiar sound of unwrapping candy. Jade kept a jar on her desk.

"Not this time. I want to leave readers thinking, remember? Dark and twisty. Maybe a surprise. Lots of themes and imagery. A real book that utilizes my skills, my education."

Jade sucked on her candy.

"We've been over this. Please wish me well and don't give me a hard time."

"Are you sure all of this can't be resolved with a quick pop into a therapist's office? I can loan you mine because this is daddy issues, hon, clear as day."

Millie made ready to argue, but Jade continued. "Shall we go over the numbers again, because numbers don't lie. Or I can simply remind you how fricking successful you are and how much you love your job. I have back-to-back meetings starting five minutes ago, but I'll sit right here and tell you. I love you that much."

Millie explained that she did not need the numbers. After a few more laughs and a suggestion that "inspiration is all around," Jade kiss-kissed and ran off to her meetings. Still chuckling, Millie replaced her now-cold coffee and was once again grateful for her double-threat friend. Not only was she a relentless champion as Millie's agent, but she was the most take-me-as-I-am person. Millie didn't have many friends — more specifically, she had one true friend. She was so lucky to have found Jade. They were both lucky, she supposed.

An hour later, Millie still had an unfinished outline, but she had a new Pinterest board. A little annoyed with herself for procrastinating and, of course, looking for more procrastination to ease her disappointment, she peeked through the blinds at the sound of fishing boats arriving. Drake was back on the dock and walking toward a very tall woman, who hopped off one of the boats like she did it every day. Even from a distance, Millie could see Drake's huge smile. Millie nodded. She seemed his type. Long legs, athletic, and gorgeous.

Yeah, Millie would have written his love that way too.

Chapter Five

*D*rake tried not to feel responsible for the circles under his sister's eyes as she jumped onto the dock, but she needed a break. He knew firsthand what it took to run Branch Fishing. He'd reluctantly done it for a while. Nowhere near as well as Jules, who outshined him by a mile all while raising an incredible human being, but he knew the job. Drake was the big brother by birth, but Jules taught him every day about getting up and getting on with it.

Catching the bow line, she noticed him standing on the dock and smiled. He held up her breakfast and a thermos of coffee, rewarded when her toothy grin chased some of the fatigue from her eyes.

"You are my favorite brother," she said as he walked toward her down the dock.

"Only brother." Drake stood back as the rest of her crew finished tying off the boats.

Lips curving like she had the most exciting secret, she lifted her sunglasses to her head and brushed the shoulder of his T-shirt. "Doesn't matter. You'd still be my favorite even if I had ten brothers."

"Ten, huh?"

She nodded. "How are you today?"

"I'm good—"

"Great even," she finished his response in her standard gruff man impression. Jules worked exclusively with gruff men, so she had the voice down.

Drake laughed.

"Your canned answers are always so insightful. I'll be more specific. How's your arm since last month's adjustment? Has the weird rubbing spot healed?"

"Holy shit. Go interrogate your crew or say goodbye to your passengers." Drake gestured with the doughnut bag, almost cracking up as her nose followed the smell. "Go. They need you."

Jules shook hands and expressed appreciation to the six men she'd taken out that morning for whale watching. From the looks of things, they'd had a good morning. She gestured to her guys to finish up as she grabbed her backpack and headed back up the dock. Taking the thermos of coffee Drake handed her, she closed her eyes and mouthed a "Thank you, God," before taking a sip.

"Where were we?" She shifted her backpack and swatted Drake's hand away when he tried to take it from her. "Oh, when does the gallery open?"

"Not for a while. Tyler is working on the plans."

"And the music?" Clad head to toe in gear he used to wear himself, she surveyed him.

"It's handled."

"How? I heard the new renter is complaining."

Drake shook his head. "How do you know these things?"

She smiled and waited for his answer.

"She's the one renting. The music stays. That's how." Drake tried to keep it simple. He'd grown up with two sisters. He should have known better.

"Wow, look at you, all badass man of the town. Did you explain that—"

"Did I explain that I whimper like a girl at the—"

"Hey."

"Sorry. Whimper like a boy. Did I explain the details of my life to a total stranger?"

"Yeah." Jules grabbed the bag, pulled out a doughnut, and took a bite.

Drake shook his head. "You drive me nuts."

"I'm sure, but I'll bet if you'd explained that instead of wagging your balls, she would understand."

"She's accepted the music. She hasn't been back. I won. Now, can we please talk about something else?"

"Maybe you should go see that doctor," she said as they continued walking. "You know, the one who helped you with the nightmares."

"I don't have nightmares anymore."

"So, it could still be related. They can give you tools." They stopped at the benches before the end of the dock. "I read this article on PTSD. Maybe your accident caused—"

"Jules." He snatched the paper bag back from her. "These are the new doughnuts from The Roastery. I stood in line for them this morning."

She licked her fingers. "They're delicious," she mumbled through the last bite and focused on the second one still in the bag.

"I will give this back to you if you promise never to mention my accident and PTSD in the same sentence ever again."

She seemed ready to argue, but he held the bag closer.

"I'm fixed. The music works. Let's not elevate my stupidity to something more heroic, deal?"

"The music is a Band-Aid, not a fix." Jules snatched the bag. "You can't avoid things. Believe me, I know."

He went to grab the bag back but was too late. She munched into the second doughnut like a woman who needed a break from being a single mom with a dickhead ex and two fishing boats to manage. He had no idea where she found the energy to give him a hard time too.

"What does that mean? I'm having one issue."

"Bella said you told her she was beautiful and offered to beat up anyone who wasn't nice to her," she said with a full mouth as they stood in the parking lot.

"Don't do that. Don't change the subject. Are you saying I have more than one issue?"

"You avoid… a few things. Totally normal."

Neither one of them said a word as Jules took another bite. Drake could have pushed, gotten his sister to spill, but he suddenly changed his mind. There was no way he was still— there couldn't be that many things he was avoiding, could there?

"Let's talk about Bella." Jules took another gulp of coffee.

Birds from the same nest, Drake thought for a beat before gladly changing direction. "She is beautiful. And I said I would 'take care of' anyone who was giving her a hard time. Are kids messing with her?"

"No." Jules washed down the last bit of doughnut. "Well, not anymore. There's this kid who keeps pulling her braids and saying, 'Bella Smella.'" She rolled her eyes. "Not incredibly original, but I'm pissed that when I spoke to Mrs. Flake, she said she thought Kyle—"

"Stanton?"

She nodded and tossed her backpack into the truck. "She thinks Kyle 'has a little crush' on Bella, and that's why he teases her."

"And embarrasses her?"

Jules pulled her suspenders down and sipped her coffee. "Yeah. Like pulling her hair and being mean is some kind of twisted fifth-grade courting."

Drake shook his head and took the empty paper bag from her. "That's—"

"Fucked up." Jules swallowed. "That's what it is. And we wonder why girls grow up with issues. I thought about telling Bella to kick him in the balls, and then she could bat her eyes in the office and say she was just loving on him."

"You seem ball-obsessed." Drake smiled. "Like more than usual."

"I know. I'm surrounded by balls." Jules twisted the thermos closed.

"Did you talk to Mrs. Flake?" he asked, imagining his sister up in Betsy Flake's face.

"I did. Well, I left out the profanity and the ball-kick idea so I wouldn't get a lecture from Mom, but I told her if that little twiglet touches my daughter again, I'll meet with the principal next."

"Twiglet?"

"Yeah, us moms need to be creative without our big girl words."

Drake nodded. "Very resourceful. You could always talk to his parents. You went to prom with his dad."

"Ugh, that's a hard pass." She shook her head. "I can't stand them."

"Don't hold back, Jules."

Her face twisted some more as she handed him the empty thermos. "They're so... matching pajamas, ya know?"

"I did not know their pajamas matched, and I'm not sure I want to know how you got that information."

She swatted him. "Mom and Dad get their Christmas card every year." She pulled on a sweatshirt from her truck. "Christ, I need to move out of our parents' house."

"You could live with me."

"In the trailer?"

"It's an Airstream."

"It's a shiny trailer. A shiny trailer with one bed."

He laughed. "Probably not the best plan."

"Yeah, we'd kill each other. Or you and Bella would gang up on me."

"That's exactly what would happen."

"I'll figure something out."

Drake held the door for her even though she rolled her eyes, and she kissed him on the cheek before climbing into her truck.

"Thank you," she said. "You know you don't have to keep meeting me. I mean, I love you and you're the only man I want to start my mornings with, but if you're doing this because—"

Drake closed the truck door. "Because I love you and you're such a joy to be around." He patted the metal. "Now, get out of here and go take a shower." He sniffed her. "You smell like fish." He turned and switched his mind back to his list for the day.

"Seriously? I wonder why?" she called after him.

Drake pulled his keys from his pocket.

"I love you, Iron Man."

He pumped his left arm in the air as the engine of his sister's truck roared to life.

~

Entering the studio, Drake first noticed the music was turned down. For the first time since Chase moved in next door, Drake wondered if his music bothered anyone else. If Jules was right and it was a Band-Aid.

Drake knew Esteban wore earplugs sometimes, but did the need for noise make everyone miserable? The thought hit him center chest and he was suddenly questioning if the people in his life were still making accommodations for him. Years after his family and Tyler had turned their lives upside down, Drake was confident he'd made amends. But, was it possible he was still screwed up?

You blast music at a million decibels because you can't tolerate the sound of grinding metal. Yeah, that's still screwed up.

Flipping the page in his tattered notebook, he struggled to get Jules out of his head and focus on his list for the day. Things were relatively quiet at Chase's place. Drake had no idea how long the peace would last, but he was not touching the volume unless he needed to.

Glancing up, he noticed Tyler, who gestured that he was on the phone. Where did Tyler make calls when they were working, when the music was full volume?

Holy crap. One complaint from the nosy renter and he was in full reevaluate mode. He grabbed both buckets, thankful for his routine, when Esteban and Hazel arrived.

"Mija, it sounds good to me. Maybe ask Mama to help when we get home." Esteban stopped his daughter by tugging on her backpack. "I'm sure they're going to love you," he said, kissing Hazel on the forehead.

She rolled her eyes. "Pop, you think everyone is going to love me."

"No. We *know* everyone is going to love you." Drake set the buckets aside. He was still eleven minutes ahead of schedule. "What's the problem?"

"Berkeley is the problem." She pulled her backpack off with that barely adult huff Drake still remembered so well.

"Three essays. We have to write on three of the seven prompts. I have all the test scores. I'm second in my class, and"—she slapped both hands on the work counter—"I have a 4.2 in all my community college classes. I work a full-time job. Why does it matter what I feel I'm bringing to their school or why I'm passionate about anything?"

"Wow." Drake looked at Esteban, who sighed with the resolve of a man who'd listened to his daughter all the way into work and probably every day since she'd downloaded her application. "Well, you're passionate about not writing essays." He laughed. Hazel did not and Esteban shook his head with a slight grin.

Scrambling for an answer, Drake did what he'd done since the accident had knocked some sense into him: he surveyed all available resources. "Tyler," he said as random as his thoughts.

"Yeah?" He looked up from his desk and quickly pulled his reading glasses off, as if hiding them meant he didn't need them.

"You're smart," Drake said.

"Aww." He batted his eyes.

"I'm serious. Hazel needs help with her essays."

"I don't need help," she said. "I need them to go away."

"College entrance essays?" Tyler cringed. "I barely survived mine. They're the worst." He put his glasses back on and returned to his reports. "Maybe ask the renter. She's a writer," he said.

"She is?" They all replied in concert.

"Yeah. I Googled her. She writes romance. Am I the only one who pays attention around here?"

"She writes romance?" Hazel asked.

Tyler nodded, still into his reports.

"You Googled her?" Drake set the buckets down again. Two minutes until he was truly behind schedule.

"Yes." He looked up. "Stranger comes to town, needs quiet, working on a serious project. That screams Google. Her writer name is Millie Hart. She's a big deal."

"Define big?" Drake asked.

Tyler took off the glasses again. "Pretty big. *New York Times* best seller. She's on a bunch of must-read lists. Profiles in major newspapers. Big."

Drake crossed his arms like that was enough to disguise his interest.

Hazel was eyes into her phone. "Wow. Big is right. She's got a book coming out in a couple months. Fancy website, book tour. I wonder if Nikki knows her?"

"If it's romance, Nikki knows her." Drake grabbed the buckets. Time was up. He had a schedule to keep.

"Maybe she's hiding and doesn't want anyone to know she's here. I'll bet she's famous." Hazel kept scanning her phone.

Esteban, who'd lost interest at the mention of Tyler's Google search, finished placing equipment at their benches.

"Or she has weird rituals," Tyler said. "Writers are reclusive, you know?"

Drake stopped just shy of the door and turned. "How the hell would I know? Do we know any writers?"

"We do now." Tyler grinned. "In fact, we've seen one in her pajamas." He waggled his brows and dropped his reading glasses back on.

Drake shook his head before pushing his back into the door and welcoming the fresh air. This day needed to settle down because so far it had been nuts.

On some universal cue, Chase's shop fired up their equipment and began tearing through sheet metal or steel. It didn't matter. It all brought the same clench to Drake's chest. As he'd closed his eyes to focus on breathing, the music from inside the studio went full blast. The eighties. Good choice. Drake opened his eyes. Yeah, he was still totally screwed up and apparently, he was the only one still unaware.

Chapter Six

*A*listair Holt was on his second cigarette. The sky was—Millie's hands hovered over her keyboard—*the sky was blue.*

She closed her eyes as the Go-Go's, whose harmonizing permeated every inch of her tiny space even with the windows and blinds shut tight, wailed about their vacation. She was sure the sky over the bay was blue, and now she knew it was clear skies in Go-Go land too. They wouldn't shut up about it.

Taking a deep breath and trying to focus on the sweet purr of Pop-Tart in her lap, Millie realized she was going to have to compromise with this guy. She'd been in Bodega Bay one week, survived five playlists, and accomplished next to nothing. Shutting things out had not proved as easy as she'd thought. Something had to change. She'd spent a lot of money on a four-month rental and needed this to work.

Yesterday's playlist was techno, which on the outset was more tolerable, but by the end of the day, the thumping had given her a headache. The day before was mostly Queen. She loved Queen, but not when she was trying to remember the sequence of an autopsy. She'd never written anything close to an autopsy, so it was already a struggle. It proved near impossible while humming along to "Another One Bites the Dust."

Today he was back to the eighties, and she would challenge any writer regardless of genre or education to find inspiration in the Go-Go's. Pulling on her sweatpants and a bra this time, Millie set out again across the path to BP Glass Works.

He would probably make her out to be some weirdo who didn't like music. She loved music. She had playlists for all her books. She didn't listen to them while she wrote, but she understood musical inspiration. Readers followed her playlists on social media, but this book was different. It required more from her, so much more that she'd packed up and moved away from her life for peace and quiet.

Four measly months. That was all she needed to work, seriously work, and this one man was going to be her undoing. This had to be a test, or maybe it was a struggle she needed to endure and produce her best story. Ugh, she'd always hated that kind of suffer-for-your-art drivel, but Sir Francis Drake was pushing all her limits.

Wrapped in thought, Millie slipped on the grass again but recovered like a pro this time as she came around the corner and almost ran straight into the music man himself.

"Morning," he said right outside the front door and surveying her in that way that had Millie smoothing her hands down her oversized sweater and sweatpants.

"I realized I was not all that forthcoming when I first got here." She stepped closer as he set two buckets up on a bench. "I thought I'd clarify my situation."

His brow furrowed. "Okay."

"I'm a writer. I write... things." Millie blinked rapidly, like her mind was a bug-infested windshield that would work as soon as she cleared it. There wasn't enough blinking to help her, so she stopped and tried again. "I'm renting the cottage because I have four short months to get my next—"

"Thing?"

"Yes. My next thing started. I know you need the music for your creative space and I completely respect that—"

He was about to say something, but she held up her hand. She wanted to get this all out before his next retort. "And, I know that

I'm from out of town, which I'm sure is annoying. But." She went up on her toes to achieve as close to eye level as possible. He smiled, a little, and she took that as a good sign. "Now that you know I am not sleeping with a married man, nor am I some vacuous debutante on a bender, can we please strike a deal so we can both create?"

"What's your book about?"

Worst question in the world, Millie thought but fumbled through an answer anyway. "My protagonist... a professor named Alistair, dies in the first chapter. Then the story flashes forward and he's not dead. Well, he's alive. So, it's sorting out how he came back or if he's still dead or if he was ever killed." So many bugs. The eternal optimist, she blinked again.

"You kill your main guy at the beginning of the book?"

Millie nodded and felt the drop. God, she hated the drop. She'd had it for as long as she could remember. That sense at her center that she was making a mistake, not brave enough to be a true creative. She could blame her father for this professional insecurity, but that seemed too easy. She was a grown woman. At some point, she needed to own her life. Maybe that's what this book was—a professional stare down. She'd ultimately need to embrace the drop, but not today. She must have waited too long to answer, or she was blinking again because the guy looked almost remorseful.

"I didn't mean to critique." He crouched and unraveled a hose.

"It's okay. I'm used to it. Comes with the job." She rolled her shoulders back, faking it until, well, as long as it took. "Yes, I kill off Alistair in the first chapter."

"Cool. Not all that romantic, but way to be different."

"It's not supposed to be romantic. Why would it be—"

"Tyler Googled you."

Millie tried to play it off like she didn't care. Like she wasn't hoping she'd left her profile and book reviews back in the city with her giant and sorely-missed television.

Drake shrugged. "Small-town people are nosy." He turned on the hose.

"Right."

There went her privacy along with any hope of peace and quiet. Temporarily defeated, she turned to regroup.

"My aunt, well she's not actually my aunt but we call her Auntie N." He moved the hose to the empty bucket. "Irrelevant. Anyway, her name is Nikki and she owns Swept Away Books in town."

"There's a bookstore in Bodega Bay too?"

The universe was clearly trying to tell her something.

"Get a grip," she muttered.

"Sorry?"

She shook her head. "Nothing, not you. You were saying?"

"Yeah, she owns a bookstore and I'm sure she'd love to meet you."

Millie hadn't realized she was shaking her head. He thought she was crazy, no doubt. There was that sympathy look again.

"You know, everyone thinks running away to a small town is the answer and it—"

"I'm not running away."

"No? Well, everyone but you then thinks it's the answer, and it never works out. People have a better shot disappearing in a big city."

"Great. I live in the city, so you're saying I should have just stayed home?" Millie turned the hose off and coiled it on the stand. She needed something to do. Something that had an answer, because at the moment it looked like all her latest decisions had been the wrong ones.

"Thank you," Drake said, seemingly thrown by her pitching in. It was only a hose.

She wanted to exclaim that she was super nice. That if he would just lower his music, she would leave him and his nosy small town alone forever. They'd barely know she was holed up along their precious bay.

"Wait. Why would your aunt want to meet me? I thought you were all allergic to tourists."

"Swept Away is a specialty bookstore. My aunt only carries certain kinds of books."

"Okay."

He lifted one bucket and waited.

46

"You're kidding."

"She's famous or notorious, depending on who you talk to, for her love of romance."

"I don't even... What are the chances? Only romance?"

Drake nodded, sliding the door open and setting the bucket just inside before returning for the second. "She's committed."

"Why are you filling buckets of water?" She was again grasping for a topic change. It didn't matter that there was a romance bookstore in town. Un-freaking-believable, but not the prevailing problem. She needed quiet. Quiet was the goal.

"We use wooden blocks to shape the glass. They have to soak in water to stay cool. I fill them every morning at this time."

"The same time every morning?"

"I like a schedule."

"Interesting," she said, soothed by someone else's details. "Isn't it Auntie Em? Wizard of Oz, right?"

"Yea, but she's Nikki. It's a—"

"Play on words. Got it. So, back to my—"

He set the second bucket inside the door and returned. It felt a bit like she wasn't invited back into his studio, but that was ridiculous. Wasn't it?

"Okay, well maybe if you take a break, you can stop by and see Nikki. I'm sure she knows your work." He smiled like he was dodging the Girl Scout cookie table outside a coffee shop. "Speaking of work, I need to get back in there."

"So, that's a no on the creative compromise?"

Drake turned. "Any thoughts on why you chose Bodega Bay in April? Does your book take place here?"

She shook her head. "London. Well, and Vienna."

He snorted. "Yeah, that figures."

"What's that supposed to mean?" Millie made to follow him into the studio, but he stopped short and she nearly ran into the back of him.

Herbal and ocean. How does a man smell like ocean?

She stepped back as a screech of metal cut through the lull of silence in the playlist.

"Yikes. That's almost as bad as your music. Who knew small towns were so freaking loud?"

Drake closed his eyes and took a deep breath.

Good God, was it so hard to turn down the music? Clearly his other neighbors didn't care, but Millie was baffled that she'd wasted more than a courtesy visit, one neighbor to another, on this topic.

He opened his eyes as the next song started. "Here's the thing." Drake slid the door closed, which didn't diminish the music, so she wasn't sure why he bothered.

"I have no idea how much rent you laid out to the Millers for four months, but maybe you should cut your losses and go to London. Our busy season is only a few weeks away, so it's only going to get worse for you."

She couldn't imagine that was possible. What, did they march a band up the beach during high season?

"People come here to have fun, eat crab, shuck oysters. We like beer, music, and festivals." He looked her up and down with an unexpected elitist snark with which she was all too familiar. "We're not big on serious writers who wear their pajamas all day."

What in the hell is this guy's problem?

Her face flushed hot as she glanced down to confirm she was wearing the sweatpants she specifically changed into for this round of nightmare neighbor. When she looked up again, he was gone.

As a rule, Millie avoided confrontation. She let Jade fight most of her professional battles and the occasional personal one too. The water heater in her apartment had been replaced within twenty-four hours instead of the proposed 7-10 days thanks to her dear friend. And it was true that Millie shied away from her own assistant. She wasn't scared of Karen, but Millie chose her battles. Most things weren't worth spilling her half-full-glass attitude over, so she dodged or compromised.

But this crap was officially ridiculous. She had been dismissed for a large chunk of her life by a man she cared about a hell of a lot more than some music-blaring, control freak townie. She would, of course, do a quick edit of her word choice before sharing that with him, but there was no way she was running scared now.

~

Drake thought that went well. He might have been a little harsh, but seriously, it wasn't his problem that she'd ordered a quiet beach town in her mind and gotten his reality instead. Granted, his metal-grinding realism was a bit over the top these days, but this was still his town and he was a local business. Millie Hart would be gone soon enough. A few months early would benefit them both, he thought, changing out the buckets and helping Esteban finish up a glass pitcher.

Tyler and Hazel were back with lunch a few minutes later. Drake silenced the music and walked to the front.

"Look who we found pacing outside?" Tyler set bags on the counter as Millie walked through the door.

"I wasn't pacing. I was editing."

Tyler raised a brow, nodded at Drake, and closed the door.

"Hey, Millie." Hazel pulled the containers of potato salad from the giant paper bag. "We can call you that now, right? Now that Tyler has stalked you," she clarified.

Millie nodded, glaring at Drake. He knew he was an adult, but he glared right back.

"Sorry about that," Tyler said, setting out the napkins and utensils.

Esteban introduced himself and grabbed his lunch.

"We won't tell anyone outside the studio in case you're hiding out," Hazel took her usual turkey on a poppy seed bagel.

"It's fine. I am not hiding out. Not running from the cops or having an affair either. And I don't always wear pajamas." More glaring. "These are sweatpants and I am wearing a—" She shook her head. "Forget it."

Tyler glanced at Millie and back at Drake, who joined them at the front counter but kept quiet.

"We had not thought about the cops, but—" He gestured to Drake again. This time he leveled a glare he hoped communicated that he was not up for a friendly lunch chat with their neighbor.

"Sandwich?" Tyler asked. Millie accepted but held it unopened. She was probably humoring them, hoping Drake would finally give in on the music. Yeah, not happening.

His heart hammered in his chest. Sure, she'd dropped into their quaint and quiet town for her own reasons, but she certainly wasn't the worst tourist he'd ever encountered. Jules was probably right that he was being inhospitable, but he couldn't remember being so aggravated.

"Millie, since you're a professional," Hazel said over a full mouth. She swallowed. "Could you please tell my dad that writers are born? You either have it or you don't, and I don't have it."

Millie finally stopped glaring at Drake and looked to Esteban for some explanation or an answer he was looking for her to give. Esteban shook his head and Millie opened her sandwich, seemingly buying time. "I think everyone has the ability to write, not necessarily fiction, but something. What are you trying to write?"

Hazel explained about her college entrance essays. There was a fair amount of whining, but their neighbor morphed into a less-annoying version of herself who was listening attentively to a young woman she'd just met. Drake imagined since Millie was such a "big deal" that she'd perfected her listening, not quite listening, expression, but that's not what this was. She was truly present, which struck Drake as rare: local or out of town.

"I don't know why Berkeley can't save the essays for English majors and give me a question that relates to my field. I'm a biology major, not Shakespeare."

Millie laughed. "Well, even biology majors need to express themselves, right? Reports, presentations. What are your questions?" She folded her sandwich into the paper and followed Hazel, who rooted around in her backpack, producing a stapled stack of paper.

Drake focused on his sandwich because if he gave Millie any more thought, he might realize he'd been unfair. That she wasn't some pseudo celebrity bent on molding the locals for her few months of peace. He hoped she truly was obnoxious because he hated being wrong.

"I think she's my favorite renter," Tyler said quietly at Drake's side.

He glanced over as his friend chewed his lunch like they were watching the same movie. "Is that a thing we are doing now? Favorite renters?"

Tyler nodded.

"She's good with kids, that's a plus," Esteban added at Drake's other shoulder.

Drake's brow furrowed. "Hazel is twenty."

He shrugged. "Still. I like her too."

The three men stood shoulder to shoulder while Millie and Hazel's conversation grew more animated. Both women laughed like they'd talked more than twice in the last week. Millie was... different. Relaxed maybe, or more energized? He couldn't tell because he was trying not to look at her, but discussing college entrance essays agreed with her.

"What do you think about her?" Esteban asked.

Drake side-eyed both men and continued facing front. "I think she's renting the Millers' cottage."

"And?" Tyler asked.

"And... she's annoying the crap out of me. The music thing was supposed to be just... a fix, and now it's like every other day. Lower the music. What about the music?" Drake was mocking a whiney voice and was pretty sure Millie and Hazel had joined them again because Tyler and Esteban were silent. On a deep breath, he glanced up.

Yup, she was right there glaring again, this time with a bit of humor in those gorgeous eyes, so that was something.

Always happy to entertain, Drake crumpled his lunch trash and tossed it in the bin. "Party's over. We have work to do." He moved past Millie. The jolt of annoyance didn't go away until he started his second project of the day. At some point, their new little lunch group dispersed because when he glanced toward the front of the studio again, Millie was gone, Esteban was working on his own order, and the infamous music was on full blast where it belonged.

Chapter Seven

The following Thursday, Millie woke inadvertently humming "Smells Like Teen Spirit" by Nirvana, which was surprisingly hummable for nineties grunge. She lay in bed enjoying the morning without worrying about the time. She'd slept in, but she wasn't all that concerned.

She was going soft since she'd met with Hazel two days ago to work on her first of three essays. The time had started perfectly normal, Millie spent a few minutes giving a bit of a pep talk about writing and they worked through a new prompt from an app Millie had on her phone. That got Hazel writing about something other than why she was the best candidate for Berkeley, and she relaxed. Defenses down, Hazel proved to be an excellent technical writer with clear points and valid support. She was obviously entrenched in science so she was never going to wax poetic, but Millie was optimistic with a few more sessions, Hazel would kill the essay portion of her application.

Millie had never collaborated with a writers' group or in plotting sessions she'd seen other authors discuss on social media. Maybe it was the only child in her or that writing often felt intimate and private, but whatever the reason, Millie wrote alone. So, she was surprised how gratifying it was to bat ideas around and assist Hazel in finding her voice. It was fun and had stimulated Millie's own creativity.

Then she'd found out through that same helpful prompt that her obnoxious neighbor wasn't obnoxious at all. The prompt was—write about when you were the most scared. Hazel's brainstorming revealed that she was scared her sister Sofia wouldn't recover after she tore her shoulder and lost her softball scholarship. She wrote about the stress it put on her family, but mostly how she "lost" her sister for a while and that was the most scared she'd ever been.

Sofia had gone to physical therapy, and that's how her dad met Drake.

"He was in a nasty motorcycle accident like six years ago. Way scarier than my sister's shoulder. They didn't think he was going to live," Hazel said.

For a second Millie had thought about moving on to another prompt because sharing their own memories was one thing, but knowing things about Drake without him being there felt intrusive. But Hazel went on to say that Drake losing the lower half of his arm and pushing through was inspiring and showed her and Sofia real strength. Millie couldn't stop her and felt the jaw often clenched for her neighbor begin to soften.

"Then he and Tyler hired my dad. I've been his apprentice for a couple of years. He's overcome a lot."

"How's your sister?"

"She's a swimmer, well she's in medical school now, but when she couldn't throw anymore, she swam in college."

Millie tried not to acknowledge the details of her insufferable neighbor's life because they made him human. She wasn't ready for the guy who was making it near impossible to work to be a human being, much less an inspiring human, so she gently redirected Hazel back to how she could use people in her life to inspire her essay.

She continued on about how incredible Drake was and all the brilliant things he did for their community. He'd started a fishing conservancy group in his dad's name, and he met his sister every morning when she brought her boats in. Millie ignored the twinge in her stomach at the knowledge that the woman on the dock was not his lover but his sister.

"He still struggles, but he's awesome." Hazel beamed.

"Doesn't seem like he's struggling at all," Millie joked as they wrapped up and Hazel zipped her backpack.

"Probably not supposed to share this, but it's nuts that he's not telling anyone."

Alone in her bed now, Millie still wasn't sure why she'd held her breath as they walked to the door of the cottage, but even gossip seemed more dramatic in a small town.

"Drake let Chase move in next door because his family is going through tough times."

Millie had nodded, acknowledged another point for sainted Drake.

"The noise from Chase's shop like... triggers something in Drake. My dad says it reminds him of the accident or something. Anyway, that's why we blast the music."

Millie's hand must have gone to her chest because Hazel begged her not to make a big deal out of it. Drake didn't like fuss and if he knew she'd told a stranger, he'd feel "extra nuts."

She'd closed the door after arranging to meet with Hazel again and gone completely soft. Nothing was black and white. She knew that from her own writing. Millie finished humming along with Nirvana. She still wasn't sure what to make of Drake Branch, but he certainly wasn't nuts. Deciding to give in to the music for a little while anyway now that she knew the reason behind it, and emboldened by her time with Hazel, Millie gave herself some room to breathe too.

She knew from experience that she couldn't force a story that wasn't ready to be told. So, she spent a couple of days cleaning the cottage and putting away snacks she'd ordered online. Yesterday she did laundry and casually took some notes on setting before going to bed early and finishing someone else's book set in London.

It had been on her to-be-read list forever and she wanted to get it out of the way before she started getting serious about her own writing. It was a romance, which she'd sworn off for her time in Bodega, but when she'd found it had been left behind in her bag, she rationalized the intrinsic value to her current project. It took place in London. Nineteenth-century London. A gorgeous, steamy, perfectly-crafted love story that had nothing to do with stamps or a guy who was dead and not dead, but still... London.

Remembering she'd fallen asleep thinking about her own story, Millie patted the bed for her notebook. She pushed her hair out of her face and scanned the pages for the notes she'd made last night. She wasn't normally inspired in the moments before bed, but three books ago she'd written a whole meet-cute after waking up in the middle of the night to use the bathroom. That book had gone on to be a reader favorite, so she'd kept a notebook by her bed ever since. Maybe she'd written something brilliant, she thought, still flipping through old notes. On the last sheet she read—*Make things seem more mysterious, like Jack the Ripper or Sherlock.*

That was it? Beneath an oiled stain she suspected was peanut butter, one line encouraging her toward literary derivation?

Millie sighed and looked around for Pop-Tart, who was stretched out enjoying her favorite blotch of morning sunlight.

"A lot of help you are."

She threw herself back in the bed and tried to ignore the disappointment. She'd loosened the reins, let her creative flag fly, and still nothing. Damn it. Millie lifted her pad overhead hoping some magic might produce different words.

"Make things more mysterious," she read aloud. "Jesus Christ, what is happening to me? Make things more mysterious?" She laughed a sort of pained howl before tossing the pad aside and getting up to make coffee.

Scowling at her poor, innocent cat before pushing the button on the coffee grinder, Millie went through the steps of what had become her morning routine. Although now she had cinnamon bread for her toast.

"It's come to this, Pop?" she said as her cat sauntered into the kitchen hoping for breakfast. "I'm aspiring to be a dollar-store version of Sir Arthur Conan Doyle and the highlight of my morning is cinnamon toast."

Buttering her toast, she rolled her right shoulder, which acted up when she slept on it wrong or typed too much. It was clearly the former since she had typed diddly squat during her be-free-no-pressure experiment.

Mashing cat food into Pop's bowl and setting it down, she decided it was time to put the pressure back on and get her ass in the chair. Time to focus and write about... death. Yes, today would be the death scene. The chapter leading up to it and the moment he—

She crunched her toast.

"Despair. Hopelessness," she said, grabbing a paper towel to wipe her hands before sitting down at her now-clean and organized desk.

Alistair would miss blue-sky days like this when he was gone, she typed and then backspaced. *It was blue-sky days like this Alistair would miss the most. Days where the blue was so blue that he...*

Millie slouched down in the chair and tried to imagine her own death. What would she miss? Who would miss her? Maybe she could start there instead of following the outline verbatim. Yes, she could even work backward. The funeral, Alistair's funeral. Who would be there and what—

Nothing. She took another bite of toast.

She had no point of connection. The birds were chirping outside. Her coffee smelled great and the cinnamon toast was yummy. Pop-Tart was now purring a breakfast thank-you in her lap. In her present mood, she wondered if death was even all the doom and gloom people made it out to be. Maybe it was simply a surprise, like a broken water heater or a flat tire. Maybe those around Alistair are shocked, but they got on with it. That wasn't a full book. More like a pamphlet in a psychologist's office. Millie set Pop down and stood to refill her coffee. Research, she decided, she needed research.

She called Jade.

"Do you think that woman we used a couple of years ago, the one with the llamas or—"

"Goats," Jade said. Millie could hear her clicking at her keyboard.

"Right, goats. Do you think we, or I or someone could ask her for research on death? Near-death experiences, or mostly what it feels like to lose a person, watch them slip away, you know? I'm going to start with Alistair's family and what they've lost. They're at his funeral and it's like nothing, numb. You know?"

Jade was quiet.

"Are you there?"

"I am... writing a... finishing an email, and bam." Millie could hear her agent hit the enter key. "I am all yours. Research on death. Okay, maybe have Karen contact goat-lady. I'm sure she still has the contact information."

"Hmm."

"What's hmm? You want to contact goat-woman directly? Have you read any of those books you bought? That psychology one looked dark and boring. It might be helpful. Or maybe you don't need that much structure. How about journaling or draw on your own experiences?"

Millie shook her head again before remembering she was on the phone. "I closed my eyes and tried to get all death-y, but it's charming here in Candy Land. I'm not sure what I would journal. Maybe I need to interview people, or reading more is a good idea." She pulled up an email and typed some notes for Karen.

"What have you read so far?"

"Um, well I'm halfway through that the boring psychology book, but I haven't read much else."

"You're always reading. What was the last book you finished? Maybe there's something in there to draw on."

"*Wicked and the Wallflower,*" Millie mumbled.

Jade was silent. No keystrokes. No laughter. Millie knew her friend was deciding whether or not to judge. It was the perfect moment to declare that this whole project was a joke.

"Sarah MacLean's *Wicked and the Wallflower?*"

"No. Wicked and the Wallflower—a study of naughty flowers. Of course it's MacLean's."

"Brilliant, right?"

Millie sighed. "So brilliant. That opening balcony scene? My God."

They chatted about the book and a few others Jade had read recently, including an advanced copy of Beverly Jenkins's new one. Millie had only seen the magnificent cover and didn't want spoilers, so they moved on. Lying on the couch, she was filled with pure joy. She loved books and romance, especially with— *What the hell are you doing?*

"Okay, that's enough about that," she said like a school teacher.

Jade whined. "No, no, please. Can't I have a few more minutes of you before you slip back under the black cloak?"

Millie stifled a laugh. "Death. Let's talk death."

"What about your mom?" Jade said on an exhale.

"What about her?" She sat up.

"Mil, you lost your mom when you were twelve. You were there. I would think you know a lot about death and what comes after loss."

"I'd...never thought that like—" Millie stood, suddenly needing to walk around the tiny living room. "I was young, and I don't picture my mom that way."

"Maybe you should. We can talk about it when you come into town next week."

She bit her lower lip, amazed at how things could turn so quickly. "I'm not... I need other death stories. Real ones."

After a long pause, Jade said, "Okay."

"Great." Millie held her eyes open wide and shook off the sudden flood of unwelcome emotion. "Thanks. In the meantime, I think I'll try baking something."

Jade laughed. "That could be dangerous," she said. "You could take a walk instead. Give Alistair a sex scene. Better yet, have your own sex."

"Does your mind always go there?"

"I represent a lot of erotica authors, Mil. The sex is epic. I'm hoping the Bumble thing works out in a few months because I'm so ready to teach a man."

Millie laughed as they disconnected and dropped back onto the couch. No music from next door. It was quiet now. Probably lunchtime, she thought. Touching her phone, she brought up pictures of her mom.

Her father had given her a box of loose snapshots when he sent her to boarding school two weeks after the funeral. Millie had misplaced the box and was in the throes of a full panic attack when one of the school psychologists suggested that while keeping her mom's memory alive through pictures was "honorable," she needed to avoid pretending her mother was still alive. She needed to put the pictures away and grieve the loss. Go through the pain.

Millie eventually found the box and had since scanned the pictures. She knew her mom was gone. She was reminded every time she pulled up a photo and saw her vibrant face frozen in a time long gone. Next year, Millie would be thirty-three. A year older than her mom when she died.

She bit the inside of her bottom lip at the thought. The psychologist was wrong. It was possible to have the pictures and the pain. Millie touched the screen and quickly swiped her phone to the blue bubbles of her background. Pearl Jam. She knew this one. As the music filled in around the cracks of her space, Millie wiped her eyes. For the first time since she'd arrived, she was grateful for the noise.

$\sim$

Drake was sick of the nineties by one o'clock, but Chase had a big project and they were working all hours lately, so there wasn't time to be picky. He wasn't sure if it was all the attention brought to the music lately or his sister's comment about avoidance, but Drake was starting to believe the music Band-Aid, as Jules called it, had a shelf life. He needed to think of a Plan B.

His first option was to find Chase another space, which wasn't a viable option even with their new contract to build batting cages for the new elementary school and the park. Chase was back on his feet and making more money, but not ready to make a move. So, that left Drake with option two—work through the noise.

Tyler took his glasses off and rubbed the bridge of his nose. His tell. Drake grabbed the remote and muted Pearl Jam. When they were kids, Drake used to think his friend rubbed his nose because his glasses bothered him, but he eventually learned Tyler rubbed his nose at the on-set of a migraine. He'd dealt with headaches for as long as Drake knew him, but this one felt like his fault.

"The Airstream is freezing, and I've got that fancy cold water you drink in my fridge."

"I'm fine."

"You're not. Is it the music?"

"We've been over this. Music has nothing to do with it. I took something." He glanced up. "I'm good," he said, eyes narrowed in obvious pain as he grabbed his phone and keys. "I'm going to be late and you have a ton of work."

The sounds from next door screamed to life. Tyler picked up the remote and returned them to the nineties before switching out his reading glasses for sunglasses and nodding goodbye.

Drake had forgotten all about Tyler's migraines. How was that possible? The idea that his shit was still eclipsing everyone else's details was unsettling. He checked his notebook and grabbed a pipe.

Maybe he could go back to acupuncture. That had helped with the nightmares, but returning to something he'd done before felt like, well going backward. Maybe if he tackled some of the other things he'd been avoiding, he could work his way forward to silence in the studio or at least a normal volume. The problem was he wasn't sure what he'd been avoiding. He'd thought he was a total success story until Chase moved in and Jules alluded to other Band-Aids. It was unnerving to be told, even in a roundabout way, that he was fooling himself.

Unclenching his jaw from the thought of further discussion with his sister, Drake let out a slow breath and turned his attention to the second half of his list.

Esteban and Hazel were at a financial aid seminar at the community college, and Tyler would be in meetings all afternoon negotiating the new gallery space they'd decided to rent in town. Tyler wanted a more "artsy" place to showcase and sell their work to tourists. Drake was happy to take over the vacant space next to Swept Away before some fast food chain or gaudy souvenir shop tried to muscle into Bodega Bay.

Tyler would handle most of the details. For now, Drake had the studio to himself, so he dropped the safety glasses over his eyes, checked and preheated his pipe, and went to the furnace for his first gather.

By the time he'd blown a small bubble of air into what would become the first of a twenty-four-glass online order, Drake found his normal. Each step, from the dip of his pipe to the thread of green he ran along the base was singular, specific, and therapeutic. Step by step, that was how Drake crawled back from loss. Why wasn't it enough anymore? Why couldn't he get wrapped up in the process like he had initially and step his way out of Chase's noise?

Esteban taught Drake to blow glass years ago when they met in the waiting room of the physical therapist. He was there for his oldest daughter who had shoulder problems from pitching softball and Drake, among other things, was learning to use his arm. Esteban became his friend, his teacher, and when Drake and Tyler opened the studio, their first employee.

"It's a dance, man. Molding fire," Esteban had said that first day. "It will take over your mind if you let it and walk you right out of whatever is troubling you."

Drake was reluctant at first. So much of glass blowing involved coordination and back in those days he felt a lot of things. Coordinated was not one of them. But after one class in an open-to-the-public glass studio, he was hooked on the challenge. Calmed by the rhythm.

Now, after years of frustration and more than his share of failed projects, blowing glass was as much a part of him as breathing. He joked he could do it in his sleep. Running the back of a jack along the base of the glass, Drake kept turning. Once it was right where he liked it, he carefully tapped the glass off into a cushioned mitt they'd designed for solo work.

The afternoon sun softened the steel edges of the studio as he set the pipe aside and picked up his latest creation. All this time and he still marveled at the way sunlight played with glass. Setting what their fancy website called "tea time" into the kiln to cool, Drake rolled his neck and started again.

Twelve glasses later, Esteban and Hazel returned with tons of information on federal forms and timelines.

Esteban declared he was "happy to be back at something he understood" and took over for Drake, who grabbed his water and listened to Hazel chatter on about her growing list and the trials of "adulting" as she called it.

"At least my first essay is almost done."

"Yeah? That's great. You discovered your inner writer after all."

"I wouldn't go that far," she said, still unenthusiastic. "Millie had me write about something else to loosen me up, and that helped. She'll review my final draft next week, but I think it's pretty good for a science geek."

"Millie?"

"Yeah. She's great. I mean she should be, right? She's a professional, but she is smart. And nice too." Hazel pulled her hair back and put her Cal hat on backward. "One down, two to go."

She practically bounced with excitement as she joined her dad at the furnace, her entire future ahead of her. Only after a long gulp of water was he able to process that Millie Hart, an outsider with nothing to gain and her own work, was helping Hazel step boldly into that future. He'd have to thank her. For the first time since meeting their new neighbor, he was sorry for making her life difficult.

Drake exhaled and got back to work. He'd figure it out. Adapt. Hell, adapt was practically his middle name.

In the early years after he lost his arm, therapists both physical and psychological threw around words like "fluid" and "flexible." Drake had joked that he'd had enough f-words to last a lifetime. After a while, he realized they were all telling him that what he knew as normal no longer existed. He'd learned to reprogram the simplest tasks first followed by things like contact with other people and "allowing his personality back into his movements and gestures."

Some days it felt like he was relearning everything and others he almost forgot something was missing. Drake learned so much about himself in those years and to the delight of his mom, he became an expert at putting things back where they belonged and where they were easiest to access.

He imagined there were plenty of amputees who resumed a modified version of their old selves, but that's not how things "manifested," as his psychologist liked to say, for Drake. The accident had changed him inside and out. He cleared his mind of anything he didn't need to get up in the morning, and then he cleared out all the other crap. Once a man with a collection of watches, he became an enthusiastic minimalist. He streamlined everything from the clothes he wore to the food he ate. He was right-handed so unlike a lot of people with greater challenges, he still had full use of his dominant hand.

His left hand was a state-of-the-art piece of machinery thanks to his mom's relentless calls to their insurance company and what Drake knew had been at least part of the second mortgage, which paid the rest of his medical bills. He was fitted two years after his accident and had cherished his arm like a sports car.

He'd been to every seminar, watched every video, and asked all the questions. Last year he even went to a medical conference in the city to demonstrate the potential of his Artemis 6000. He was the poster child for prosthetic arms, which made the realization he still had work to do even more annoying.

He'd known the risks in letting Chase move in. He wasn't denying he had triggers or that the sound of grinding metal was up toward the top. But Chase went to school with his little sister, Sistine. Their family had fallen behind on payments after a nonexistent fishing season threatened everyone in Bodega Bay. They never recovered and lost their boat. Then they almost lost their home to foreclosure the following year.

Drake could help Chase with rent-free space, so he did.

After the first day of working next door, he knew he'd be uncomfortable, planned for some anxiety, but it had proven too much and while he was able to dim the noise through a slew of meditation techniques he'd learned, he wasn't getting any work done. That's when Tyler came up with the idea to mask it with music. For almost a year now, it had worked. Hazel, Esteban, and even Tyler had grown used to their playlists, and they were all productive as hell with a soundtrack.

"The power of music," Tyler had joked.

But Jules was right—it was a Band-Aid over a problem he'd need to deal with, but for now, the next time Millie Hart barged into his studio, and she definitely would, Drake would go a little easier on her and let her know he was grateful. That would have to be enough.

Chapter Eight

*M*illie was repeating herself. She stood from her desk and walked around the living room, eventually sliding on her socks like an ice skater before tossing herself onto the couch. She needed a TV. What had she been thinking renting a place without a television?

You were thinking that you'd write more than two hundred and fifty words a day. That's what you were thinking.

Pulling the carrot-shaped throw pillow over her face, she screamed and remembered her childhood psychologists. They were the only support after her mom died. Millie had never been away from her parents, let alone to a boarding school, when her father sent her packing. Mrs. Ethan and Miss Blanc were like surrogate parents those first few years. Miss Blanc passed away recently, and Millie drove up for the funeral. She still sent Mrs. Ethan a signed copy of her books prior to every release day. Family, she learned the hard way, wasn't always blood.

She screamed again, put the pillow at her waist, and tried to figure out how and why she was going to get Alistair on that train.

He hated flying? No, too obvious. *Trains were in his background?* Maybe. She tossed the pillow aside and sat up.

"His father was a conductor." She scoffed and grabbed a handful of popcorn off a spindly table in front of the couch. "His... great-aunt was struck by a train carrying secret messages for the French."

"The Russians?" she asked Pop-Tart, who was now calmly cleaning her paws on the other side of the couch. On a groan, Millie inhaled the last of the popcorn in her hand. "The Russians don't have to pass envelopes anymore. They just get on Facebook," she said, still chewing.

Pop-Tart moved to the chair.

"Maybe." She stood, grabbed another handful of popcorn, and sock-skated back to her desk. "Maybe the train is a metaphor."

Millie nodded and started typing. Fast and furious like they always depict writers in the movies, yet two minutes into realizing she was typing garbage, she stopped. Closing her eyes, she mindlessly searched her bag for her smartphone. She'd shut it off and shoved it all the way to the bottom because she'd recently started playing *Two Dots*, which was a mistake, but something told her if she could reach the top of that little Swiss Alp-looking mountain, she would discover the meaning of life. Maybe even figure out how to write an entire freaking paragraph. Without finding her phone, she looked back at her laptop

The train swooshed by like so many memories—she closed the lid.

"Swooshed. Always stop when you're swooshing, right Pop?"

Her cat deigned a glance in her direction before returning her focus to the moths hovering around the light outside the kitchen window now that the sun had set.

Maybe tomorrow Millie should return to the outline. Things were getting off track and if she added one more character, she was going to start buying wine online. In bulk. No wonder Hemingway drank, she thought, opening the refrigerator, only to close it again.

She craved something warm and cooked. She missed the city most around dinnertime, which wasn't fair since she hadn't even been into Bodega Bay yet. Maybe Jade was right and there was a quaint little restaurant where she could sit by a window and look out over the water. A retired chef running a five-table bistro with perfect risotto.

Millie shook her head, knowing she was spinning glitter around reality again. Reality was, she'd settle for a piece of pizza. Maybe two.

Kissing Pop-Tart and pulling on a sweatshirt, she stepped outside the cottage. Town was probably close enough to walk, but it was dark, so she hopped in the car. It was amazing how quickly days, weeks even, could go by when she was holed up in her head. The morning before she left the city, she'd spoken with a neighbor in her apartment building elevator. The woman explained that she was finally feeling better after being sick and said, "I have not left the house for three days. Three whole days. Can you believe it?"

Millie could. She wasn't sure what her record was for consecutive days in her head, eating popcorn, and sometimes forgetting to shower, but three was amateur level. She didn't say that to her neighbor, of course, because people rarely understood writer oddities. She learned that early on at her first book signing when she'd exclaimed that she was grateful for events with readers or she might never shave her legs. They'd all fake laughed, but it was awkward. Not that Millie cared, but she did learn it wasn't necessary to share.

She never minded the isolation of writing. That probably had a lot to do with her childhood but turning onto what looked like the only illuminated street, she wasn't in the mood to think about anything other than melted cheese. Did they have takeout in Bodega Bay? Snagging a parking spot in a small gravel lot, Millie was about to find out.

~

Drake found a table outside Dough Bird, the new pizza place in town, while Jules grabbed their beers. Over the years, they'd seen a lot of places come and close. Dreamy tourists intent on living the vacation, working remotely from their sleepy town, or savvy venture capital firms determined to beat the seasonal odds. In what seemed like another life now, Drake worked with Tyler in wealth management. He understood the appeal of investing in the cozy culture of Bodega Bay, but few survived once the coastal buzz wore off and the chill of the off-season arrived. So far, Dough Bird—clever name—was busy before the full flood of vacationers. A good sign.

A few bites into his first slice, he understood the line at the pickup window. Before he could offer his opinion, Jules declared, "They'll be gone by next winter." She took another bite. "The sauce is too… salty maybe?"

Drake finished his first slice and washed it down with a regional beer, another good sign. "The only other pizza place that's survived is Crusty's, and I'm not sure their cheese is from an actual food group. This is good. I'm not complaining."

She huffed and he took another slice.

"And, they've got good beer." He folded his pizza. "I vote they stay. Salty sauce or not."

"It's salty, right?"

Jules finished and took another one. Drake masked his smile behind a swig of beer. "It's good. Quit expecting a problem."

She shrugged. "Yeah, well, that's what I do. I'm a defensive lifer. Is that a word? Lifer. I live defensively, like driving."

"I get it. Eat your pizza." Drake took another bite and reminded himself Jules appreciated the direct approach, so he jumped right in. "When you said I avoid 'other things' last week. What did you mean by that?"

She eyed him mid-bite and started shaking her head before she even swallowed. "I should not have said that. You know me, I'm incapable of being normal."

"I think you're very normal."

She scoffed and drank her beer.

"Well, kind of normal. Come on, what did you mean? Do I have other weird Band-Aids?"

Jules wiped her mouth. "Weird? No."

"What then?"

"I… think some things are always going to be a challenge and others you just avoid. Rightly so."

"Like what?"

"I don't know."

He waited her out.

"Fine. Like you haven't been out on the boat since before your accident. Which is not a big deal."

Drake knew this one. He wasn't exactly avoiding going out on the boat with her or his dad. He'd been busy. It had seemed like something he would do eventually until that moment and the realization that so much time had passed.

"This is ridiculous. I'm sorry I said anything about the music. What do I know? You almost died. Who cares if you're not doing everything you used to do? You've had a lot going on."

"For six years?"

"Has it been that long?"

"Jules."

"Drake."

She shook her head. "Please, give yourself a break. You were in a horrible accident. That changes a guy. Please don't start some crusade."

"What else don't I do?"

She chewed and took a long pull of her beer. "You don't swim in the bay. You relearned how to swim after the accident, but you don't jump off the dock. You don't swim like you used to."

"Wow. You do have a list."

"I pay attention and I'd like to say again that maybe your doctors—"

"I can't pull myself back onto the dock with one arm," he said, not sure that was solid reasoning but going with it anyway. "I don't jump off because I can't get back up."

"Dad built you a ladder."

"Are you listening to yourself?"

"Stop. It's a..."

"Modification. Yeah, I know."

"It's not like some big eyesore that says, 'Drake lost his arm.' You can't even see it. It's underwater."

He finished his beer in silence and discomfort he hadn't sat with for a while.

"Okay, this is good. I'm great with lists. I'll knock off this little stuff and... that will help me rip off the last big Band-Aid."

"Oh God. See? Crusade." She shook her head and took another piece of pizza.

"No, a quick jump off the dock and getting on the boat. If I tackle those—" He stopped when Jules raised a brow as she reached for a napkin. "Shit, there's more?"

"You asked and I'm telling."

"What?"

She shrugged. "You don't date."

"Not true. I went on... two dates with the woman Tyler set me up with."

"Oh, right," she said with her mouth full. "What was her name again?"

Drake had no idea.

"Exactly." Jules took another swig of beer. "You don't date."

"That one doesn't count because I... am completely focused on bettering myself."

Jules laughed.

"It's true. There is no room on the list."

It was not the best time to notice Millie Hart standing in line at the take-out counter, but surprise at seeing her away from their battleground won out. Jules followed his line of sight.

"Ooh, that's her?"

He nodded.

"The famous and reclusive writer. Kind of intimidating, right?"

Drake snorted. "Oh yeah, she's extremely intimidating."

"She's pretty," Jules said, craning her neck, which was more for effect since she was almost as tall as he was.

Drake said nothing as his sister eyed him and then the counter.

"No," he said, spotting the mischief in her expression.

Jules wiped her hands and set her napkin to the side. A sure sign she was getting up. Drake put a hand on her shoulder to hold her in place, unsure why he bothered. She shrugged free.

"Calm down. Wow, you're a little... jumpy around your new neighbor."

He shook his head. "Your powers will not work on her. She hates me."

Jules leaned over, met his eyes, and looked almost as young as Bella. He laughed and grabbed the last slice of pizza.

"Are you blushing?"

"I am not. You are reading into things again." He finished off his beer and kept his eyes on their table. Jules was a heat-seeking missile. If she sensed even a glimmer of interest, he was toast. Both his sisters were nosy, but Jules had superpowers.

"She may hate your taste in music, but you're... interested, aren't you?"

Drake kept chewing and shook his head. "Have you heard anything about plans for Mom and Dad's birthday?"

"Are you sure? Not even a little intrigued?" She tried to catch his eyes, which was comical.

Drake chuckled and wiped his mouth. "We have traded insults. Nothing more. She seems like a typical entitled tourist."

Jules patted him on the shoulder and Drake knew he was screwed. "Less is more. You know that's rule number one of the lying game. I'm disappointed." She pursed her lips. "My sources tell me that our new writer in residence is helping Hazel with her entrance essays. Millie Hart has been to your studio at least twice and both times there were... sparks."

Son of a bitch.

"My sources also tell me that she is nothing at all like an entitled tourist and you"—she pointed, enjoying her little reveal—"are the one being less than welcoming. I wonder why?"

"Your sources? Let me guess... Tyler?"

"Surprisingly no. I haven't seen Fancy Pants lately. Esteban is my man on the inside, if you must know."

Drake almost choked. "Seriously?"

She nodded.

"It's always the quiet ones."

Laughter broke out at the take-out counter, and Drake glanced over at the same time Millie looked up. That was all the encouragement Jules needed.

As she swung her legs around to get up, Drake went for the Hail Mary.

"If you move from this spot, I'm going to announce to everyone that you laughed so hard at Christmas that you peed your pants." He raised his brows in defiance.

Jules shook her head. "How the mighty have fallen. That's all you've got?" She stood, ponytail flipping around her neck. "It's hard to believe you once taught us all the skills. No one cares if I peed my pants, and it was a tiny bit, just to clarify. I had a baby. People know your pee control is all screwed up after that."

Drake couldn't hold back the laughter. Every time he thought his sister had said it all, there was more. She tsked and left to cause trouble.

"Millie."

Drake took a deep breath as Jules approached the counter like she'd run into a long-lost friend. Millie smiled as Jules bounded toward her. Christ, there were those eyes again. Drake pulled out his phone, suddenly busy.

"I'm Jules, your neighbor's sister," Jules said in a chipper tone Drake had not heard in years, maybe ever.

"I didn't know Drake had a sister."

He glanced up and put his phone away. Jules was practically dancing a jig at Millie's familiar use of his first name.

"Interesting that you didn't know that Drake Mortimer Branch had a sister. He has two, in fact."

And there it was, his middle name. Perfect. The humiliation was in full swing.

"He likes to keep me a secret."

Millie seemed hesitant as Jules pulled her toward their table, but so far, she was handling herself well. Most people shriveled at the full force of Jules. He wondered if Millie was taking mental notes again. Insane siblings probably led to great story ideas too.

"Look who I found, big brother?"

Drake stood, tried to come across friendlier outside of his studio, and nodded a greeting.

"Big brother?" He scowled at Jules.

"I call you that."

"You have never called me that."

"Oh, well. Here's your neighbor." She presented Millie like a surprise package. "Your adorable, great hair, friendly, and surprisingly down-to-earth neighbor."

"She's afraid of you. That's why she's being friendly." He met Millie's eyes but looked away when she laughed. He'd handled the cats playing poker and even dismissed her plea for a 'creative compromise' with barely a shrug, but in-town Millie was relaxed. The streetlights making her eyes glitter, joy he'd only caught glimpses of was now front and center.

"Your eyes are so blue, aren't they, Drake?"

Superpowers, the woman's ability to find weakness was legendary.

"They are." Drake threw out their trash.

"Mortimer?" Millie said quietly. "Kind of an old man's name, don't you think?"

His back to them, Drake grinned. Yeah, he had that one coming. "I'm afraid to ask your middle name." He rejoined them. "It'll probably put you solidly in the grandma category."

"Amherst."

He faltered.

"My mom's maiden name."

"Good name." Something in her expression at the mention of her mother told him to drop the sarcasm. When she smiled and said, "It is a good name," Drake gave himself what Tyler referred to as a "mental pat on the back."

Jules watched like she was expecting them to break into song at any moment. She was a defensive lifer and a reluctant romantic. She'd been dragged through the mud so he couldn't blame her for either, but even at his expense, it was nice to see she still knew how to be silly. He guessed Bella kept those parts of her mom safe.

"Have we arrived at the portion of the show where you pretend you have somewhere important to be?" Drake asked.

Jules held up her finger with dramatic flair and grabbed her bag off the table. "Funny you mention that because Dad"—she looked toward their parents' house for effect—"um, needs me."

"Yeah? Did he send a smoke signal?"

"It's a sense." She fumbled with her phone. "And, he texted me."

"Did he? Let's see what he needs." Drake leaned toward her.

Jules pocketed her phone and grinned at Millie.

He laughed. "Leave."

"Have a wonderful night." She kissed him on the shoulder. "So great meeting you, Millie."

"Nice meeting you too."

"If you can get away from your..." Jules mimed typing.

Another first: his sister miming. *Unbelievable.*

"You should come to Fish Fest."

"Goodnight, Jules."

"It's in a few weeks. All the fishing boats. Crazy fun. I'm sure Drake will tell you about it and invite you. Maybe you can make it a—."

"You have no shame."

"I do not." She winked at him. "Listen to your sister and remember the list. You asked." She ran toward her truck and was gone, leaving Drake standing with his neighbor, nothing but a pizza box between them this time.

～

He gestured for her to join him. It was the polite thing to do, and he wasn't quite ready to go back to his trailer alone and stew over what he wasn't yet sure how to fix.

"Unless you need to get back or you're still pissed at me."

Millie glanced over her shoulder, and he wondered if she drove into town. "I've never been good at staying mad."

"Could have fooled me," he mumbled.

"Do you realize people can hear you when you say smart-ass things under your breath?"

"At least I don't outright talk to myself."

She huffed, and he could feel them sliding back into pettiness.

"Let's sit." He made room for her pizza on the table and held the chair.

She narrowed her eyes.

"What? Your hands are full. Just because I like loud music doesn't mean I don't pull out chairs for old ladies."

"And we're back." She sat, opened her box, and folded one slice, only to open it again and add peppers. "Your sister's nice."

"She is."

"Do you two come here a lot?" She took a bite and pulled a napkin from the holder in the center of the table.

"They've only been open about a month."

She nodded and finished chewing. "Good pizza."

"Some people think it's too salty. There's better pizza in the city."

"Are you in the city a lot?" She took another bite.

"I used to work—Well, when I was younger, yeah."

She met his eyes, curious but seemingly aware when a person didn't want to elaborate, before swallowing.

"True. The city does have better pizza, but"—she set her slice down and wiped her mouth—"I didn't have to wait an hour and this view is less... intimidating here."

There was that word again.

Millie looked over the bay, and her gaze traveled to the homes and storefronts surrounding them in that same way she'd scoured his studio. She seemed to take in everything like it all deserved attention and was totally comfortable in the silence.

Fine. Not a typical tourist, but clearly from out of town. Jules was half-right. There was no point in pretending he didn't find Millie Hart interesting, but he had no intention of more than surface conversation with a woman who was only passing through. He'd made plenty of mistakes in his life, but he tried not to bang his head on the same wall twice.

"Hungry?" He handed her another napkin.

"Starving," she said, adding more hot peppers and moaning. "Much better with more pepper." She wiped her hands.

"Hazel mentioned she was finished with one essay," Drake said.

Millie smiled, her hair was loose and riding every breeze in a swirl around her now-pink cheeks. She explained Hazel's newfound confidence and how helping her had been a boost to her own creativity.

"I've never... mentored, I guess, someone like that. She's so excited about school and life. It's kind of contagious, you know?"

He did but nodded instead of searching for the right words. Amid the muffled chatter of a Friday night, he was taken by how good his town looked on her. He wondered if it helped eclipse some of her frustration at not getting the peace she was clearly promised. Not that he was bringing that topic up anytime soon.

"Thank you for helping her," he said instead.

Millie nodded, seemingly surprised by his sincerity. She swallowed the last of her pizza. "You're welcome. It's my pleasure."

Their eyes held. Saving them both, her gaze slid once more toward the bay before she shrugged and stood. Drake took that as his cue they were done.

Tossing her box, they stepped out from under the restaurant awning. Millie began walking in the wrong direction. He could have mentioned her car was the other way, but he shoved a hand into his pocket and fell into step beside her.

"Have you lived here your whole life?" she asked, pulling the hood of her sweatshirt farther up her neck.

"I have." A simple answer to a question that would have surely made him feel small town back before he knew better.

"Lucky," she said, her voice so soft Drake almost missed it.

Chapter Nine

*E*xpect the unexpected. Millie had almost forgotten one of her mom's favorite lines. Laughter and joy at life's twists and surprises had been so much a part of those first twelve years that after her mom was gone, Millie was certain she'd left behind enough magic to last a lifetime. But lately, her mom's insight and the way she made Millie feel like there was nothing in the world she couldn't do had faded.

Her mom would have loved what the locals called "in-town." She would have never spent three weeks holed up indoors before pulling Millie from shop to shop, trying on sunglasses and crazy hats. She would have chatted with everyone and barged right into Swept Away to declare her daughter was a fabulous romance writer. She was that person, that way. Millie swallowed back the pain of what she could no longer touch and barely access, instead focusing on the unexpected charm of Drake Mortimer Branch.

Her ease with him could be explained away as finally getting out of the cottage and pizza. Pizza made everything better. Or maybe she was able to appreciate Drake now that she understood his motivation. Hazel's reveal about the music had given Millie context and, as with her fictional men, she had a soft spot for men who pushed through and made the best of things. Those guys were always more interesting than some one-dimensional jerk who enjoyed torturing renters with his blaring tunes.

"You'd better be careful, Mortimer, or I might actually think you're a decent guy," she said as they walked past the darkened shops.

"Just like that? I pull out one chair and thank you for helping Hazel?"

"And you pointed me toward Buzz even though I showed up in your town in the middle of the night. Kind of a big deal." She glanced over at him, mocking but so aware how easy he was to be around, especially without the frickin Go-Go's. She'd never thought about it before, but she supposed all people raised in these gorgeous towns were entitled to a little attitude toward tourists, especially the ones who swooped in to gentrify everything locals had known for genera-tions. Millie was lost in what it must be like to have that kind of permanence.

"You named the gnome?" Drake asked.

"Of course. I was going to call him the Key Master, but that felt ominous even for my serious project."

"Ah, yes. How is the serious project coming along?"

She stopped walking, "So nice of you to ask, kind neighbor. It turns out I can write with a bit of music, an unexpected surprise" — she smiled this time at the memory of her mom — "and I'm confident that Alistair is not working for the Russians."

"That's great news." Drake's expression was wide-eyed. "Were we concerned about the Russians?"

"It was touch and go this morning."

They continued on. Millie realized she was nowhere near her car but was enjoying the newness between them. She wasn't ready for the evening to end.

"Did you know Alfred Hitchcock's *The Birds* was filmed in Bodega and Bodega Bay?"

She had not known that little piece of trivia, and he must have seen it on her face because his expression grew lighthearted in a way Millie had not realized she was craving. She'd vowed to close herself off in the name of more serious work, but in truth, without her love stories, she was lonelier than she'd been in a very long time. Sadness was draining, even in fiction.

"I can see you are not the typical tourist."

"Thank you for finally admitting that."

"So, you are eligible for the grand tour of our 'slice of heaven,' as my mom calls it."

Millie's heart tripped at the present tense of his mother. The casual mention and the absence of pain were fascinating, and Millie's mind flooded with questions. *Are his parents married? What does his mom do in her favorite town? Maybe she's the mayor. Is she as tall as Drake's sister?*

No way she was pulling him into her mental swirl, so she went with, "Ooh, I like that visual."

"She does too. She and Nikki had T-shirts made when they were in high school."

Millie grinned. *So, his mom was raised in Bodega Bay too.*

"Does Jules get her... enthusiasm from your mom?"

Drake laughed. "Jules isn't usually *that* enthusiastic."

Something crossed his eyes. Love. Regret. Before she could tell, it was gone.

"Do you have other siblings?" she asked as they stopped in front of a house built into the hill.

"I have two sisters. Jules is the middle Branch and our sister Sistine is the youngest. She lives in Petaluma."

"That explains 'big brother.' You're the oldest." Millie tried to temper the usual mental puzzle she played when getting to know people, but she was drawn to his details.

"I am and she honestly never calls me that, but back to the grand tour. I give you the Inn," he said, arm raised in presentation.

"There's an Inn. Real quick, what differentiates the 'grand' tour from the regular tour?"

He smirked. "You're cute."

She knew she flushed, but surprisingly, she wasn't up for picking herself apart. Drake seemed to have his defenses down, so she gave her internal editor a break.

"The Inn," he said, more playful than she would have thought possible on the morning they met. "The grand tour includes the Inn."

They both laughed, and Millie wondered if he too had grown more comfortable with her or if sharing his home simply brought out the best in him. She had always been most at home in her head. Drake's passion was clearly his reality.

They stood shoulder to shoulder looking up at a huge house built into a fall of mud and green. It lorded over several smaller homes with an enormous wraparound porch that reminded Millie of a crown. The Inn on The Bay, the sign at street level read.

"It's lovely," she said, noticing she could see her breath before sliding her hands into the pockets of her jeans.

"It is. It was built for Miss Crabtree by her fiancé Mr. Levinson back in 1923."

Millie pursed her lips and nodded a bit like she remembered her father doing during museum tours before her mom died.

"I can tell you picked up on the crab reference. Glad you're paying attention. Anyway, Mr. Levinson was marrying up the social ladder and wanted to build his woman a grand house. Story goes he did most of the work himself and was on site for two weeks straight by the end of construction to make sure it was finished in time for her birthday celebration."

"I don't have a good feeling about this story." She winced.

Drake continued. "Showered and shaved, he returned to San Francisco to bring Miss Crabtree up to see her new vacation home."

"He was early or unexpected, wasn't he?"

"He was."

"Oh, poor Mr. Levinson."

"Long story short. Crabtree married Levinson's millionaire boss and Mr. Levinson became a full-time resident of Bodega Bay."

Millie shook her head.

"But."

Millie glanced up hopeful.

"Levinson married an awesome woman who appreciated the garden out back, and they had two sons. Oh, and she used to make all of us caramel apples every Halloween while she was alive, so it worked out for him. Now the house is the Inn, but rumor has it Mr. Levinson is not well these days. So his granddaughter stays with him on and off. Not sure what's going to happen there."

"Still, a happy ending." Millie clapped her hands together. Her father never clapped during tours even back before he'd turned to stone.

"I suppose it is a happy ending. Jules loves that story."

They walked on.

"Okay." He cleared his throat. "Bodega Bay has a population of one thousand and seventy-seven."

"That's more than I thought."

"Yeah, well we're trendy these days. People are buying up our little homes and moving in, but I'm on a roll so I'll stay positive."

"Please do. Let's not get crabby."

Drake tilted his head at her reference and smiled. She might have written him with a forced smile if she'd had to describe him at their first meeting. But now, with his full mouth curved and the crinkles at his eyes, she realized he was a man who smiled often. Maybe not at her initially, but he had things to smile about. And she found she was glad for that.

Millie grew up in the city. She could shuffle and bustle with the best of them and while she'd never mastered what Jade referred to as a "resting bitch face," she wasn't overly friendly with strangers either. None of that mattered as she stood with him, intoxicated by the simple belonging.

They made their way back toward the pizza place. Drake waved to an older couple who were leaving before pointing out Farrah's Florist, which resembled so many pictures Millie had saved in Pinterest. Certain Drake did not have a Pinterest and couldn't relate, she listened as he highlighted another hill where a father and son owned a surf shop as well as the "world famous" taffy shop that she had not noticed on her initial trip into town. He pointed out that the building was pink, white, and hard to miss, but she reminded him that she'd arrived at night and had not left her cottage before her trip out for pizza. She was strangely unaware of how much time she'd wasted.

Drake took a seat on the bench outside the bookstore.

Millie sat too, both of them facing the water.

"And that concludes the tour." He folded both arms over his head.

"That's not much of a grand tour. You haven't told me about the rest of the shops."

"I assumed you were not interested in the bookstore." He propped his legs out in front of him and crossed at the ankles.

Millie glanced over her shoulder at the darkened windows of Swept Away – Books and More before kicking her own feet out, her Converse glowing orange and reminding her of that first morning she'd paired them with her PJs

"You're right. It was a bad grand tour," he said on a breath while they both watched the water.

"It wasn't the worst tour I've ever been on."

"There's a lot more to the town. We have a great roastery."

"I noticed. I have a sixth sense when it comes to tracking down coffee." She looked up at the stars.

"Have you tried it?"

"The Millers left me a couple of bags in the cottage."

"That's right," he said. "I know that they do that because of Lou."

"Coming for you Mother Nature, Lou?"

"The one and only. He brought his bag of coffee over to the studio. Said it was the worst crap he'd ever tasted."

Millie looked over. "That is strange. Why not set it aside and not drink it?"

Drake lifted his brows and waited for her to answer her own question.

"Tourists," they both said.

He let out another deep breath and narrowed his eyes in observation.

"Do you have any siblings, Millie?"

Jolted out of her comfort at the mention of her reality, Millie felt her jaw tighten. "No."

"Huh, only child. Did you grow up in San Francisco?"

"I did."

Drake focused back on the bay. She knew she wasn't forthcoming, but she didn't have anything to add to the loveliness of his town or his life. He would never understand a world like hers, so ending the evening discussing her details was a bit like mixing drinks. He lived within walking distance of everything he loved. What must that be like? Interesting jobs, friends and family who not only shared a childhood but were still around for pizza on a Friday night. Millie could only make up that kind of solid security for her characters.

No one's life was perfect. There were obviously dents and dings in Drake's life, but sitting next to him, the warmth of his body chasing the evening chill, it sure seemed like the rest of his world made whole any remaining scars.

Her life was different. Fractured. No one shared fractured willingly. Drake didn't push and as impossible as it seemed a few days ago, she liked him.

"Tell me about the bookstore, tour guide."

Arms still overhead, he met her eyes. The night sky lit his features and Millie's breath caught. He was a story. A laughter and tear-down-the-cheek story. She could not remember the last time she was this intrigued by a real person.

Drake cleared his throat again and looked over his shoulder. "The bookstore is"— Drake cleared his throat and broke eye contact— "Well, Nikki is my mom's best friend. They grew up together. She's godmother to all three of us."

"Wow. A super best friend."

"Yeah. She might as well be my aunt. She used to be the English teacher at our elementary school. Her husband, Uncle Bart, died only a few years after they were married."

Perhaps there was a sad story attached to every bookstore, she thought but managed to keep to herself.

"He left her with some money, and she opened her store."

"Was it always romance?" Millie asked.

"It didn't even start out as a bookstore." He tapped the heel of one boot on the toe of the other. "At first, she had a gift shop with a small book section, but she chatted with visitors and locals about books all the time, especially romance. The book section became a wall, and by the time we were in high school, the seashell art and souvenir T-shirt racks were gone. Swept Away – Books and More was born." He held up his hands in presentation again.

"You have serious tour guide skills." She grinned.

Drake stood and bowed, so she clapped and got up too.

"Another fascinating fact," he said as they moved back toward the shop windows. "Most of our residents are older, like in their fifties, and we have slightly more men than women."

"How do you—"

"Tyler sits on the town council. He talks town facts and stats for fun."

Millie nodded. She could see that in Tyler.

"What else would you like to know about?" He put his hand back into his pocket.

Everything, she wanted to say but didn't. She peeked into the bookstore window. Even in the darkness, she noticed a couple of large chairs in the back. Trinkets and baskets on the front counter near the register and books on every other surface. Hardback titles written by women, all of whom she recognized and some she considered friends, were artfully propped among the front window display.

Romancelandia was a tight-knit group. Writers could be cut-throat and backstabbing like any other industry, but for the most part, romance writers told stories about love, tried to lead with the same energy, and had the absolute best readers. Swept Away was nothing like her father's bookstore. It was joyful even in the darkness.

She was struck by Drake's reflection in the shop window. So close to hers they almost overlapped. Were she writing a book, she would note the beauty of two very separate people somehow softer and joined in reflection. In her real life though, Millie had spent more time reaching across reflections in a desperate attempt at connection. She needed to remember this wasn't fiction. Bodega Bay was not some made-up town from her imagination and the man standing next to her was real. Millie stepped away. Break time was over. Alistair was the only man in her life these days, and he was dead. Kind of.

86

~

Drake had never shown anyone around Bodega Bay before. He had memories of his parents welcoming and touring with relatives or friends who had moved away, but he'd spent more time rolling his eyes at tourists than anything else. They seemed to descend and run when the weather wasn't just right, or the antiquing not up to their standards. He knew it wasn't fair to generalize, but he'd witnessed enough out-of-towners behaving badly to sway his opinion. Millie, on the other hand, seemed downright enchanted, and he would admit it was fun giving the grand tour.

He'd expected a normal Friday. Dinner with Jules while his parents had movie night with Bella. His sister did most of the talking, sometimes they firmed up plans for Bella's school events or things going on with their parents, and then he went home. This round of Jules's dating game had left him entertaining a woman, which was something he had not done in some time. Not wanting to think about how long it had been since he'd been out with a woman or that his sister's list was spot-on, Drake focused instead on Millie's reflection in the bookstore window. Her errant curls had a life of their own and her still-indescribable blue eyes had so much going on behind them that he found her fascinating and exhausting at the same time.

"Do you enjoy reading?" she asked, still glued to the window like it was her first time seeing a bookstore.

"I like biographies."

"Truly?"

He nodded. "Mostly guys with more money or bigger balls. That seems to be my genre."

She laughed.

"I just finished this massive book by one of our former senators that pissed me off, which I guess is the sign of a good book, right?"

Millie faced him. "I'm not sure that's how it works with nonfiction. Maybe he just pissed you off."

Drake shrugged as they walked toward the gravel lot where they'd parked.

"I also like spy novels, well, some of them. Villains with one arm or a bionic leg, that kind of thing. I think I've always liked the idea of being a villain, even before my hardware." He patted his prosthesis and she nodded.

"There are some heroes with hardware. Iron Man." She scrunched her face in thought. "Thor has the hammer, but that's not a part of him."

He shook his head. "The villains get almost all the hardware."

Their eyes held again.

"You don't read romance?" she asked, a little breathier now.

If he stepped closer, he could—he shook his head, which would have been enough to answer her question and his own sudden need, but he added, "I'm not all that romantic." Like an idiot.

Millie laughed. "Well, at least you're honest."

"That came out wrong. I've never considered myself the kind of person who would read about romance." He tried to salvage some of his cool. Jules would have a field day with this. "They're mostly for women, right?"

"Generally speaking, yes. More women read romance than men, but we have a growing male readership."

"I'm not sure I'd be into reading about two other people falling in love."

"Probably not a romance reader then. You have to be up for the love, the relationship. From there, you can go in a million directions. There are so many subgenres. Like historical. You can even find spy novel romance. Senators, maybe the less-annoying kind, are in romance. It's anything and everything under the umbrella of a happy ending."

"Always."

She nodded as they both moved toward their own cars. "Most of the time. There are always rebels of course, and not all romance has to be happily-ever-after. Some end on a happy-for-now."

Drake wasn't a fan of the for-now endings for reasons he would not be sharing no matter how much he was fumbling over himself.

"But it's kind of a promise romance makes to its readers. We'll take you on a journey. There may be twists and even darkness, but we will always deliver you safely back home with a deep sigh and the relief that things worked out."

"Sounds nice." He'd walked away from his truck and was now back in front of her, inches from those eyes.

"It is," she whispered. Which of course brought him to her lips. Drake stepped back.

So, what was the problem, he wondered. She was practically glowing. Why write about dead-not-dead guys? Maybe she'd given up on happy endings. She'd probably had her heart broken or at least stomped on. He could relate, and somehow that thought steadied him. Neither one of them wanted romance in real life, so that was good. Good news.

"Something wrong?" she asked, and he realized he was nodding.

"No." He looked toward the bay because holy shit his face was on fire.

"It's nice that you've had one place. This place, your whole life," she said, the crunch of gravel beneath their feet as they shifted amplified now that the night had quieted down.

"It has its advantages and disadvantages, same as anywhere else."

He had lived in Bodega Bay his whole life and despite his often-high-speed attempts to break free of childhood and obligations he didn't appreciate when he was young and stupid, this was his place. By choice or "mental speed bumps" as his physical therapist called them, this was where he belonged. He knew nothing about Millie's upbringing or her life as a "big deal" writer, but standing in the parking lot of Bodega's newest pizza place, she looked a little lost. He knew that feeling too.

"Well," she said. "It's getting late and I'm sure you have things to do. And I"—she hesitated and when his eyes met hers—"Thank you for eating pizza with me and for the grand tour."

"Not all that grand," he said.

Neither of them moved. A strand of hair crossed her cheek. Drake fought the urge and balled his hand at his side. She tucked the curl behind her ear.

"I'm sick of the nineties. Any suggestions for tomorrow?" He grabbed the handle of his truck, returning to where they'd started because things made a hell of a lot more sense when she was another annoying renter.

"Tomorrow is Saturday." She opened her car door. "BP Glass Works is closed on Saturday. The sign is posted right by the door."

"You are correct. The sign is posted."

"So I've been told." She ran her hands down her jeans. "Oh, and for the record, I'm not always in my pajamas. Tonight, I even have a bra on."

He lost all sarcasm at the image of Millie in her bra. She was suddenly not the only one with an active imagination. "I do not want to think about your bra," he said out loud like an idiot.

Her face pinked. "Why not? I have great bras." She turned toward her car with joking and dramatic flair as the keys to her rental car flew from her hand.

Drake practically charged to pick them up. So did she. At the touch of her hand, his mind was right back to the bra, specifically taking said bra off and—He pulled his hand back.

Millie stood without a word. They were barely inches apart again, her head bowed this time and super interested in the plastic of the keychain.

"Okay, well, have..." She met his eyes and quickly looked away. "Enjoy your weekend, Drake."

Holy crap, his heart was banging at his chest. Was that heat? Did she look like she wanted—

"Millie?"

Her car door was open before she turned.

"Should I be—" This was nuts. He ran a hand through his hair and tried again. "I'm sure your bras are great."

She smiled and the heat in her eyes was still there. "They are. Glad we got that straight. Goodnight, Drake," she said and was gone inside the car.

On a nod, he closed his door and sat in the quiet warmth of his truck watching Millie back out and head to her cottage. When she drove off, he dropped his forehead to the steering wheel.

I'm sure your bras are great?

He lifted his head and started his truck.

"Christ." He backed out and headed home, admitting only to himself that dating was solidly on the things-he-now-sucked-at list.

Chapter Ten

"The first one was only easy because we did that distraction thing, but I'm telling you I'm not going to make it through two more of these," Hazel said, plopping down on the Millers' couch. "I'm the wrong side of the brain, like the left or maybe it's the right. Which one is science?"

At their second meeting last week, Millie had asked Hazel to make a list of words that described the best parts of her life. Hazel, no longer the confident writer-in-training she'd been after their first two meetings, handed over her list.

"Right brain," Millie confirmed as she looked over Hazel's list of words to build her second, and decidedly more difficult, essay. "And everyone has both sides of the brain, Hazel. One happens to be more dominant."

"Are you sure?"

"I'm positive. I was a train wreck in every math class, but if I didn't have at least a little math sense, I'd be overdrawing my bank account every day." She circled a few words.

"Don't you just use an app for your checking?" Hazel peered over the paper.

"Okay, fine, yes."

They both laughed.

"But you can write." She held Hazel by the shoulders. "You've already written one great essay. Now, let's do it again."

They moved back to the table and Millie set a spiral notebook in front of Hazel, who groaned. "We are going to remove the pressure again. No pressure. The words will help break things down into small pieces. Have you ever heard the·expression about eating an elephant?"

Hazel raised a brow. A perfect brow, Millie noted and kept to herself.

"Okay. Forget the elephant. Maybe you should hold Pop-Tart for comfort." She couldn't find her trusty writing companion, so she moved on. No one understood writing angst more than she did these days, but she knew a bit about Hazel now and the small steps would work. "No wrong or right answers. What do you bring to UC Berkeley?"

"I have no idea. That's the problem. What is the right answer?"

"You tell me." Millie went to the kitchen to refill their popcorn.

"Anything?"

She nodded.

"My parents' money? My gorgeous face and my science mind that might one day cure cancer?"

"Yes." Millie set the popcorn down and pointed to the words she circled on the list.

"Yes? That's it?" Hazel glanced down at her own words.

"Not quite, but this is where we start. These are your truths."

"My truths." She nodded. "Yeah, I like that."

"Words are powerful, Hazel. Don't be so quick to turn your back on them." She grabbed a handful of popcorn, a superfood in Millie's mind. "You will need words for research grants and even texts home thanking your parents for all the opportunities you're about to realize."

It struck Millie that she had become an adult—a woman with information younger women might not have or had not yet experienced. She'd sculpted characters in her head, known where they were going before they did, but helping Hazel was tangible and somehow Millie knew things. What a gift it was to discover she was no longer an insecure child. That even outside of her writing, she'd become strong enough to help another girl find her magic.

"And the money," Hazel said. "The words are important, but the school wants the money too."

Millie laughed. "Right, and the money," she said. "How about investment or commitment instead."

Hazel finally picked up a pen and added those words to her list.

"There's more than one way to say things, several ways actually."

"You probably have a million ways of saying things." Hazel took some popcorn.

"Not lately, believe me." The clench of her own insecurity surfaced, which Millie reasoned away as humility. "So, we have family, confidence—"

A rap on the door stopped Millie midsentence, and she glanced at Hazel like maybe she was expecting a visitor.

She shrugged, as did Millie, and then she shuffled to the door to find Drake and a cat that looked remarkably like—"Pop-Tart. What are you doing?" Millie glanced back in the cottage as if deciphering a magic trick. Her perfect cat had never escaped before.

"Does she ever answer you when you ask her questions?" Drake laughed, Pop-Tart tucked into his arm like she belonged there instead of inside in her favorite sunshine spot.

Fresh out of the shower, Millie noted, moving on to the man in her doorway now that Pop was safe. Wet hair, more herbal than ocean. After a quick intake of breath at that unhelpful and surprisingly vivid image of her less-obnoxious neighbor in a steaming shower, she could hardly blame Pop-Tart. Millie wouldn't mind tucking herself into—*Focus!*

"How, did you? Sorry, I'm stunned that she is... that you're standing at my door."

Like magnets to all things embarrassing, his eyes traveled toward her feet. Not in the mood for mocking, she reached out and took his chin. "No. Eyes right here, mister. This is a writer-friendly zone. No judging. It's all about comfort and fun while we are weaving the words. Do you understand?"

The smile reached right up into his eyes. Distracted for a moment by the scar on his chin, made more noticeable by his clean-shaven face, she remembered she was not alone and pulled back.

"Will there be more bra discussion in the judgement-free zone or only"—he took a closer look for effect—"narwhal slippers. Those are narwhals, right?"

"Yes. Thanks for my cat." She reached for Pop-Tart. Drake handed her over.

"It is news that you have a cat." Still in the doorway, he scratched Pop's head. Always a flirt, she purred and stretched back to give him better access. Well done, Pop, she almost said out loud.

"I do. How did you know she was mine?"

Drake pointed to her pink and black collar. "I recognized the collar. You have a bracelet that's the same colors."

Millie tried to not acknowledge that he too was observant and then ignored her wonderings about the state of her hair. She'd planned on spending the day writing with Hazel, not devoting time to the man who'd gone from showing her the door to imagining her bra in one grand tour.

"Pop-Tart, this is the neighbor who wakes us up every morning. Neighbor, this is Pop-Tart."

"Pop-Tart Hart." There was the smile. "Cute."

Hazel cleared her throat. Millie blinked.

"Right. Um... Hazel is here, so come on in... neighbor."

Drake's expression went wide. "Is she? That is..." He craned his neck and waved as he stepped inside. "It's great that Hazel is here. Hard at work, I hope."

They both sounded like they were in a Public Service Announcement. About what, Millie had no idea, but there they stood while Hazel shook her head and smiled.

"How's it going?" Drake cleared his throat, obviously struggling for his regular voice and flicked Hazel's ponytail before joining her at the table.

"Good." Millie also tried for casual and was less successful, so she sat down.

Hazel let the awkward fall away. "I'm speaking my truth." She grabbed some more popcorn from the bowl.

Drake nodded and looked at Millie for confirmation.

"Hazel brings a commitment to family, her confidence, and her eagerness to make a difference in the world to UC Berkeley."

Her mouth still full, Hazel looked at Drake, whose eyes were wide with interest.

"That's incredible." She swallowed. "I did not say that. I only wrote words, but that's a great answer."

Millie wrote it down above her words. "It's always easier to see a person from the outside."

"That's how you see me?"

"It is." She handed the notebook back to Hazel.

Her expression warmed. "Wow. Thank you."

Millie's chest swelled with pride. In her own writing, it had been a fleeting flutter after a swoon-worthy epilogue or even a great fight scene. Pride did not occupy a permanent place in Millie's psyche, but witnessing Hazel discover herself and all she was capable of was solid and deep in Millie's heart like it might stay for a few minutes.

"Okay, so now what? I need more than one great line. Where do we start?"

"We don't yet."

"No, not the write-but-don't-write thing."

Millie laughed and tried to focus on Hazel as Drake grabbed a handful of popcorn.

"Take those three topics: family, confidence, and desire to make a difference. Write ten words for each—ten words that come to mind when you think about those ideas. Don't worry about my sentence."

Hazel groaned and stuck the notebook and her papers into her backpack.

"Hey, you only have two more to go and then it's done," Drake said.

She stole the last few pieces of his popcorn. "Are you going to tell me what doesn't kill me makes me stronger again?"

"I will if it'll help."

She shook her head, stood, and tossed her backpack over one shoulder before a heavy sigh. "Wednesday?"

"Looking forward to it." Millie opened her arms and Hazel hugged her. "Ten words, and I promise we'll have a rough draft of that second essay next week."

"Are you sure?"

Millie nodded. "I'm a professional. Remember?" She glanced at Drake, who smiled.

"No pressure." Hazel opened the front door.

"That's right."

"Thank you," she said before glancing at Drake. "See you tomorrow?"

"I'll be there." Drake stood. "Boy bands?"

Hazel tilted her head, indifferent.

"I will be in the city tomorrow," Millie said, "so you can break out your very worst playlists."

They both nodded and said, "Hair bands," in harmony.

Hazel laughed. They all did. And then she left for home and "real" homework. Millie walked Drake out right as the sunset touched the bay. She took in a deep breath and despite having again written next to nothing of her own work, she was filled with the most delightful sense of accomplishment.

She wondered if helping was part of being a family, part of a community. She and Jade helped one another. Millie gave to various causes here and there, but she wondered if this kind of one-on-one gave people more of a richer life. She shivered, at first sure it was the evening chill, then realizing Drake was standing beside her.

~

"So, you like popcorn." Drake had no clue what he was saying or why he was still standing outside the Millers' cottage. Cat returned. It was Sunday and he had things to do on Sunday. Didn't he?

She nodded. "So much popcorn." Millie looked at him.

"Are you off to the city for work, or are you going stir crazy in there?" He gestured with his head back toward the cottage.

"No." She looked out at the bay again. "I mean, yes I have some meetings, but no I'm not going crazy. It's... special here."

A grumble of thunder shook the dimming sky.

"Looks like you might get some rain for your dark and stormy story in... London, was it?"

Oh, come on. You know exactly where her book is set. Do better, loser.

"Yes. London. Oddly enough, I'm not a big fan of the rain."

He wanted to laugh, but this was the longest they'd been civil since she arrived and he didn't want to ruin the streak with a few poorly-chosen words. He was sure he would do that several times in the coming months. For now, their mutual appreciation of the setting sun was enough. Instead, he allowed both the silence between them and his growing interest in Millie.

"It was depressing when I was a little girl and now as an adult, it's more trouble than it's worth. I've written some pretty memorable rain scenes, but in the real world, rain can be isolating, right?"

"It can be." He'd spent months in a hospital bed after his accident and several more in his parents' house recovering. It had rained a lot, but overcast days were never the ones that bothered him. "Sunny days are rough too though if you can't go outside."

She glanced at him, the fleeting bits of daylight sweeping across the rounds of her cheeks. He could almost see her fighting back the questions begging to come out. In that moment, he was suddenly eager to answer anything she asked so long as they stayed right where they were.

More thunder and the wind picked up. Millie tucked her hair behind her ears, eventually using an elastic at her wrist to pull it off her face.

The urge to bury his fingers in her hair was surprising. Stupid, but it was there. What then? He was going to kiss her and carry her away to his trailer like some scarred-up villain in one of her romance novels. Or better yet, he'd kiss her, fall all over himself for her, and she'd dump him like a broken bastard. Yeah, he'd been there and done that. So, he'd keep his hands to himself. Enjoying Millie Hart no longer seemed optional, but he had an ever-growing list and she had a whole other life he knew nothing about.

"I see that Pop-Tart Hart is a winker," he said, keeping with safe topics.

"She is. A winker, I like that. Most people lead with 'Aw, what happened to her eye?' I mean, I guess her missing eye is the obvious conversation starter, but her nose is three shades of pink, all four of her paws are a different pattern, and her tail is crazy long and so silky. Why are people automatically drawn to what's missing?" She glanced at him, the obvious similarities he shared with her cat dawning before she shook her head.

Drake laughed.

"Damn it. Scratch all of that. I was rambling and well, it's true, but I was not drawing parallels." She brought her hands to her face. "So not my intention." She peeked at him through her fingers.

"I didn't think you were... drawing parallels. Do you always edit yourself like that? In real time?"

Millie thought about the question. "I guess I do. Wait, are you making fun of me?"

He shook his head. "No. Just enjoying you."

Thunder rolled overhead again, this time louder. He knew this bay like his own heartbeat. It would rain within ten minutes. Guaranteed.

Startled at the noise, she stepped into him, her hand touching his shoulder. Their eyes met and a section of her hair broke free of the elastic. It made no sense that they were still standing there, but—

"I should go," Millie said, pulling her hand back. Maybe she could read minds.

～

Her heart was doing that little dance it did right before someone introduced her or she knew she had to speak next. Not a full gallop like when she was on, but the hop of anticipation when she was on deck. The wind had picked up, plastering Drake's shirt to his chest.

She'd touched him again. She couldn't seem to control herself or her mouth apparently. That bit where she compared a grown man to her cat was brilliant. *Well done.* Millie prepared to leave before she said something else ridiculous.

"Hemingway had cats," he said, still facing her but stepping backward toward his home.

She smiled, taking two steps back too. "He did. But he named his after famous people."

"And they had six toes."

She nodded. "Maybe that's what I need. An army of six-toed cats."

He grinned. "I don't know, you two seem to be doing fine as you are."

The wind messed his hair, his expression playful as he took another step away from her. She nodded and did the same, careful not to trip over the paver she now knew was uneven. She was, of course, still in her narwhal slippers, so that was extra.

"Well." His hand was in his pocket now. "One Pop-Tart Hart returned safely," he said, eyes still on her. Christ, the man was good at eye contact. "Goodnight."

"Goodnight. Thank you for rescuing her," Millie's voice was louder now that she was competing with the howling wind. It was probably going to rain any minute and yet she was still blindly backing up, not ready to leave.

"My pleasure." His voice was louder too.

"Mine too," Millie thought. Out loud. *For God sake, turn and leave.*

"Sorry, I didn't get the last thing you said." Drake was a few steps from his home and the thunder cracked again.

"Oh, nothing. Just... enjoying you too."

Drake laughed and came to stand under the awning of his Airstream. She was now at the cottage gate. She gave a quick wave and opened the gate.

"You know Virginia Woolf wrote most of her stuff standing up. Maybe give that a shot," he was yelling now.

Millie smiled like a fool, her back still to him as she stood at her own front door. This had turned into a game. Silly and fun.

"I did know that, but I can't write standing. Where is this spring of literary knowledge coming from?" She turned, her back resting on the door.

"I made it through English Lit classes in college by hanging onto little things I found interesting. The rest bored me to tears. I would have failed without Hemingway. I wrote my final paper on his cats."

"Where did you go to college?"

"Berkeley."

"Me too."

"I know." He opened his screen door.

"How did you—"

"Google," he said.

"I need to up my Google game," Millie yelled.

Drake smiled and it began to rain.

Just enjoying you. She couldn't have made that up if she'd tried.

Chapter Eleven

*D*rake sat on the dock as the sun rose the next morning. He'd woken up to the sound of Millie driving off a little after five, pulled on his swim trunks, and grabbed a sweatshirt. He didn't have to meet Bella for an hour and a half, plenty of time to knock off what he'd decided would be the easiest on the list. He'd managed subtle flirting without sounding like an idiot and normal conversation with Millie, but he was still a far cry from tackling dating, so jumping off the dock it was.

Legs now dangling over the edge of the worn planks, he knew with or without two arms, one thing was for certain: the water was going to be "as cold as a witch's tit." Another memorable gem from Jules. Drake grinned at the thought of his sister out in the early morning ocean. He was blessed with so many great people in his life, but Jules was his hero. Or heroine? He was sure she'd correct him if he ever had the nerve to share that mushy revelation with her.

First, he needed to stand up, give himself a running start, and jump into Bodega Bay. Still seated and contemplating his approach, he shivered. It had been a few years, but the shock of Bodega Bay water, before July mellowed it out a little, was impossible to forget. Drake looked down into the dark blue and then back up at the shimmering horizon.

He'd sat in this exact spot hundreds of times. From the minute he could swim, which was as far back as his memories went, he'd come barreling down this dock, legs flailing or pulled tight against his chest for the biggest splash. Wood docks held a special kind of warmth deep in their fibers. First splinter, first busted lip when his knee hit his face during an intense round of greatest cannonball. These docks were where he went to think when he fought with his parents or his sisters. He sat with both his prom dates on the edge of these docks to make out and then lie back watching the stars until the sun came up the next morning.

Why hadn't he remembered that story instead of telling Millie he wasn't romantic? He was an old-school romantic.

These docks had welcomed him home after his accident. He spent a year watching them from a distance while his leg and the rest of his body healed. He'd cursed pain, meditated, and learned a solid yoga practice until he recognized himself again. This wood, he thought, running his hand along the grain now, held his secrets and most of his memories. So why was he still sitting there?

It's nice that you've had one place. This place, your whole life. Millie's words whispered through the morning mist, loosening his grip on the dock.

Drake rested his weight back on his right arm and wondered what a grand tour of Millie's life would be like. Was she raised in a world of wealth and privilege, flying off to new places at her parents' whim? Money or not, what was it like to be an only child? Was she close with her mother? Maybe it was the Google search or that it was agreed she was a "big deal," but Drake imagined her life was more glamorous than little old Bodega Bay.

Drake had focused on himself most of his life, first out of arrogance and then to survive. He'd learned to care for and nurture his family and friends. His life was full of knowns, schedules, and lists. He and the people he cared most about were safe.

Maybe that's why he wasn't willing to push his luck. Maybe that's why he was holding back. Maybe that's why the more he wondered about Millie, the more his heart raced. She made him feel that rush, had him marveling at what was right around the next corner, and that, like jumping off a dock he didn't need to jump off anymore, scared the crap out of him.

Closing his eyes as the rising sun chased away the chill, Drake tried to remember the last time he'd run right off the edge and into the bay. It was two nights before his accident. Jules and her then-husband, whom Drake now not-so-affectionately called Ass Hat, and Sistine had all flown in from Seattle for their parents' anniversary. Drake had worked the morning shift on the boats and gone into the city for back-to-back meetings. He was late for the party, two hours late, he remembered now because Jules kept holding up two fingers while they cut the cake. She was relentless back then too.

So many things about those days had blurred together for him now. Too grown up, too busy, and way too intent on kicking off the dirt and salty smell of the town that raised him, the people who loved him. Tired of listening to his sisters give him a hard time that day, Drake grabbed two beers and went down to the dock. It was ink dark that night—weird, the things he remembered.

He was a beer and a half in when Jules and Sistine came barreling down the dock fully clothed and jumped in on either side of him, splashing water all down the front of his clothes. Drake had tossed out his bottles and made like he was leaving, but stopped short, ran down the dock, and flipped into the water to the squeals and delight of his younger sisters. He'd done some cool big-brother things in their childhood, but that night was unexpected.

Drake opened his eyes and rubbed at his left shoulder. Suddenly nothing felt easy. He wasn't that guy anymore. That confidence, arrogance. There was nothing he couldn't do, or at least nothing he didn't think he could do in those days. Before he crashed his bike, he'd never thought about dying or even the possibility of a misstep. Life was an open road, and everything was his for the taking.

That life plan had landed him face down on the asphalt. Before the accident, he'd never stopped to see what he had, what he might be risking in reaching for more. That kind of entitled comfort was even more dangerous than a bike. And now there he sat trying to convince himself it would be simple to surrender what little regained control he had over to the deep blue of the bay. Gripping the wood, he acknowledged the fear, respected it even.

On an exhale, Drake checked his watch. He needed to get moving if he was going to stop for breakfast and be on time to pick up Bella.

"Maybe some other time," he said, patting the dock like an old friend who would understand. He got to his feet and glanced over his shoulder one more time before returning to shore.

~

Millie pulled into the parking garage of Pickman-Brown Literary. She was fifteen minutes early even with her quick detour to enjoy the sunrise near Point Reyes. Tilting the rearview mirror, she smoothed her hair and put on lipstick that had been buried in the bottom of her bag for almost a month. There was no denying the waistband on her skirt was pinching into her sides a little, but her freckles were out and the curls around her face were flecked with bits of gold. A fair trade, she thought, blotting at her lips to soften a color she was no longer sure suited her.

Even with her fierce determination to be absorbed into Alistair's world of dreary skies and woolen overcoats, the sunshine still found her, kissed her cheeks even. She smiled into the small mirror and despite a rough night with little sleep and darkness she hadn't let in for some time, she could still reach the warm memories of her mom. A woman who loved the sunshine and her freckles.

Millie ignored her growling stomach and returned the rearview to its proper angle. She'd been up since three in the morning and still had no appetite for breakfast. Normally a sound sleeper, even with noisy neighbors, she sat bolt right up in the middle of the night. No loud noise or bad dream, she was just wide awake. After staring at the ceiling of the cottage without drifting back to sleep, she'd propped herself up and opened her laptop convinced it was a burst of inspiration. Just the kind of quirky tale she might tell NPR or the LA Book Review when they asked her about a specific ah-ha moment while writing her award-winning novel. Yup, she'd managed that bit of personal fiction right there in bed before turning her attention to said novel.

Alistair's hand lay limp over the cold railing of his hospital bed and—she had not gotten any further before she remembered the trash can in her mom's hospital room. Millie had pushed her laptop aside at the unwelcome memory, squeezed her eyes closed, and begged for sleep. But that trash persisted.

It was a ridiculous thing to recall, but that was all it took for the stinging reality of her mother's final hours to push Alistair aside.

Shallow breath in, shallow breath out. A delicate face hollowed out, chapped lips, and the liquid condensation of a Styrofoam cup filled with melting ice chips. Lying in the bed last night, Millie had tried to push all of it back into the locked room of her mind, but there was her mom's red hair, same color as her own, except dull and brushed smooth against an antiseptic white pillow case.

By three thirty, Millie's eyes were burning as she clutched a yellow gingham pillow and wondered why she couldn't conjure up the sunlight through the blinds of the hospital room that day or the tons of flowers people had sent? Why a trash can of all things? The memory opened up a bit more before she realized she'd spent a lot of time looking at that metal corner can with the clear liner bag. She had tried to be brave and hold her mom's hand tight, as the nurses came in to poke and medicate the woman her little girl mind couldn't fathom living without. She struggled not to cry, but when those days had proved too much, she had looked away, and focused on the trash can.

Where had her father been? That was the last thought Millie allowed in before wiping her adult tears, getting out of bed, and taking a shower.

Sitting in the still early morning quiet of her rental car now, she decided her subconscious was to blame. After Hazel left and Millie had finally pulled herself away from Drake, she'd spent the rest of the night listening to the melancholy taps of rain and reading about death. Before her cheeks had stopped hurting from smiling so much, she'd pulled up the new information she had on death hoping to remind herself why she was in Bodega Bay.

Unable to decide why she hadn't allowed herself to keep smiling, if that was self-sabotage or a true reality check, Millie grabbed her bag off the passenger seat, locked the rental car, and walked to the elevator, her feet already protesting high heels over narwhal slippers.

There were five stages of grief according to the website links Karen had "curated" for her. Denial, anger, bargaining, depression, and acceptance. She'd done some work plotting how to work those into the minor arcs of Alistair's family. She had not yet decided if each phase would manifest itself through weather or all colors in her story, but the research was valuable. It had helped her get into the space of loss. The space she'd told Jade she wanted to find.

Millie pushed the button for the twentieth floor.

"Denial in blue and then maybe yellow for acceptance," she mumbled, patting her leather bag to ensure she'd remembered the pound of coffee she had promised to bring and ignoring the wonder if she herself had ever made it to acceptance. Her father had disappeared somewhere between anger and depression, but when Jade had suggested Millie use her own life experiences to get closer to Alistair's death, she had been genuinely clueless for a moment. That was absurd, wasn't it? Had she forgotten that her mom died? The elevator dinged, Millie rolled back her shoulders, and did what she'd apparently done since before she got her braces off: she focused on the good bits and rewrote the rest.

Chapter Twelve

"Maybe I should grab this kid by the shirt with my Iron Man arm, or better yet, I have a claw attachment. I'll bet that would make him stop messing with you." Drake said as he closed the door behind Bella and they headed off to school.

She bit into her cinnamon roll before shaking her head and grinned.

"I'm serious." He stretched his arm and engaged the fingers. "Or how about this idea? The guy in the book I'm reading is Search and Rescue. Do you know what that is?"

She nodded, licking her fingers so much like her mom it squeezed Drake's heart.

"The men at Fish Fest who fly in the helicopter." She scrunched her face in thought. "And... Tyler's brother."

"Yes. Exactly those guys. So, in the book, the hero..." He used quotes for effect, oddly proud that he'd learned the lingo from Auntie N. "He's pushed from a helicopter by the bad guy and he's like dangling outside this helicopter from his belt loop."

Drake's storytelling skills were in full effect and Bella belly laughed.

"You're going to hang Kyle from his belt? From his belt in a helicopter because he's calling me names?" She stopped walking and quirked a brow. "I think we might go to the principal for that."

Drake quirked his brow back at her. "Ya think?" He rubbed his jaw and they continued on their way to school. "Okay, well something else. I'll keep reading."

Bella shook her head. "That's a book. A story. You're not going to find answers in there."

"Why not?"

"We can't do things that are in books. They're make-believe," she said, throwing her trash away as they approached the gate. "If we could, then"—she tapped the side of her head—"we would buy a wand."

"I like where this is going. I'm sure Amazon has wands. We could have one by midweek. Go on."

Her eyes went wide with the idea. "With a wand we could Riddikulus him." She made a swirling motion and brushed her hands together like all her problems were solved. Drake wished he could make life that simple for her.

"Okay, true, but that's assuming Kyle is a boggart."

When Bella and Jules moved home, Drake had Auntie N make a romance exception and order all the Harry Potter books. Bella was almost five, but she only had half-day kindergarten, so when she got home, she would grab her blanket and meet Drake on the couch. He was a permanent fixture on his parents' couch that first year, so she always knew where to find him.

It started with him reading to her and eventually they were alternating. Drake used to say that J. K. Rowling was Bella's reading teacher and that's why she had such an "enchanted" vocabulary, but even with that, he was still surprised she'd remembered the details after all these years.

"Is he the thing you fear most, Beauty?" Drake's pulse quickened because if his sweet niece told him this Kyle guy was her boggart, he wasn't sure what he was going to do, but it would be a hell of a lot more than magic.

"Nah, he's only a boy."

Drake exhaled and handed Bella her trumpet. He wanted to tell her that boys often grew up to be boggarts but decided to save that discussion for when she was much older.

"So, back to me pinning him to the wall with my Iron Man claw?"

She shook her head, and Drake leaned down so she could kiss him on the cheek. "Let's keep things in the real world, okay?" She patted him on the shoulder and agreed to let her and the teacher handle Kyle. For now.

With Bella safely delivered, Drake got to the studio, cranked up a seventies playlist, and worked through the day's projects with Esteban and Hazel. After dropping the outgoing online orders off at the post office barely under their five o'clock cutoff, Drake met Tyler at the new gallery space. It was barely eight hundred square feet, but it still felt like a big step.

"So, we're going to do this?" Drake said when the realtor left to grab the paperwork.

"We are. Second thoughts?"

"No. Not exactly. I've never pictured my stuff as gallery material, ya know? We make things people use."

"Aesthetically pleasing things people use, and we already have inventory. Those vases and the bowl you made last year. We can mix in some functional pieces too. They all deserve a space."

Deserve.

He wondered if Jules would add that to her list too. Drake had been out of practice deserving anything since the accident. Something about escaping death made a guy feel like he was on borrowed time and deserving of nothing extra.

"Deserve is a strong word."

Tyler shook his head. "Don't do that. Your work deserves a great space."

Drake shrugged.

"Okay. How about... I'll have an office if I ever decide *I* deserve one, and there are a bunch of shelves where we can store your functional stuff. Maybe people will buy some of it. Better?"

Drake grinned. "Better."

"This doesn't have to be pressure. How long have we known each other?"

"Forever."

"Have I ever steered you wrong?"

Drake raised a brow, and he waited for Tyler's memory to kick in.

"Other than that time," he scoffed. "I had no way of knowing my very attractive coworker would turn out to be a stalker. Even you"—he pointed—"thought she was stable in the beginning."

Drake laughed. "It was unexpected. So, no. You have never steered me wrong where it counts."

"So, we're signing?"

Drake ran a hand along the painted block of the back wall and nodded. "Yeah. Two years?"

Tyler nodded.

They signed the papers, shook hands, and after a quick rundown of the alarm system, they were again alone.

"Do you have room on that notepad of yours to get a beer? I think this calls for at least one toast."

"I'm done for the day." Drake faced him. "One more thing. I'm not going to have to dig up my old suits and walk around telling people about my process, am I? Tiny sandwiches and champagne?"

"Yeah," Tyler deadpanned it. "That's exactly what I had in mind. Bodega being such a highbrow crowd and all, definitely the tiny sandwiches."

"You know what I mean."

"Twist yourself into one of your poses and breathe, man. This is simply another avenue to sell your work."

"Our work."

"Drake, it's your work. Christ, it's been years. You can give yourself something. Our business, but your work. This doesn't change anything. We will hire someone to work the gallery and tourists will love you."

Sensing Tyler's segue, Drake turned to leave.

"Some might say the tourists are already taking an interest." His less-than-subtle friend closed the door they would refinish at some point with a custom piece inlay.

Drake ignored the comment. "Where are we getting a beer?"

"One of the same two places we always get beer."

"Oysters or burgers?"

"Burgers. Fish Fest is next weekend and we'll be up to our asses in oysters."

Drake agreed and clicked open his truck.

"So, do you think we'll have a busy tourist season?" Tyler asked.

Drake stopped short of climbing in, stepped up on the running board and glared at Tyler's big stupid grin over the top of the cab. "Drop it or I'll tell Jules you had a crush on her for all of fourth grade."

Tyler busted out laughing, but he was still blushing. "Does this blackmail shit you pull ever work?"

They both slid into the truck.

"Seriously, has anyone ever said, 'Oh, no. Don't tell anyone. I promise to—'" Tyler stopped short when he nearly closed the door on his leg. "Goddamn it."

"It's working right now. Look at you all flustered and much less annoying."

Tyler shook his head and brushed at his pant leg. The awkward his friend had dealt with growing up was barely visible now under his expensive clothes. Loosening his tie, he made to lower the window right as Auntie N knocked, scaring the crap out of them both. Her red-rimmed glasses and multicolored scarf accented her dark hair with a shock of white in the front.

His heart rate seemingly back to normal, Tyler lowered the window.

"Took you long enough. What'd you think I was, a carjacker?" She pushed a wrapped banana bread, the only baked good she made, and a card into the cab of the truck.

"Sorry. I was... struck speechless by your gorgeous scarf," Tyler said.

Auntie N batted her eyelashes and mussed Tyler's hair. "Oh hush, you. The card and my hard work in the kitchen are to welcome you two boys to the neighborhood."

"Thank you," Drake said while Tyler fixed his hair.

"I'm excited to have some strong labor next door."

"We're opening a gallery." Tyler smelled the banana bread.

"Don't get all toity with me. Gallery owners can still lift books. I'm remodeling."

Tyler's eyes shot up. "Again?"

"Business is booming. People love love."

Drake could see the need for gossip in his godmother's eyes before she said another word and if he didn't know she would chase them both down, he would have driven away. The last thing he needed after Tyler's little jabs was for her to—

"Speaking of love books, are you enjoying Millie's?"

And there it was.

Drake nodded and Tyler grinned like a guy who, well had some dirt on his best friend.

"It's interesting," Drake said, thinking he might save this. "I'm about halfway through and the stuff about Search and Rescue is great."

"Millie always writes awesome careers. Before this one, well the brothers are twins, you picked up on that, right?"

Drake nodded. Tyler raised his hand like they were in school, barely able to contain the smugness. "Sorry to interrupt, but what is the name of Millie's action-packed and incredibly-masculine book?"

"*Rescue Me.*"

Drake closed his eyes. When he opened them, Tyler was still brows up, lips pursed, and nodding.

"So, the one you're reading is the second book," Auntie N continued, oblivious to Drake's humiliation at not only reading a romance, but one written by the very neighbor he was attempting to downplay. "The first one is about his brother who is a forensic pathologist. Unbelievable how she adds just enough detail and then the romance. God, have you met Nat yet?"

"I have."

"She's smart as a whip and boy does she put Brix in his place. He thinks he's tough, but she's tougher."

Tyler looked at Drake.

"What? It's a good book."

Tyler mouthed *Rescue Me* and put his hand under his chin. Drake laughed.

Auntie N patted the truck. "All right, well I need to get back in for book club. You two behave."

They waved and drove up the road in silence.

"Okay, so this is progress. We've now established that you're into the new neighbor."

"It's a book." The first rule of lying: less is more. Drake remembered this time.

"Uh-huh." Tyler let him off easy. "Anyway, back to our new space. We're kind of the official now, right? I mean who would have thought Pace and Branch—"

"Branch and Pace," Drake clarified.

"It sounds better the other way. It's not an ego thing, purely—"

"The way it trips off the tongue," they both said on a laugh.

Drake took his first deep breath since they'd shook hands with the realtor. BP Glass Works was a success. They'd built everything on a friendship that started in the first grade and had never faltered. From Drake getting his first black eye their freshman year in high school when Danny Morris pushed Tyler against the lockers and asked if his mom bought her clothes at the thrift store too, all the way up to Tyler picking Drake up, literally, for at least a year after his accident.

This business wasn't a fleeting whim, he reminded himself as they parked. They had made it past the three-year mark. They were brothers in every way that counted, and they never let the other feel sorry for himself or bow his head. Ever. They'd sat shoulder to shoulder through twenty-seven years of life. Some of it awful, but most of it a blast. A little gallery expansion changed nothing.

~

Millie had a habit of avoiding headshots and publicity photos, which explained why even before she'd left for Bodega Bay, Jade had locked down a morning full of too much eye makeup and blouses never to be worn again. After the photographer left, Millie made a long overdue Facebook Live appearance on her VIP reader page, signed advanced copies won in a promo the publisher put on, and answered questions for three blog interviews due out on the book's release day. By the time she and Jade made it to a late lunch, Millie was exhausted and even though she missed the friend side of Jade, the agent part was relentless. After nearly a month at the Candy Land cottage, it seemed difficult to resume life as she'd left it in the city. That had nothing to do with Drake, she told herself. Alistair was the reason she was in Bodega Bay. Drake was a flirtation, a distraction and nothing more.

"So, how's the grumpy book coming?" Jade asked after they'd finished their pasta and the waiter refilled their wineglasses.

"Good. You know, early stages, but good."

"You look fantastic. That little cottage agrees with you."

Millie fluffed her hair and pursed her lips.

"Are you sure there aren't any hot fishermen I need to know about?"

Millie nodded and sipped her wine. "Just me and the gnomes."

After catching up on all the agency gossip and reviewing the changes to her upcoming tour schedule, Jade grew serious.

"Now that you won and are settled in, would you mind telling me what prompted this change of direction? I know your father is involved, but did something extra happen because he's been a pain in your—"

"Last Christmas Eve," Millie blurted before she had time to change her mind. She hadn't told a soul why she chose to step away from romance but being in Bodega and after last night's dive into death, something in her wanted to share. At the concern in Jade's expression, Millie changed her mind.

"Mil, I'm usually fine with your recoil, but please let me in on this one."

"Last Christmas Eve," Millie started but paused for a sip of wine, hoping it might give her courage to tell what she knew was going to sound absurd. "I found myself on Brompton by my father's bookstore. I walk that street every two weeks or so. Sometimes I stop in, but mostly I walk by and check from the window that he's still alive." She took another sip. "It was around eight o'clock and unusually cold. I remember because my nose was kind of runny and I'd worn a scarf that was too thin."

The waiter dropped off their desserts.

Millie picked up her fork in the hope she could stop mid-story. "And?"

She sighed and continued. "That night I had decided to go in. I'd picked up my father's favorite Pinot Noir and wanted to wish him a Merry Christmas."

Jade inhaled like she already knew the ending, and Millie felt like poor predictable Mr. Levinson mindlessly building a dream house for Miss Crabtree. Everyone seemed to know Millie's father couldn't care less, except Millie.

"Anyway, I'm sure you've guessed the rest. I stopped short before I crossed the street. He was having a holiday party. Thirty or so people, lots of turtlenecks, and they already had red wine."

Jade gulped the rest of her wine like she needed it.

"Are you sure you want to hear the rest? We're having a lovely time and this next part is where I sound pathetic."

Jade gestured with her hand. Millie continued.

"In fairness to my sad self, the ambiance was kind of great. The shop glowed like one of those houses in a winter painting and I... was glued to that window. Freezing my ass off, but glued. I'd walked by thousands of times and it always aches, but there was something about that night. This perfect lilt of music, laughter I could hear from the street, and my father, one hip propped on that couch in his front room. Do you remember the couch?"

Jade cleared her throat and gave a small nod.

"He was in deep conversation with a woman in a velvet blazer. Then more laughter and a big toast. They were all telling stories I couldn't hear, eating food on little plates I couldn't taste." Millie realized she was twisting her napkin.

"The only way I can explain it is my normal longing turned desperate. I sat on that bench across from his store and cried like a baby. A sad, left-behind baby."

Jade bit the inside of her lip, her face trying to stay neutral for Millie's sake but still scrunched at her brow.

"That night I went home and decided if I could write the right book, win the right awards, maybe I could get my father back. Maybe he would laugh with me. Love me." Millie let go of the napkin, cleared her throat, and took a bite of her cannoli. She didn't want Jade to say anything. There was nothing to say.

"There it is. The sad truth." She wiped her mouth and finally met her friend's eyes.

Jade paused for a minute, and Millie knew she was searching for something to say. This awkward scramble for the right words was exactly why Millie usually kept the ugly parts of her life to herself. Everyone had problems. Dysfunctional families, sickness, and sadness were everywhere. Jade could certainly relate to life being not as she'd planned, so that wasn't what kept Millie from sharing. It was that even compared to most of the ups and downs of living, her story was heartbreaking and so senseless.

She wanted things to be different. Her mom was gone. There was no changing that, but part of Millie believed there was a chance, if she tried hard enough, she could write her way back into her father's heart.

"I don't expect you to understand," she finally said, hoping to rescue her friend.

Jade pushed her wineglass away and poured them both coffee. "Listen, no one has more faith in you than me." She reached across the table and took Millie's hand. "You are the most brilliant and brave woman I know and if you—" She let go when her eyes welled, shook her head at whatever else she was going to say, and poured cream into her coffee instead.

Millie swallowed back her own emotions. She was so tired of crying over the past. "The good news," she said, taking another bite of her cannoli, "is that I'm pushing my creative boundaries."

"True." Jade nodded.

"And it is good for me to get out and explore new settings."

"Also, true." Jade ate her dessert. "But let us agree that it's super selfish of you to leave me all alone."

Millie laughed and the sadness fell away. Jade truly did always know how to fix things.

"I mean come on. Yesterday I went to the movies alone. Do you know how hard that is on a recently-divorced woman?"

"You've been divorced for two years."

Jade shrugged. "I need a date, and I'm not doing it without you."

"Stop. You can wait. I've already paid for the cottage and I'm working. I have an outline and everything. My main character is named Alistair and he's lovely so far. Dead, but he'll be lovely in flashbacks."

"I hate flashbacks."

"You'll love these."

Jade was a great agent: intuitive and dialed into Millie like no one else. For those same reasons, she was a nosy friend. The waiter refilled their coffee, buying Millie a bit of time, but she knew she wasn't getting off that easy.

"I still think you're holding out on me," she said, dabbing at the powdered sugar on her plate and bringing it to her mouth. "No hot guys? Are you sure?"

Millie broke and told Jade about Drake and the rest of the people she'd met in Bodega Bay with as little detail as her persistent friend would allow. It was a relief to end on a happy note. Even in the city, the bay's happy rubbed off.

They walked back to the office and Millie promised to keep Jade posted on her progress.

"Alistair's and maybe your own story," she said before kissing Millie on both cheeks and heading off to another round of meetings they both knew would take her well into the evening.

Millie should have taken her valet ticket straight to the garage and gone back to Bodega Bay, but childhood gripped like steel, and even though she knew better, she went for a walk and tried again.

Chapter Thirteen

*H*azel lowered the music. Drake and Esteban both looked up quickly before returning to the pitcher they were working on together. Sheers were always tough for Drake, as was anything that required a lot of detail in his fingering. He could turn forever, but he needed Esteban or Hazel's help cutting glass and adding most flourishes.

"What's up?" Drake asked as Esteban cut off the piece they'd added.

"I need your thumbprints on these," she said, gesturing with her head toward the glasses she finished for the new gallery. The first glasses BP Glass Works ever sold were pints dented with a slight thumb imprint that made them easier to hold. They were still the most popular item on their website, and Tyler wanted some in the new space.

"Use your print." Drake grabbed a piece of wet newsprint to shape the base of the pitcher, his aching shoulders reminding him why custom orders were a bitch.

"Actually?" Hazel said. He glanced up quickly and noticed the honor right there in her expression. She was a great kid, well, young lady. It was fitting that her thumbprints would be in the gallery since she'd probably set the world on fire one day soon.

Drake nodded as he adjusted his angle so Esteban could place the handle.

"Cool. Thanks."

"Don't screw them up." He glanced over at her again with as serious of an expression as he could muster, but her eyes went wide, and he cracked up.

She laughed too.

"Hey," Esteban said, setting the long ornate handle. "There's no laughing in glassblowing."

At that, they all laughed, and Esteban admired their latest creation.

"What are we laughing about today?" Tyler arrived holding a roll of what Drake knew were build-out plans for the new space. "Nice pitcher." He tossed his bag onto a chair and the plans on his desk.

Esteban reiterated his no-laughing-in-glassblowing joke and Tyler shared his adventures in construction, complete with a story of him almost tripping and falling flat on his face in front of the lead contractor.

"I think it's time we addressed the elephant in the studio," he said, out of nowhere and giving Drake no time to prepare. "According to Nikki, who heard it from a reliable source, someone was not only out on a Friday night past his bedtime, but on a date." Tyler crossed his leg for dramatic effect. Navy blue pants today and a plaid shirt that reminded Drake of a Creamsicle.

"With who?" Hazel asked before figuring it out and pointing. "Ooh, Millie."

"Mildred," Esteban said.

"No, we're not doing that anymore. Keep up, Pop." She kissed his cheek and sat next to Drake like proximity gave her a larger slice of the gossip.

He took the clipboard off Tyler's desk and began checking orders. At the silence and the spin of noise from next door, he looked up to find all three of them still waiting for a response. Drake had grown up in a house full of nosy women and an even nosier father. He was a pro at this "rumor has it" game.

"Why are you looking at me?" He shrugged for added casualness. "Tyler's playing make-believe again. Speaking from the real world. Those wineglasses are done and ready to go out."

"I'm not making anything up. Were you or were you not eating pizza with our new—"

"She's not that new anymore. She's been here a month now. And I have some tea to add when you're done," Hazel said.

"Tea?" they all said. Drake was temporarily grateful for the distraction.

"Yeah, tea. Spill the tea?" She rolled her eyes. "Gossip. Wow, you guys are so old."

"Okay, well hold your tea, but first, were you eating pizza on Friday, Drake?"

"With our new pretty neighbor," Esteban added.

"At night and under the stars." Hazel batted her eyelashes.

Drake laughed. They were good. "Not that it is any of your business, but nothing is getting done until I come clean, so here goes. Yes, I was eating at Dough Bird on Friday night with... my sister."

"Ooh, how is the new place?" Esteban asked, again a potential reprieve. If anyone was going to take them off topic, it would be Esteban. Although he was Jules's source, so it was hard to trust anyone these days.

"Not bad. Jules thinks it's salty, but she's picky." Drake kept it simple.

Tyler snorted.

"What? What was that snort?"

"Basic farm animal acknowledgment that your sister is picky. No need for redirect. Back to our question."

"Our neighbor ordered takeout and Jules went over to introduce herself."

"And?" Hazel scooted closer.

"And Jules pretended she had somewhere to be, so I gave Millie a quick tour and we both drove away in separate cars."

"Wait, so when did you talk about her bra?"

Esteban and Tyler gasped like they were watching a movie while Hazel nodded. "That's the tea! Millie was helping me with my essay and Drake rescued Pop-Tart."

Both men looked confused.

"Her cat."

They nodded.

Holy shit!

Drake exhaled. "There was no pizza date. Her cat did get out when Hazel went over to work on her essay, that part is true."

"And the bra?" Tyler asked.

"When we were walking to the parking lot, she joked about writers occasionally wearing bras in public. That's all I'm saying. You are all clearly in need of excitement. It was innocent."

Tyler started to add something.

"And"—Drake held up his hand—"yes, I am reading her book. It's called *Rescue Me*. It is a romance and it's good." He exhaled again. "Anybody else?"

"Does she have a boyfriend back home?" Hazel always was the brave one.

"I don't know."

"You don't know, or you didn't ask?" Tyler smirked, clearly enjoying himself.

"Both."

"What did you two talk about after I left the other day?" Hazel asked.

"Her new book."

"Did you pay for her pizza?" Esteban set a box and the wineglasses on the table for packing.

"I did not."

"What about... you know? Did you?" Tyler waggled his eyebrows.

"Ogle her like a creepy stalker? No." Drake closed up the box.

Tyler grabbed the tape. "I don't know. Kind of sounds like things are heating up."

"But he didn't pay, and he didn't kiss her," Esteban, Drake's new best friend even if he was a spy, added.

Drake's face warmed at the mention of kissing Millie, but he laughed it off before anyone noticed.

"He did give her a tour in the moonlight," Hazel added with a dreaminess she didn't often let show. "He can't stand most tourists and we still have the bra."

"Eh, I think he can do better." Esteban loaded the box onto the cart. "Let's wait for the real date."

Tyler glanced over and pointed. "Why are you smiling?"

Drake grabbed the remote and turned up the music even though Chase had probably left for lunch already. Tyler said something else, but Drake held a hand to his ear in a sorry-can't-hear-you gesture.

~

The familiar ding from somewhere in the air of Hartfield's Books should have been comforting. It should have welcomed her home and into a space where her father, the man who raised her after her mom died, toiled away his days and most nights. That's how Millie would have written the opening scene, but instead, her neck tightened as the door closed and the bite of the air conditioning reminded her that things were rarely as they should be.

Cancer, ovarian to be specific, had taught Millie a lot about the downside of expectation. Taught her father too, she supposed, not that they'd ever discussed her mom's death or any emotion that seeped past a quick pat on her head during the funeral. After her mom had "passed on" as someone who read at the funeral put it, Millie and her father had come to a fork in the road. She hadn't known it then, but as she got older and spent some time looking at why things were as they were, sometimes with a nice lady in an armchair, she'd come to understand that her father chose the darkness. He seemed to thrive in it. His heart broke at having love snatched away from him, the same psychologist hypothesized, and Millie took the other road.

Somehow in her twelve-year-old wisdom, she had figured out that life was short, and so explained her "zest for life." She too thrived in her choice. She'd held tight to the good memories of her mom and made every effort to see the glass half-full. All of that sounded great in the comfortable beige and ivory office, but in practice it meant that she and her father became strangers.

The upside was that Millie parlayed her "zest" into writing and surrounding herself with love and happiness. Even if she hadn't found her person yet, she'd created stories of love and fun. Brought people to life who struggled, sometimes made bad decisions, but found the joy.

Later in life, another therapist had once asked Millie if she thought losing her mother had brought her to write the kinds of books she wrote. Millie thought about it and replied, "I think having my mother for the short time I did brought me to writing the books I write."

Dragging her hand down the tightly-packed spines along the shelves of her father's bookstore, Millie smiled at the thought of her mom. Lavender and uncontrollable curls like her own. She was spontaneous before Millie knew what that word meant. She was forts made from bedsheets and picking flowers. She was—

"Mildred. Well, this is an unexpected pleasure." Her father came out from the back office.

Judy Marie Amherst-Hartfield was nothing like the man she'd married. Although Millie remembered a time when her father was, well, her dad, he was simply that stranger she'd left at the fork in their road.

Leaning forward, she kissed her father on the cheek. Smooth and soap. Nothing unexpected, not one hair out of place. "Hi Dad. I'm in town for the day and I thought I would—"

"Drop by unannounced. Is your phone not working? You insisted I buy one of those blasted things. I'd think you could use it to at least prepare me for your arrival."

"Prepare?"

His brow crinkled in confusion, like he'd missed some custom of which he was unaware.

Millie didn't bother arguing. She had wasted far too many hours taking that route in her teen years. She'd come to accept what she couldn't change. Another therapy nugget. Christ, she was the picture of control with all the answers to the whys and hows of their unhappy little relationship. So why did she still want to shake him and yell, "What happened to you? Why are you so—"

"Tea?" Her father asked, stepping behind the small counter toward the back of the store. Millie nodded and ran her hand along the marble swirls of wood. When she was little, she used to get lost in the curves before they disappeared behind the counter.

"Do you still do that sugar nonsense?"

Millie nodded again. No need for real words; she'd played this scene with her father hundreds of times.

"How many?"

She held up three fingers.

"Three lumps of sugar for one small cup of tea?"

More nodding. Millie scratched her head. Maybe she'd break out in hives and collapse right in front of him. Maybe he'd stop critiquing her then. There she went with the maybes again. She truly was the eternal optimist.

Her father set a teacup on the counter in front of her and stirred his own while he leaned on the wall where he kept posters of upcoming readings and events. He took his tea black, so she never understood what he was stirring. When she'd asked him about it one day he had told her that he enjoyed the sound. It had grated on her ever since.

There was a small round table near the travel books. They could sit there, share a cup of tea, and catch up. They could, but instead they stood as they always did and tried to navigate the silence.

"I heard you had Stephen Marshall in to read his latest last week." Nothing.

"He's one of your favorites, isn't he?" she asked.

Her father shrugged and sipped his tea. "His last two efforts were strictly commercial and he's a drunk."

Wow. Millie almost spilled her tea.

"I thought drunks were good. Dark and brooding."

"What's that supposed to mean? When have I ever said excessive drinking was an admirable trait?"

"You haven't. Can we sit?" She gestured toward the table.

"I don't have time." He finished his tea and motioned for her cup. Millie took one last sip and returned the cup to him half full. "I have a meeting in fifteen minutes and a reading to prepare for. You should have called."

"Who's reading tonight?" she asked, ignoring the rest of what he said.

"Casandra Rye." He returned after setting the cups in the back sink.

"Ooh, mystery. Fun."

"You read her?" He walked toward the front of the store, stacked a group of magazines that did not need stacking before not so subtly nudged her out.

"I read her first one. What was it? Something about a kayak, I think."

"A Single Canoe."

"Right."

"Not all that difficult of a name," he muttered.

Millie rarely found things in common with her father, but they both muttered. Or maybe he muttered, and she mumbled. It would follow suit that even that would be different.

"It was short-listed for the Booker Prize."

"I remember."

"Just not the title."

"I'm sorry?" She knew what he meant, but sometimes she enjoyed throwing pompous back at her father. It was a little game she played to ease some of that grab-him-and-shake-him tension. He never assumed she was smart enough to mock him, so it worked out well.

"You remembered the short list, but not the name of the book."

She let the comment go and said what she had come to say.

"I took four months off before my next book tour to write a literary novel. Turn of the century London and present day."

Her father pursed his lips. "Interesting."

She nodded. "I've finished an exhaustive outline."

Her father was barely listening, and Millie felt like a child explaining a painted pasta necklace she was making in school. Another memory of the Mother's Day she had actually presented a pasta necklace teased at the cold center of her father's store.

"Not now," she said out loud and then lost her train of thought. Her book, her real book, right. "So," she rolled her shoulders back and followed her father, who was now adjusting a display of cookbooks toward the front window.

"I'm thinking of using color for the—"

He spun around, a large book with golden loaves of bread on the glossy cover in his hand. "You know, Mildred, I'm surprised you're not married yet."

He might as well have said he was a Russian spy. The shock she knew was on her face would have been the same.

"This talk of real writing will certainly require you to go back to school, and maybe that time has passed for you." He propped the cookbook up on one hand. "A better investment might be getting married and parlaying your... talents into something like this. Cookbooks are big and certainly more respectable than what you're currently writing."

"What did you just say to me?"

Her father rolled his eyes and returned the book to the display. "It was a suggestion. Good God, there's no need to get hysterical."

Millie stepped back like she'd been struck and scrambled to order her thoughts. There were so many things she'd thought to say to him over the years. He'd basically told her she had a better chance of whoring herself out to the first willing man and baking fricking bread than she did writing a literary novel. Setting aside what an insult his misogynistic scenario was to cookbook authors, every part of her pride demanded that she stand up for herself. Now.

At a minimum she needed to represent the rich and delightful world of romance that had given her so much. But he'd been insulting her craft for years along with every author who stood proudly in the genre and Millie had never done more than dodge and ignore. He couldn't hold a candle to any of those writers or their readers, and yet there she stood.

"You have never once—" *supported me, never once even asked about my writing or my reviews. I've spent years celebrating every milestone and accomplishment with Jade or alone.*

Millie couldn't breathe and if she did manage to find oxygen, she was going to cry and that could not happen. She might not be able to form a complete sentence and she was surely leaving without her pride, but she would not cry in front of this man.

"Take care, Dad."

"You as well, Mildred. Give my suggestion some thought." He nodded, and like a cue for a prearranged scene change, she stumbled out as customers arrived, morphing her father into a human being. A bookshop owner thrilled to discuss preferences with perfect strangers.

The sun was setting and she again longed for the solitude of Candy Land. Like the pitiful child she clearly still was, Millie watched her father from his store window. Alone now in his own world, his eyes sparkled in conversation as he offered a book from the Owner Recommendations shelf.

The woman took the hardback. Millie couldn't make out the title, but her companion said something and the three of them laughed. As they moved toward the register, her father noticed her watching from the street. His face dropped for an almost imperceptible beat. For the seemingly millionth time, Millie wondered what caused that drop. What was he thinking watching his only child standing on the edge of a world he'd quietly escorted her from when she'd needed him most? Was his heart broken too as the psychologist had said? Did she remind him of his pain or was she truly foolish and it was as simple as he'd detested her all along? Millie ignored the tears that again threatened her still camera-ready eye makeup and walked away.

All her life, she had infused people with emotions beyond their capabilities. At least, that's what her last boyfriend told her while he packed his things and left. She questioned their connection. Told him she didn't think they were truly in love. He'd laughed at her and told her she needed to grow up before any guy would think about marrying her.

Before any guy would think about marrying her.

That's what he'd said wasn't it? Or maybe it was "consider" marrying her.

Given her father's words, it was a short leap for her mind to recall other failed relationships. She didn't have a tremendous history with men in the nonfiction sense. The few guys she had dated inevitably felt stunted when up against her limitless feelings. Millie had believed that people loved with their whole heart and often, not that she thought about it much anymore, that had left her the fool when things ended.

Fool or not, none of it mattered as long as she had her writing. Turned out her teachers were wrong when they said writing would help Millie sort through her loss. Writing had given her a back door to her pain. Her stories were not about sadness or the everyday cruel things people did to one another. Instead, they were the pure delight that emerged from the bits of love Millie remembered and still clung to with all her might.

Maybe at the fork in the road Millie hadn't chosen a different path. Maybe she'd slipped out that back door before her father had a chance to pull her under. Maybe she did that with all the ugly in her life. Worst of all, maybe she was "pushing sugar-dusted schlock," as he'd once said, while the rest of the world was rooted in reality. Whatever the reason, he was embarrassed by her unwillingness to shut down her feelings, that she'd gotten "hysterical."

As she drove over the bridge toward Bodega Bay, Millie felt certain there wasn't a best-seller list in the world that would ever change his mind.

She arrived back at the cottage in a daze. It was a little after four, but she changed into her pajamas anyway and made a fresh batch of popcorn before crawling into bed with her laptop. The Millers seriously needed a television. Pop-Tart curled at Millie's side and they watched Netflix until they both fell asleep.

Chapter Fourteen

The next morning, Millie barely noticed the disco playlist as she flipped to a clean page in her journal and began, as she'd instructed Hazel, finding her truth. Teaching and doing proved to be very different things as she slowly unpacked her memories. She had not revisited her own story beyond the best sellers and fun facts found on her website for a long time. The little girl who stayed at school during holidays, eventually sharing Thanksgiving dinner with her teacher's family instead of her father was a tale that only evoked pity, so she'd stopped telling it.

Millie had not wanted the life she was left with after her mom died or the sympathy from her classmates when they received cards on birthdays and just-because dinners with their parents throughout the year. Instead, she wanted to be seen for who she was, so she'd changed the narrative.

She supposed those were her first stories. When she was old enough to travel unaccompanied, she bought her own ticket and showed up on her father's doorstep, explaining to her friends meeting their families at the airport that her dad couldn't pick her up because he was "opening the cabin for ski season" or "tending to a beloved grandmother who had taken ill." It had been easy to embellish the blank notebook left behind after her mother died because Millie was the only one telling the stories. Back then, her father handled her much the same way he did now: with an air of inconvenience and minimal effort, but the cruelty was new.

Sitting on the couch with Pop-Tart, Millie edited her life down to what was real and found she had a mixed bag. The terror of finding her mom collapsed on the kitchen floor with a burning fever after her last round of chemotherapy mixed with the smell of their old car on a summer day and trips to the ice cream parlor, the one that handed out balloons. Memories of tubes, needles, and what she recognized at twelve as exhaustion on her mom's face were eased by the Rules for Chewing Bubble Gum and Eating Oreos the same woman had posted on their refrigerator.

Good and bad, even when her mom was sick. Millie turned the page, kept writing. An hour later, she could barely breathe because it turned out that the single most tragic event in her life was not her mom's illness or her early death, as Millie had always been led to believe. No, back then, the good and bad mixed together to form a life. The single tragedy of her life so far had been the loss of her father and her fruitless efforts to bring him back.

Even after years of neglect, she still called and "hounded" him until he agreed to dinner, sent him cards and presents for his birthday and Christmas, receiving nothing in return but an eye roll and a "This was unnecessary."

Unable to bear the thought that this time she'd turned her life upside down not for the love of writing or even to "push her creative boundaries" as she'd told Jade, but to gain approval from a man who didn't want her, Millie pulled on her shoes and stood. Was it possible to play make-believe for so many years? Writing love stories without ever truly experiencing love? Convincing herself that she could research real struggle while keeping her own packed up tight? If it was possible, she wanted to go back and never leave the sunny world she'd built around herself ever again.

What had she done? What did it say about her that she had no roots of her own? That her life could be so easily flipped on a grab for acceptance?

She felt trapped, her mind scrambling to put things back where they were before and struggling with the idea that her life was nothing more than mismatched and discarded pieces. Millie stepped outside for a gulp of air and her sadness turned to anger.

Not wanting to be in the confined space of a car, she grabbed a dilapidated bike resting on the side of the cottage and started pedaling. She needed life, other people's lives and problems smaller than her own. She would get ice cream for lunch and gum—lots and lots of bubble gum. Oreos too, and with any luck, the general store carried fashion magazines like her mom used to read because there was no way she was looking in the bookstore. No matter how freaking cute it looked from the outside, Millie might never go into another bookstore again. She was going to gather up every good memory she had until she felt better again, until she found her way back to pretending.

By the time Millie parked the bike in the alleyway adjacent to the market, she was numb. How ridiculous she'd been giving lip service to dark and moody, pulling the blinds like that's all it took to understand the things that brought people to their knees. The truth was darkness had come for her right there on the street outside her father's shop and instead of welcoming it into her creative process as she'd said she would, she ran. Back to Bodega Bay, someone else's hometown. Nothing she'd admired about Drake's upbringing was hers to have, but she needed to belong somewhere for at least a little while.

Millie made a beeline for the bubble gum—sugar-filled, obnoxious bubble gum. It had always been her go-to when her father pissed her off. The smell of it alone as she added it to the green plastic shopper she'd picked up at the entrance brought forward another memory.

She'd returned home on break from boarding school only to be whisked off to some dinner party. In the middle of a room full of her father's so-called friends, he stopped the conversation she was trying to have and told her to go throw out her gum. "It's tacky, Mildred. Cows chew, not young ladies."

The crowd had laughed, and that marked the first time Millie wanted to be anywhere but home. Her father's corrections in the name of propriety went from mildly embarrassing to flat-out rude. By the time she was in college, she'd stopped coming home altogether. When her father didn't call or check on her, she grew concerned. Worried he might be lonely or need her, she had always been the one to break first. She'd call or stop by. Thus began the cycle that had again found her tossed out on the curb.

She'd been holding tight to the pieces of her life that she'd only now noticed her heart was bleeding and she had no idea how to stop it.

Shoving the memory back where it belonged, she loaded up her basket and got in line.

"She's the writer," a woman behind her whispered.

Millie felt expectation scrape up her spine and wondered at the likelihood of people noticing her right in the middle of her disastrous epiphany.

"Yeah? Like a real writer? Do I know her?"

Odds were pretty good, it turned out. Millie considered dropping her shopping spree at the counter and making a quick exit, but she absolutely needed bubble gum.

"She writes books. Well, not book books, but romance," the woman said a little louder this time, clearly not giving a crap that the veiled insult might be overheard.

Finally next in line, Millie set her basket in front of the teenager behind the register and asked a higher power to get her out of this situation without either punching someone in this lovely small town, or worse, completely losing her mind and ending up as some salacious story for the next amateur tour guide.

"Romance like *Fifty Shades of Grey*? My God, I loved those books. Ask her if she knows the author," one of them whispered.

Don't do it. Please.

"Excuse me." A woman tapped Millie on the shoulder right as she handed the cashier her card.

"Yes." She glanced in their direction, striving for casual despite her clenched jaw.

"We were wondering since you write romance too." Both women looked at one another like they'd had thunder beads up their asses too. Thankfully Millie did not vocalize that thought. The store was spinning. "Do you know E. R. James?"

"I do not."

"Bummer," the one in the sweatshirt said.

It is a bummer since E. L. James is the author, dipshit. Another observation she kept to herself and even managed a smile this time. She was on a roll.

"Well, she's super famous so yeah... long shot."

"There are a ton of these writers, like cranking out books," the other one said.

"Right?" Both women giggled.

Millie couldn't even chronicle their features. They were swirled into a generic blur of judgment with which she was intimately familiar. No longer concerned with her public persona or even being polite, Millie turned back to the register and pleaded with her only savior who was "kinda new."

"We should totally write romance."

"We'd make a killing."

They tapped her on the shoulder again right as the kid figured out the card machine. Millie entered her PIN and side-eyed the women.

"Sorry." More giggling. "We're doing some research. Like how long does it take you to write one of your books?"

"Yeah, like a couple of weeks? Months? Ooh, and where do you get your ideas?"

"Great question." The two women high-fived.

Millie took her bags without another word but spun on both women before she left. The step they took back was a testament to the crazy that must have been all over her face. She wanted to say something she would regret just to say she'd done it. This one time, she wanted the last word, but it wasn't fair to unload a lifetime of pain on two strangers, so she clutched her bags tighter and walked out.

$\sim$

Tuesday was Drake's day to pick up lunch. The sun was out again, so he decided to leave his truck and jog up to the Santori Brothers. "Best subs in town." That was their tagline. Their only competition was the prewrapped mystery subs at the gas station, so more like "only" subs in town. But they were great, so Drake never pointed out the obvious.

He'd paid and shoved some of the mints Tyler liked into the bag when he saw Millie outside the mini-market. She set two full bags on the basket of a bike that looked like the one the Millers kept propped on the side of the cottage. He hoped she wasn't trying to ride that thing because—

Before he could finish his thought, the basket broke. Drake made to cross the street, but when she put her face in her hands and slid down the side of the building until she was seated, his heart sank.

She didn't look up as he crouched to put her things back into the bags. She stayed in a ball, hugging her legs to her chest. All he could see was her back pulsing with sobs so powerful that he was afraid for her. Without a word, he brought her to her feet and moved her back into the alley for what little privacy Main Street allowed.

"Breathe." He rubbed her back, the full weight of her resting on his chest. Drake needed a plan, but for the moment remained quiet. Was she in pain? Afraid? Before he'd come up with what to do, she lifted her head. Eyes rimmed in red, she wiped at her tear-soaked cheeks and sniffed. To his relief, her breathing settled to a more natural rhythm.

After a minute or two, she patted his chest to in some way assure him she was okay before meeting his eyes, an expression filled with sadness he hadn't known her capable of until that moment.

Not that he knew her. Everyone had sadness, but from the looks of her and the panic thundering in his own chest, Drake thought her level of sadness might be more than most. Relying on instinct since there was no way he was coming up with a plan when she was looking at him like that, Drake held her shoulders.

"Let's take this slow. Are you okay? Do I need to call the police or take you to a hospital?" She closed her eyes, pulled her bottom lip between her teeth, and shook her head.

"Good. Very good news." He took both of her hands in his one hand, only wanting to touch her with warmth.

Her expression grew concerned and she took his other hand like it was made of skin and bone. Of course she did. Drake's heart lurched again. His focus shifted to the bag of sandwiches tossed at the entrance to the alley. Every bit of him struggled between his need to restore order and holding her steady.

"I'm fine." She stepped back. "Truly. I just... I'm sorry." She let his hands go and tucked hers into the pockets of her sweatshirt. She was dressed casual in jeans, but what looked like it had once been eye makeup was now smudged under those incredible eyes.

She glanced at the bike. Drake was probably staring again, but he couldn't think of a thing to say. Did he ask her what happened? Should he leave it alone? Whatever made her cry was none of his business, and it didn't seem like she was ready to share. The silence growing more awkward, Drake fell back on the Branch family standard in times of crisis—humor.

"You know? I told the Millers they needed to fix that basket."

Her lips curved. Not a smile and nowhere near a laugh, but considering she'd been in a ball moments ago, it was a start. Slow progress was still progress, Drake remembered being told years ago.

"Why," she croaked before clearing her throat. "Why do I not believe that?" She walked toward the bike, steadier now on her feet.

"Okay, you caught me, but they shouldn't leave that thing propped there like it actually works."

She bent to pick up her bags.

"Can I—"

She lifted both bags and sniffed again, this time with a lift of her chin he felt certain she'd done a lot in her life. It was a pride thing. He recognized it right away.

"I need to get back. I'll walk."

No way he was going to grab his lunch and part ways like nothing had happened. Cursing his decision to leave his truck back at the studio, he peeked into one of her bags. "That's a lot of food. Wait, are those Oreos?"

She met his eyes, a little more of a smile this time. "Yes. Three packages."

"Nice." He lifted the bike, checked the tires, then the handlebars. "Give me those magazines so the bag isn't so heavy." He swung his leg over the seat.

"What are you doing?"

Drake bounced his weight on the wide vinyl seat and with his good hand, checked that the elastic on the panel behind the seat was in better shape than the basket. He held the straps and gestured with his head for Millie to slide the magazines in the back. She did, and he snapped the elastic straps back into place. One thing taken care of, he ran through a quick list of things that could go wrong, noting that he had not ridden any kind of bike since the accident and hoped he could still remember those days when he rode his bike with one hand or no hands.

Millie was still waiting for him to explain what he was doing, so he adjusted his prosthesis, and not wanting to remember which muscle to fire, manually clamped the fingers around the handlebar. He took a deep breath and hoped he looked like he knew what he was doing.

"Here's how this works," he finally said in a tone more confident than he felt.

There was no reason for Millie to know that he hadn't done this since he was in high school, back when both of his arms worked without complication. Channeling Bella's faith in Iron Man and ignoring the twist in his gut, Drake extended the arm not attached to the handlebars.

"Hand me your bags."

Her expression shifted from confused to exhaustion as she handed over the bags without a word.

"You're going to sit on the handlebars, facing me."

Her eyes went wide, but she wasn't arguing yet, so he continued.

"Put your feet here." He gestured with his head toward the thick support bars extending from the pedals to the front wheels. Her eyes followed and returned to his face.

Drake smiled. "This is a piece of cake on these old bikes."

He was certain this was the longest she'd gone without speaking since he'd met her and for once was grateful.

"Oh, and toss those sandwiches in one of your bags. Esteban is going to kill me if his tuna is soggy."

When people are in crisis, the mundane is their salve, he remembered a therapist telling his parents early on. He hoped that applied to all crises.

After rescuing his sandwiches, Millie stopped short of climbing on the bike.

"I'm not sure this..."

Her words trailed off as she appeared to run through the plan he'd laid out. Right when he thought she might protest, she swallowed and climbed on. When she was settled, he handed the bags back to her, explaining how she needed to rest them on her lap to free up a hand to wrap around his neck.

Drake ignored the charge her touch sent through his body. If he didn't pull this off, they were both going to be on their asses in under five minutes. Now was not the time to wonder why he had not stopped thinking about her. Making one more adjustment to the Iron Man side of the handlebars, Drake met her eyes to check that she was ready.

"I'm assuming you have experience with bikes?" she asked.

Drake laughed at the irony.

"I know I'm not in much of a position to be picky, but when was the last time you were on a bike like this? With a person on the handlebars?"

"This is like an interview? Right now?"

She nodded as though she'd hop right down if he didn't have the right credentials. Her lips curled into a grin, and Drake felt he'd scored another point over whatever or whoever had made her cry.

"You may be disappointed because I do not have specific experience transporting attractive women holding snack foods home on the handlebars of my bike."

"Oh, that's a shame." Full smile this time.

"It is, but hear me out. When I was seven, Genevieve Abbott lost her dog and I pedaled her around town on my handlebars for a couple of hours before we found him. To be clear, she was holding a puppy on the way back, not Oreos."

Her eyes were almost playful now and Drake could not explain why that made him feel like the actual Iron Man, but it did.

"You drove her through this town? These streets."

He nodded.

She shrugged. "Okay, I guess if it was good enough for Genevieve, it's good enough for me."

"She's a lawyer now."

"Even more impressive."

"Tighten your grip, Millie." Had he said her name before? It sounded different with her this close.

She adjusted the bags and held on with a strength he remembered from their first handshake.

Meeting her eyes, he said, "I will not let you fall."

"Okay."

Christ, those eyes.

"Just don't let go," he said.

All the possible meanings in such a simple statement passed between them. Drake rolled the bike up to the entrance of the alley, checked for traffic, and pushed off.

"I won't," she said softly as they wobbled a bit before his foot hit solid on the other pedal and they were moving.

Once they made it to the main drag and he was confident he wasn't going to crash, he relaxed enough to enjoy the pressure of her hand at the back of his neck. The reckless fun of bounding down an uneven sidewalk brought forward good memories: simple and innocent times when having enough money for a soda or racing the sun home before dinner were the only things on Drake's list.

They turned the corner in front of the cottage. Squeezing the right brake, he brought them to a smooth stop. Millie stayed put, smiling inches from his face. He'd never met anyone at such odds with joy and sorrow.

"Thank you."

"You're welcome." He couldn't take his eyes off her and would have gladly sat on that rickety bike all day, schedule be damned, if she promised to keep looking at him the way she was right then.

"I'm serious."

"I know."

She eased her grip on his neck but stayed put. "This was fun. And... I'm not sure how you knew, but I was pretty desperate for fun, so thank you."

Drake nodded because if he opened his mouth, he'd scare her away with questions. He'd try to fix her, break things down into steps because that's how he worked these days. Millie had every intention of walking herself home, she had not asked him to rescue her, so he stayed quiet and held the bags as she hopped down.

"How about dinner later?" He took the sandwiches from her and parked the bike back on the side of the cottage. She was curious, he knew that about her. Maybe if he gave her mind something else to think about, it would heal itself. No fixing, just food and a little more fun.

"I should get some..." She looked toward the door.

"Pizza again, nothing fancy. And I'll throw in a behind-the-scenes tour of the studio."

"Another tour. Wow, so soon."

Drake smirked, relieved to see color back in her cheeks. "So, whaddaya say? Six o'clock?"

"It was good pizza."

"Yeah, and I might even let you keep what you make."

"A souvenir? Well, now you have a deal."

"Excellent. I'll see you at six."

She nodded, holding tight to her bags.

Drake dismissed the smudges under her eyes and the pain still right behind her smile as he turned to leave.

"What happened to your arm?" she asked, standing at the door when he faced her again.

He'd answered the same questions dozens of times, but this time it felt like a test. Like she wanted him to share some of what made him different.

"I know you were in an accident, because Hazel told me and there are pictures in your studio of you younger. Before." She shook her head and Drake almost laughed.

"That sounded weird. Forget I asked."

"I'm surprised it has taken you so long to ask."

"Yeah, well I'm having trouble finding my words lately."

"I was in a motorcycle accident. The bike went one way. I went the other. Everything below my elbow on my left arm was shattered. They couldn't put me back together again. So, I became Iron Man. The nickname my niece gave me." He held up his left arm, flexing his muscles to open and close the fingers of his prosthesis.

She listened. As much as she enjoyed talking, she listened to people and he liked that. Maybe it was growing up in a loud house or always being surrounded by a small town of talkers, but her moments of silence, not like she was waiting for her next opportunity to speak, made a person feel valued. He wondered if she knew that.

"It's pretty incredible what they can do now, isn't it?" She reached out and touched the metal.

"That it is. Anything else you want to know?"

She shook her head, adjusting her bags back into both arms. "Not right now."

He nodded and she went into the cottage. Drake blew out a breath, and for the first time in his life, he looked forward to more questions. Maybe he would get some answers too.

Chapter Fifteen

The first and only time someone pulled Millie out of a panic attack or spiral, as she termed them when she got older, she was twelve. Her second week at Saint Beatrice Academy and she was drowning in grief. Eyes still puffy from crying herself to sleep, she'd gone to class only because her dorm monitor said it would be good for her to "get on with life." Millie recognized later that a dorm monitor was not the person one turned to for grief counseling, but back then she'd thrown on clothes and gone to class.

Her first period English class was reading Jane Eyre, a book Millie had not read. The class was ten chapters ahead of Millie, but the teacher asked her to read anyway. Millie began reading, and it wasn't long before she flubbed a pronunciation and then skipped words all together. She was numb and going through the motions, mostly oblivious to the whispers and giggles until one voice behind her exclaimed that Millie's shirt was on backward. That's why they were all laughing, not her reading.

After louder laughter and the teacher's how-can-I-help voice, Millie curled herself into a tight ball on the floor of the girls' bathroom, certain the walls were going to swallow her up and wondering if she would see her mom once they did.

One of the counselors, Dr. March, had found Millie and carried her to the office. "Your grief and your panic are real, Millie. You have absolutely nothing to be embarrassed about. I would like to teach you some ways to work through this if you're open to that," she said in a voice Millie could still conjure up all these years later. It was the first time anyone had acknowledged what had happened and offered to help.

Over the next year, Dr. March did what she promised. In addition to providing a safe space for Millie to talk about her feelings that didn't require her to "get on with life," she taught Millie the AWARE steps, which empowered her to work through panic attacks for the rest of her life. They were infrequent these days, another testament to the power of her father, but Millie knew how to handle anxiety. She would have worked her way through had Drake not been there, but he was there. Quiet when he needed to be, distracting when she was ready, and kind.

God, Millie had always been a sponge for kindness.

After putting her junk food away, she kicked back on the couch and ordered the largest television she could fit in Candy Land. From here on out, the rules were changing starting with Netflix, damn it. The Millers could thank her later. Millie then took a nap and a shower before kissing Pop-Tart on her sleeping head and stepping outside. Drake was sitting on the one-person porch of his Airstream. He stood when he saw her.

She'd passed by his home a few times now and was always curious how a person lived in there, but at that moment, she was drawn to his expression. Concern was all over his face. She couldn't blame him but hated it all the same. She wasn't that little girl anymore, and she'd been perfectly happy before Christmas Eve. Before the dead-not-dead book idea Millie had been safe in Romancelandia. Now, a month trying to corral Alistair into a story and a blow from her father she had to have seen coming, and Millie was a mess. She would need to sort through more than her outline, but she'd agreed to dinner. She was going to have pizza and learn to blow glass.

Drake had helped her without making her feel powerless. If that wasn't a great guy trait, she didn't know her heroes.

"Did you know glassblowing has been around for thirty-five hundred years?" she asked, reminding herself she was not good at real-life romance.

"I did know that, but I'm impressed you've done some research. Google?"

"Where all important information is housed," she said, before reaching into her back pocket. "Gum?" She held it out to him.

"Sure."

He took a piece and returned the pack. Millie watched and applied the Rules for Chewing Bubble Gum her mom had established long ago. You could tell a lot about a person by first whether they chewed bubble gum at all, second how they put it into their mouth, and third how they handled the bubble. There were lots of gum chewers, but people who chewed bubble gum were special. "Bubble gum chewers remember forever what it's like to be a kid," she'd said. And it was true. Millie had never met a child who didn't love bubble gum or an adult she liked whose eyes didn't light up when offered a piece.

Drake undid the wrapper and popped the whole pink brick into his mouth.

"That's a good sign." Again, her thoughts were vocal.

Drake glanced over, already chewing. "What's a good sign?"

"You didn't bite the gum in two before putting it in your mouth."

He scrunched his brow. "What am I, an amateur?"

He blew his first bubble and let it pop across his nose. "Damn, I'm a little rusty."

They walked the small distance separating her work from his as another orange sunset melted into the bay.

"Still impressive," she said, getting used to how easy it was to smile around him.

"Yeah?" He finished sticking the gum back into his mouth.

"You let the bubble pop on your face. You chewed quickly and got right down to blowing. Followed all the rules."

"Wow, this is serious."

She grinned, and they both faced the water as the light faded.

"I'd forgotten about bubble gum. I used to carry a pack around in my front pocket."

He touched his jeans, and Millie imagined a younger Drake.

"I always forgot about it and my mom would yell from the laundry room when it showed up in her dryer." He nodded. "Cool memory. Thanks." He touched her hand and she replayed the bike ride, the feel of his sun-warmed neck against her palm.

"You're welcome." She reached into her back pocket and handed him an unopened package. "For your pocket," she said, facing him.

The edges of his face softened, and in the purple-blue of early evening, he was beautiful. A completely overused and, according to many writers, an unimaginative descriptor, but Millie believed in the adage that sometimes one word did the job. Drake was a beautiful man. Tyler was handsome, polished, and fun to look at, a lot like his well-constructed leather bag. Drake was more of a worn leather jacket, a favorite pair of jeans. He was the sum of life experiences she'd probably never know, and she wasn't sure she'd ever had someone look so deeply into her eyes.

It should have been intimidating, but it felt more like he was trying to figure her out, put her pieces together. She might have told him not to bother. She was one of those thousand-part projects, which would take a heck of a lot longer than three months to solve.

"For this," he said, sliding the gum into his pocket, "I will not only feed you, but you will definitely get the grand tour now."

"The bubble gum tipped things in my favor, huh?"

"It's an out-of-towner special we're running."

"I thought tourists drove you nuts."

"Some do." He slid open the door and gestured her in with tour-guide flourish.

"But not me?" She walked past him into the studio.

"I'm not ready to make that call yet."

Millie laughed as Drake lifted a section of the counter that separated most of the studio. "Smart man."

Millie was more aware of the space on this side of things. She'd appreciated it from the front, but everything revealed itself now that she was inside. The wood beams in the roof and the massive columns supporting the inferno that sat center stage seemed accessible, work-worn rather than set pieces. She hadn't realized there were bits of copper swirled into the floor that sparkled like stars the closer she got to the fire. Needing to touch, she smoothed her hand over the top of a metal table, surprised that it was almost cold. There were three of what Drake called "work-benches" set up the same way with a wide L-shaped seat behind a support and a side table.

"This is where the magic happens," he said.

Millie rotated in the space one more time and smiled. "You know, in romance novels, that line rarely refers to a glassblowing studio." She tilted her head.

"Right. Well, I'm sure that's not the only difference between me and the guys in your books." He stopped at a large corner table where he'd set out pizza and wine.

"Although, I have to admit Brix and I would probably get along. Some of the Rescue Ops guys train in the bay, you know? Tyler's brother for one."

He might not have noticed when Millie gripped the table holding what looked like medieval torture tools to keep her balance, but her mouth was no doubt hanging open. Drake uncorked and poured the wine and continued like it was the most natural thing in the world to discuss one of her books.

"I have five chapters to go, but I'm guessing he gets fired or hurt. The guy is out of control and I don't think Nat is going to put up with him for much longer if he doesn't pull it together, you know?" He offered her a glass of wine. "Well, of course you know. You wrote it."

"You have five more chapters to read in *Rescue Me?*" She managed to take the glass. "You're reading my book? This is not a Google search?"

Drake took a gulp of wine. "No. Auntie N said this was a good one to start with. One thing though, not to be critical, but is the cover model supposed to actually work in Rescue Ops? Because that's like a ten-pack." He gestured for her to sit up on the giant table. She did.

"No one is getting rescued because that guy is living at the gym." He joined her with one easy lift, and they both sat cross-legged on opposite sides of the pizza box. It was like something out of a movie, only real and better and—

Holy crap, he's reading my book? Does he know what that does to a woman?

She couldn't speak. When he glanced over, Millie set her wineglass down.

"That was critical. You know what? Forget I said anything. I—"

She shook her head. "Not critical."

She could have kissed him. Not in the literal sense because she'd been sobbing and blubbering all over him mere hours ago. Kissing him would be needy and possibly desperate especially considering her father's comments. No kissing. Something else. God, when had she started analyzing her own motivations and stakes?

Maybe all those years of telling other people's stories had broken something inside her and she was incapable of living a nonfiction life. Millie shut off her editor and took a piece of pizza. She and Drake continued discussing the ending she already knew but wouldn't give away. Everything about the moment was effortless. Words flowed. There was no struggle or clashing of opinions this time. They talked about what they loved to do and laughed. Millie so needed to laugh. It was a perfect evening already, and they hadn't even gotten to the glassblowing part.

In fact, if she were writing this scene, she would kiss him. Jumped into his arms the minute he mentioned her book. Glasses would crash to the ground and he'd hold her weight with one strong masculine arm. No problem. She'd drive the kiss. She'd kiss the hell out of him and he would lay her back on this table and—

Hello, crazy writer, please report to your real life, daddy issues and all.

~

What in the fuck is wrong with me?

She was clearly going through something and Drake couldn't stop thinking about the sex scene in her book. That was next-level-creepy neighbor. It was bad enough that she'd been shocked that he was reading her book, but then he went on about the story and the guy's abs. Drake exhaled. It wasn't his fault she wrote great sex or that he wondered if any of that scene was based on actual experience. He wasn't going to ask that, of course, because hello super-creepy neighbor and it was insulting. She was a writer, probably made things up all the time. Really great scenes that he may or may not have re-read twice, but that didn't mean she expected him to kiss her like that.

Don't go there. You're barely capable of dating, remember?

Besides, what was she going to do, throw herself into his arms? Arm? Yeah, he needed to get a grip. Drake had meant what he said. He wasn't Brix Baxter or any of the other men in her books. In the real world, when guys fell down, he didn't get back up without the help of a stretcher. He needed to remember that before he went and did something stupid. Just like the few things on his sister's list, Drake didn't do stupid anymore either.

He'd barely survived stupid. He was missing part of his arm and the rest of his body was covered in scars. That wasn't hot; that was damaged. On top of that, Millie was dealing with something and he'd been there to help. That's all this dinner was, helping. Period.

In his experience, people needed pizza and wine more on the shitty days than they did when things were great. He knew how to help people in need and on occasion give them what they wanted, but he hadn't heard from his own wants and needs for a long time. He'd put all his energy into rebuilding his life, but sitting across from Millie, the need sat front and center. Unrelenting and unscheduled, he recognized stubborn, and she was talking about everything but herself.

"So, anything else you'd like to talk about?"

Her eyes met his over the rim of her wineglass and in the time it took her to swallow, she'd tucked whatever had put her on the ground next to the mini-mart behind a smile.

"Did you know that Onion was the first—"

"Ennion," he said. "He was the first glassmaker to sign his work."

"I like learning things."

"I can tell." He took another slice of pizza and waited for another chance.

"I figured you knew things about my work. Maybe if I learned stuff about yours, we could have a civil, music-free conversation. Maybe, you know…" She looked everywhere but at him. "Be friends."

Drake almost choked. "I would like that."

His dating skills were a little rusty, but he already knew he was going to fail spectacularly in the friend-zone.

"My turn," he said as they finished eating and leaned back against the wall. "Tell me about what you do."

"Very funny. You know what I do."

"You write books, I know that. But what's your process?"

She laughed. "I have no idea. I make things up and hope they make sense."

"Do you base your characters on people you know?"

"I do not," Millie said, the tension visible in her shoulders.

"Do you think you'll write about Bodega Bay?" he asked.

"Probably not." She turned the stem of her wineglass.

The studio was darker now that the sun had set. Not wanting to turn on the bright work lights just yet, Drake hopped down and grabbed a candle they'd put in one of the vases to show off the colors.

"Why not?" He set the lit candle between them and got back on the table.

She studied him. Her hair was dry now, so curls swam around her face in every direction. She tucked them behind both of her ears on a sigh before answering.

"I'm here. Living it. I'm sure my time here will inspire bits of my stories, but I don't write like that. It's not verbatim."

"What do you mean?"

"Like I might write a story about a seaside town. It may look like this town, but I'll put it in Maine. Or, I'll take this"—she closed her eyes and spread her arms wide—"this feeling or the smell of the wine, and put it on a rooftop in a big city." She opened her eyes.

"Pieces."

She nodded.

"I get it."

They sat in silence. Drake poured himself another glass of wine and went for it. "Are you okay?"

She nodded, but when she looked up, her eyes were glossy in the candlelight.

"Why are you writing a sad story?"

She blinked and swallowed. "I wanted to try something new, but I don't think it's going to work out. I mean it might, but I just don't know right this minute."

He shrugged. "That's okay."

"Is it? You seem to know exactly what you're doing."

"Within my sandbox, sure."

Her brow furrowed.

"I keep my space small on purpose, Millie."

She held out her glass and he poured.

"I like to be able to manage things. Like these benches." He pointed. "Perfect example. Everything is within reach. We lay them out the same way every day. I know what I'm doing, who I am in there. I like that."

Millie nodded.

"That's not the same as knowing what I'm doing all the time. You're trying something new."

"For the wrong reasons," she said.

He recognized the crack in the door and hoped she'd let him in.

"Do you like writing romance?"

"Love it." She crossed her arms in a hug around her body.

"But you want to challenge yourself, is that wrong?"

She shook her head and took another sip of wine. "I thought if I wrote a book that my father respected, he might respect me."

Drake didn't dare look away. If he let in even one trace of pity, she'd close up again.

"Is your father a writer too?"

"No, well he wrote one book, but he owns a bookshop in the city. Hartfield's Books," she said, her voice anxious like she was certain he knew her father's store out of all the bookstores in the city. Bold and gorgeous Millie who had barged into his studio in her cat pajamas seemed to shrink right there in the glow of candle.

Drake *had* heard of Hartfield's Books, but only because it was a few doors down from the curry place where he and Tyler used to grab lunch when they worked in the city. White building, big storefront window, two stories maybe. It was hard to tell from the street, and he'd never gone in.

"Never heard of it," he said. No way he was giving whatever or whoever lived behind that big window any more power over Millie than it already appeared to have.

She barely managed a grin and twirled her wineglass by the stem.

"Is your dad's book any good?"

"It is... ambitious. He is an extremely proficient writer."

"Okay. I'm not sure I even know what that means. It's a big book?" He chuckled a little. She did not, so he stopped.

"You didn't enjoy his book?"

"No."

"And you told him? Is that the rub?"

She shook her head. "I would never tell him anything about his book or any other book. He and his friends"—she took a deep breath and exhaled slowly, as if the words required more effort than she had—"They're... not nice."

Drake nodded.

"I'm a little sick of me," she set her wineglass down and climbed off the table.

"Have you ever thought that maybe you tell happy stories because you're happy? Why is that wrong, any less important than... ambitious books?"

"Because they're not an accurate reflection of life. People don't actually do the things I write about in my books. People don't... they don't fall headfirst into love or... jump from helicopters." She was pacing now.

"So? It's a story. People don't fly on brooms or narrowly escape exploding cars either. I don't get it. Who's reading fiction for reality?"

She smiled, but it was fake. He knew that much now. "Not sure. Listen, I appreciate this and what you did for me today."

He didn't bother with a "you're welcome" and waited for the "but."

"But, I'm fine. This is sweet and I am"—she brushed her hands on her jeans—"excited to learn about your glass."

She closed up and he couldn't read her anymore. The problem was her dad, that much was clear. Where was her mom? Was that relationship solid? He had no idea and wasn't going to push, so he followed her lead and got to his feet.

"Right. I give you, the grandest of tours."

Millie laughed. Preferring that to her sadness, Drake tried to focus on why he'd brought her there. Fire and sand were powerful, he knew firsthand. They'd given him work and purpose when he'd needed them the most. He would give her a glimpse into the magic of what he did for a living and hope she found a way back to what she loved writing. He was optimistic, but Drake knew better than anyone that the scars on the inside took the longest to heal.

Chapter Sixteen

Millie had shared too much. Other than Jade, she'd never explained the details of her relationship, or more accurately, the lack of a relationship with her father to anyone. Not that it mattered anymore. After yesterday, there would be no trying again with her father, no relationship, and nothing to share.

Focusing now on what promised to be the fun part of the evening, Millie touched the rainbow bits of glass Drake had laid out on a table. They seemed like tiny bits of crystal in every color she could imagine. "What are these?"

"Frit," Drake said, holding one of the long sticks she now knew were blowpipes.

She hoped he didn't think she knew what that meant. She'd Googled sure, but there had been no mention of—

"Sorry. Pieces of glass used to give the larger piece color."

She nodded. "Glass doesn't come in different colors? Everything in that oven—"

"Furnace," he smiled.

"Right. All the glass in that furnace is colorless?"

"It is," he said. "Most projects are the melding of pieces. Color or clear. Save a plain cylindrical tall glass or a bud vase, almost everything is a combination of separate gathers."

"Gathers being the blobs, right?"

He laughed. "Yeah, the blobs."

Drake worked in a rhythm she appreciated, a bit like he was counting steps as he pulled the pipe from the smaller furnace and examined the end. She'd asked if having her in the studio was distracting, and he'd shrugged it off like when he was working it didn't matter who was watching. Apart from the fact that Drake was lovely to watch, the process of making glass proved captivating. The movements were methodical but fluid at the same time, Millie understood Drake's connection to yoga. Brushing the bits of color from her fingers, she sat at one of the benches.

"So that was the glory hole," he said, showing her the end of the blowpipe. "We use that to warm the pipe after we've checked for any obstructions. Next is a gather, or blobs." He grinned and moved to the larger furnace.

Millie's mind was still back on glory hole. *Seriously?*

"Come stand over—"

Her expression must have given her away. That, or it was the childish giggle she couldn't contain.

Drake shook his head. "I know. There's another kind of glory hole."

Millie laughed outright now. "I'm only saying that has to be tough to say with a straight face. 'Hey Esteban, meet me at the glory hole.'"

At that, he joined her in laughter, full and echoing through the space. "I have never said that in my life. Could you please get over here and focus?"

She hopped down and stood next to him. Drake handed her the pipe and guided her toward the furnace. A few twists and he removed the pipe with a blob of glowing, sap-like liquid. A gather, she tried to be mature.

He held it near the center of the pipe with his right hand and rested the remainder on his prosthesis. Millie hadn't noticed, but he'd changed out the hand of his Iron Man arm for what looked like a clawed gardening tool. Turning the pipe effortlessly at his waist, he explained about the need for constant movement and how each rotation shaped the glass. Millie was again mesmerized, which quickly turned to panic when he handed her the blowpipe.

She did her best to mimic his movements but got trapped staring at the blob and made herself a bit dizzy. Drake calmly explained that everything, like she'd said to Hazel, took practice.

Millie had no idea how he did any of this while speaking, let alone making eye contact. All energy was on making her hands do what they were supposed to do. It seemed impossible to her that he managed with a prosthesis or that blaring music. At the same time, she understood where he'd built up his shoulders and arm muscles. Her arms ached already. And how any bit of anxiety would disrupt the flow. By fumbling her way through the first steps of glassblowing, she knew more about him, and it was way more enjoyable than twenty-questions.

Drake stood behind her and reached his right arm over to tilt the pipe up to her mouth.

"Best part," he said into her neck.

Every sensation Millie had tucked away or saved for her fictional characters raced to the surface of her skin. Nerve endings, warmth, all the things she'd used to show readers lust and passion were now dancing through her body. It was only through sheer determination that she didn't drop everything and rest her head back on his chest as he continued at her ear.

"Tilt it a little—" He reached under her arm and brought one edge of the pipe higher. "That's it," he whispered. "Easy, take—" He adjusted the pipe again. "Take your time." Did he realize his entire body was pressed into the back of hers? If he didn't, this brought focusing on work to a whole new level. Hard and herbal ocean again, save for the warm wine on his breath rendered her speechless. She honestly could have been baking bread or doing laundry. She'd forgotten whatever he was trying to explain. All she felt, could hear, or smell was him. Good God, glassblowing was absolutely going on her sexy scene list.

"Millie, are you still with me?"

She managed a nod. She was with him all right. Running through all the senses and on her way to taste.

"Great, look at me."

She did and there were his lips. Hello, taste.

"You're going to blow into this end to put a small bubble in the glass, okay?"

Lust stepped aside to make room for more angst. "How much? Maybe you should do this part. I don't want to—"

He stepped back, her body might have whimpered, and carefully took the pipe from her hands. Standing in front of her now, he put the glass back into the glory hole and when he removed it, he set the blowpipe on a stand. Still turning, he reached out and guided her next to him in front of the stand, which she assumed was some kind of support.

"You're creating something. There are no rules."

"Other than keep that thing turning."

"Other than that, but this should make it easier." He smiled. "If you can blow a bubble, you can do this, Millie. Just breathe."

"Oh, you're good. I'd like to point out there are a lot of erotic undertones to glassblowing. Are you aware?"

His expression warmed as he dipped his head to acknowledge and possibly appreciate her dirty mind, but he said nothing. More turning.

In that moment, she saw herself in his eyes. Or rather a version she knew but had relegated to wanton and frivolous under the scrutiny of those who "knew the way the world worked."

In his eyes, there was nothing ridiculous about what raced through her body, from the warmth in places she only explored herself these days to the sweeping desire most people only found on romance covers.

But this was real, she was lustful, lovely, and incredibly sexy. She could feel it down to her bones. This wasn't her getting into the mind of a heroine and then closing her laptop only to still feel broken or wrong for wanting too much. No, this was all her, sparked by the way he could not stop staring and emanating from her own truth.

Yes, they were still turning and she was still panicking, but she'd caught a glimpse of the woman she was when the critics were silenced. Strong, funny, burning with desire, brilliant, and panicking woman. God, she loved herself in his eyes.

Willing herself out of her thoughts before she burned the place down, Millie took over turning the pipe.

"Close your eyes." He stood next to her.

"What? I can't."

"Close, Millie."

She did.

"Just blow."

She did. And when she opened her eyes, he was still there. The look on his face, full of things she felt certain he would control too if he could, was still there. Drake's gaze dropped to her mouth and every reason not to kiss him fell away. As did the blowpipe, which clattered to the floor when she let go, grabbing the back of his neck, his hair, and kissing him in that way women did between the pages of those "trashy" books she loved so much.

Drake's arms wrapped around her waist and pulled her closer. She was hungry, starving for connection. She held his face, took the kiss deeper, driven by this overwhelming sense that she deserved to be kissed, which was absurd, but she'd given so many of her characters a moment or ten. This one was hers.

She had not jumped into his arms. Her legs weren't wrapped about his waist. But the groan deep in his chest as he backed her away from the furnace and drew her even closer into his own heat was her moment. His lips were soft as his tongue retreated and returned, teasing her lips in the most wonderful way before sliding along her bottom lip and back into her mouth.

Millie was gone. Moaning with pleasure so encompassing it blocked everything other than the man holding her, touching her, and… saving her.

She opened her eyes to find Drake's still closed. Dark lashes resting on his face while his mouth took more. Millie pulled away, her lungs clamoring for air and her mind stammering drunk.

Was that why she'd kissed him? It had nothing to do with being bold or the wine. She should have known nothing was ever that simple. Not in her world anyway. No, she'd kissed him for the same reason a person might put their frozen hands up to a fire or walk... into a lit-with-laughter bookshop on Christmas Eve.

Millie stepped back.

Drake was stock-still, hands up like he'd been caught doing something wrong. "Millie?"

"Oh, God. I'm—" She turned away from him to find the glass on the floor, hardened and—

"Twisted," she whispered. "I should not have kissed you. That was not what either of us needed. You were trying to,"—she pointed to the failed project—"and I." She put her hands to her mouth like she still treasured what she'd said was wrong.

Drake dropped his hands and Millie wished it had all been fiction. She could rewrite fiction, change everything except that kiss.

~

Drake hoped his brain was going to kick back in soon because Millie looked like she was about to implode, and he probably shouldn't be thinking about pulling her back in and starting all over again when that happened.

"This is not why I came here. I'm not looking for a...oh, God. Everyone knows this isn't the answer, unless." Her hands slapped to her sides. "Daddy issues. I am like textbook. Some guy I barely know is going to... want me?"

Drake commanded himself not to nod a "hell, yes."

These are rhetorical questions. Stand down.

"What, so I'll feel needed and one kiss will make it all better?"

"Millie." It was a good sign he was able to form words. He would replay that kiss for quite a while and then kick himself for letting it happen. She was vulnerable, he knew that, but when she took his mouth, she seemed a whole hell of a lot in control.

"Shit, shit, shit." Millie brushed her hands along the front of her jeans.

"Please calm down."

"I can't calm down. Drake, I was a blithering idiot only a few hours ago and now here I am practically climbing you. Don't you see what this is?" She flailed her hands between them. "No, of course you don't see because you're 'healthy.'" She was aggressive with her quotes and wild-eyed searching for her sweater or her bag, he couldn't remember what she'd brought. It was clear that she couldn't wait to get away from him.

"Okay. Stop. First of all, I have plenty of my own issues and it was a kiss. I was trying to help you and—

Yeah, the completely wrong thing to say seemed to be his special gift lately. Before he could clarify, her eyes narrowed.

"You were helping me? That's why you kissed me? What, like a community service project?"

"You kissed me," he said, not making things better. "I would have been happy with knowing your favorite color or what food other than pizza you like to eat. If we got past that, I was hoping you'd tell me what happened to you today. I'm trying to get to know you, Millie, not... climb you. Not yet anyway. You kissed me."

She snorted, found her sweater, and snatched it off the table. "You're right. I did kiss you. And like I said, it was a mistake."

"You didn't say mistake."

She flinched at the interruption.

"You said you should not have kissed me."

Her brow furrowed.

Drake shrugged. "I just think there's a difference."

Now she was nodding aggressively. "And. And...you thought that distinction needed to be made? Right now?"

Drake shrugged.

She scoffed. "Listen. I am not looking for some man. I'm not here in some little Candy Land town to hook up with the local hero."

Damn. Gloves off.

"Oh, I'm sorry. Are we not meeting your expectations here in little 'ol Bodega? I could always take off my shirt or put on some leather pants. Maybe talk dirty to you. News flash, neighbor, I'm not 'some guy.' I'm... *a* guy. A real one."

"Wow, thank you for clarifying yet again. First, you're a bad DJ, a tour guide, a counselor, and now, this just in, an expert on gender stereotypes? How do you manage all of your... little hats?"

Drake learned a long time ago how to gauge a losing battle. "This is nuts."

"Oh, I'm nuts now." She put her hand to her chest. "I'm nuts. And you're feeling stereotyped? Perfect. Maybe you should have a chat with the two locals"—aggressive quotes again—"that I ran into at the market."

He stepped back.

"The lovely women who think my life's work is handcuffs and easy money. Or, better yet, swing by and have a chat with my father since you're so keen to know more about me. He'll tell you all about stereotypes and poor sad Millie." She swallowed back something he did not understand. "I..."

If she started to cry, he might join her this time.

"I don't have time to worry about you and the poor objectified guys on my covers, who get paid a crap-ton of money, side note. Because I'm drowning"—she exhaled, only to gulp in more air—"in judgment all by myself. So, pardon me if you're just 'some guy.'"

Feeling like this was about way more than a great kiss or even what happened at the mini-mart, Drake scrambled for anything to say, but she slid the door open and walked out.

"Millie, wait." He followed.

She spun back.

"This was a mistake. There, I said it now. I should have held it together in town. I'm better than that now. I don't need anyone to make me feel better." She rolled back her shoulders. "I do not need any of this," she bellowed. "I... am not some pathetic little victim. I'm... I am huge. Successful and... smart."

He nodded and wanted to pull her back into his arms. He had no intentions of saving her or rescuing her or anything else she'd conjured up. He just wanted to hold her, but that was the last thing she needed.

"I don't... ugh, forget it." She took another step away, and the space that separated the Millers' cottage from his place went from a few pavers to a giant chasm. "You said it yourself. I'm passing through. I don't belong."

Drake thought about again clarifying that he'd never actually said she didn't belong, but that was a bad idea. So instead, he stood there like a clueless dumbass when the door to the cottage slammed closed.

He had gone from willingly participating in one hell of a kiss to "some guy" in record time. *Shit!*

He ran his hand over his face and walked toward the dock. Wine and bubble gum, her lips teasing and pulling him back. One second greedy and the next so gentle he almost lost his damn mind. Now that his brain was wide awake, he understood that she kissed like she did everything else. Pleasure and pain, rain and sunshine. Her gorgeous blue eyes lit with a fire that rivaled anything he had in the studio one minute and dim under pressure she seemed embarrassed to explain. Millie Hart didn't know which version of her story she wanted, but she'd made it clear that he was not welcome in either.

Chapter Seventeen

*D*espite acting like a complete lunatic, Millie tried to get back to her writing. It was either that or start drinking, and it was crystal clear that she was no Hemingway.

She'd managed to stay inside for three days straight, which was normal fare for her when she was on a writing roll. The problem with this hibernation was that she wasn't writing much of anything. The morning after she'd dumped exactly a lifetime of feelings onto a man she'd known mere weeks, she had met with Hazel. Millie spent the first few minutes of their essay review, hoping to all things holy that Drake was still stunned mute and had not mentioned anything to his apprentice or Esteban, or Tyler. She had a feeling small towns were not the best places to lose one's mind either.

But Hazel had not appeared to have any new gossip, which put Millie's mind at ease and allowed her to focus on the second entrance essay. A few minor changes, and Hazel had written an essay even better than the first.

"Two down, one to go," she practically sang dancing around the Millers' tiny kitchen.

After sending her reluctant protégé off with the next "annoying writer thing" in the hopes of finishing off her application to Berkeley with a bang, Millie had spent the last two days finally dealing with Alistair.

Sometime after slamming the door to a cottage she'd grown to love, on a man who'd simply tried to help, Millie came to accept that Jade was right. This entire project was decided in a bubble and a final grab for her father's attention. She'd told herself it was creative stretching or whatever other garbage her "daddy issues" allowed her to make up, but she'd been wrong. She had considered deleting everything, putting the key back under Buzz, and driving away, but in the quiet middle of the night, it dawned on her that there was no place left to run.

And scrapping Alistair now that she knew him seemed cruel. She was far enough along that he was a living and breathing person. Well, living and kind of still breathing, but the point she argued to herself and Pop-Tart that afternoon when Hazel left was that she liked her protagonist.

He chewed on a toothpick, had a weakness for cashews, and gave up playing the violin during high school. She wanted to tell Alistair's story outside of the boxes and labels. There was nothing stopping her from writing in any genre she chose. Serious or funny, murder mystery, steampunk, or romance, Millie was a storyteller and needed to at least try to give Alistair the journey he deserved. It was wrong to delete him because she had a neglectful father and she'd kissed Drake playing right into said father's "find a man" nonsense.

Drake.

There had been no music for three days. She'd been worried the following morning, but Hazel mentioned he was "trying something new." Millie had swallowed her guilt.

No matter how many writing exercises she did or journals she filled, she would never be able to explain, let alone share witty date-appropriate stories about her life, her family. He wouldn't understand and she would always feel deficient.

His life was full of love and family. He lived in the town he grew up in. Ran a business he loved with friends who made him laugh. The man read one of her books for crying out loud. He championed writing romance because his life was rooted in love. Of course, she had not told him any of that last night when he'd taken her home on a bicycle, asked her for pizza and wine, and even showed her something he loved. No, instead of telling him how she felt, she'd shared as little as possible, kissed him, and blamed him for every shitty guy in the universe.

The night had started off great, but like he'd said, Drake wanted to get to know her. He wanted more than a Google search. He wanted to know why she'd been crying. And why wouldn't he want to know? She'd practically collapsed into his arms. She was a bundle of mixed signals and now she'd woken up multiple mornings without music and wanted nothing more than to check on him.

She could practically see the reader reviews of her current situation now—*The heroine annoyed the crap out of me. The way she strung the hero along and her erratic temper tantrums almost had me closing the book.*

Millie splashed water on her face. It was Friday morning. She only knew that after looking at her phone. She fed Pop-Tart, sat on the couch, and decided to take her own advice. Like she'd told Hazel, it was time to sort her feelings and find her truth. She had no clue what stage she was in after losing her mom or why she'd allowed her father to continue, but regardless, she was ready to be happy even with her laptop closed. Happy in the real world. So, she did what every healthy woman she'd ever put to paper did and called her best friend.

~

As a neighborly gesture, and because now he cared, Drake had struggled through two days with headphones, only to step on one and knock the other into the glory hole. He'd worked without music since lunch, but either Chase was grinding a block of solid steel or Drake's "issue" was getting worse.

Leaving the remaining projects for Esteban and Hazel, he left early and went to the Crab Shack. His parents were grateful for the extra help prepping for the Fisherman's Festival and Drake was glad for the distraction, no matter how chaotic. He looked forward to the festival every year, but the day and night before was rarely a good time. The crisis this year was whether the clam chowder was too salty. By the time his parents started their third round of "Try this. Are you sure? Here, try it with the crackers," Tyler, family by proxy, had joined Drake at an outside table carrying two extra beers and a third cup of chowder from the kitchen.

"Is it this way every year?" Tyler set the paper bowl down and opened his own beer.

Drake nodded.

"Why do I say I'll come over and help every year?"

"Because you're still hoping Jules will fall in love with you."

Tyler looked back at the restaurant. "Will you stop with that?"

Drake laughed.

"Relax. She took Bella back to the house like a half hour ago."

Tyler tasted the chowder. "It tastes exactly the same as—"

"How's that batch, honey?" Drake's mom called from the door.

"It's fantastic, Muriel. I think this is the one," Tyler called back.

"Not too much salt?"

"Not at all. It's perfect."

"Perfect?"

"Absolutely." Tyler set the spoon down and rubbed his eyes after she went back inside.

"I am not doing this next year." He sipped his beer.

"Sure you are." Drake stole the rest of the chowder.

"Have you talked to Millie yet?"

"Who's Millie?" Drake's dad came out with three more beers and sat down. "I'll tell you, that woman is going to be the death of me."

"I can hear you," she called outside.

"I love you with all my heart."

Nothing.

"Did you hear that?"

"No."

His father laughed and they clinked bottles.

"So, who are we talking about?"

His dad looked at Drake and got no answer so, as always, he went to his backup son.

"The woman renting the Millers' cottage."

Drake shook his head again. "Every time," he mumbled before another swig.

"What? His stare is powerful."

Drake looked at his dad, who narrowed his eyes and laughed.

"Oh, yeah. He's terrifying."

"Tyler has the hots for the renter?" his dad asked, and Drake ignored the twist in his gut at the idea of Tyler with Millie.

Tyler shook his head and looked at Drake with a grin that was payback.

His dad looked surprised, further clarification that Drake had been avoiding dating. "Really? Is she pretty?"

Drake held back a laugh. There were times he felt older than his parents, which his dad would say was a testament to good living. "I'm young at heart," he liked to say.

"Yeah," Tyler said. "She's very pretty."

"Drake?"

"She is."

"Anything else you want to add to that?"

"She's funny."

"She is," Tyler added.

"And smart."

"Wow. You know, your mom has me watching *The Walking Dead* now. She's all about zombies these days. What was wrong with *Big Bang Theory*, you know?"

Drake shook his head and Tyler laughed. "Dad, that has never worked."

"What?"

"That thing you do where you change the subject thinking it's going to put me at ease and I'll spill my guts. It's never worked."

"Not true. That one time when you took the car. I cut the tension with my story about Doritos." He raised his eyebrows. "You caved and confessed."

Tyler nodded.

"Fine. One time it worked, but I was sixteen."

His dad shrugged and took a swig of beer. "Okay, I'll give it to you straight. You're in trouble, my son."

Drake glanced over and for not the first time became very interested in his beer bottle label. "She's only here for a few months."

"Have you asked her out?"

Tyler snorted.

"What? A pretty, funny, smart woman moves in next door. You're a single guy. You asked her out, right?"

The simple logic of his dad's mind had always fascinated Drake. Even when they were kids, his dad had a way, a straight path to happy, like he could somehow maneuver around any obstacle.

"I don't court trouble anymore."

Which was a total lie because he'd now dried trouble's tears, had pizza and wine, and kissed the hell out of trouble. Well, she kissed him first, but that was not something he would ever bring up again because she called him "some guy," which still stung. Holy crap, he was thinking like her now. Rambling and nuts.

His father nodded. "Clever play on words."

"You like that?"

"I do. But you said she was only here for a little while."

"Dad. Are you suggesting a torrid temporary affair?"

"Smart-ass."

"Now that is a constant you can count on."

His dad got up and threw their bottles away.

"I think you could use a date."

"You and everyone else." Drake stood, suddenly needing the isolation of his own space.

Tyler joined in the getaway. "Thanks for the chowder, Muriel!" he yelled over his shoulder.

Drake shook his head. "Kiss ass."

"I heard that," his mom called. "You're a sweet boy, Tyler. Thank you."

"What about me?"

"You're a smartass."

Tyler nodded. "Twice in under an hour. I wonder if Millie appreciates sarcasm."

Drake scowled.

"You really could use a date or... at least what comes after the date."

"And what exactly is that, oh master of dating?"

Tyler waggled his brows as they walked toward the bay. "Dessert."

Drake cracked up. "You're so cool."

"I know, right?"

They got to the dock a few minutes later and sat at the edge. Drake had thought about explaining Jules's list, but Tyler went on about the new gallery and the conversation turned toward work, which was good. They were moving forward. There was no need to drag Tyler down with issues he had to handle on his own anyway.

Walking back to the Airstream, he glanced over at the Millers' cottage. Her lights were still on. He could walk those ten steps to the front door and... explain or pretend nothing had happened. They could still try to be friends, couldn't they? Rubbing the back of his neck, Drake called it a night.

Chapter Eighteen

Millie woke up early, and still no music. She had thought about heading over to check on Drake, but she was still working on what to say. After sorting through her feelings, she decided the best course was to apologize. She was tired of hiding out in Candy Land and she wasn't leaving, so that left "taking ownership of her mistake" and "making amends," so said Jade.

He had done nothing more than pick her up, introduce her to the surprisingly erotic world of glassblowing, and kiss her more thoroughly than a fictional hero with all the pages in the world. Now that she'd blown the lid straight off her serious charade, maybe she'd unpack all her daddy issues. Technically it didn't get any more "dark period" than what she'd gone through with Drake, so maybe it was time to rebuild a better and more honest version of herself.

Either way, she needed to apologize. If Drake accepted her apology, maybe she'd kiss him all over again and really light up her imaginary book reviewers. *Ugh, there was NOTHING lovable about this heroine. The hero deserved so much better and I was rooting for him to get with someone else the ENTIRE book.*

Millie would wait one more day, shower maybe, and then girl-up and make her peace. Until then, she needed to work on Alistair's childhood treehouse backstory. The same treehouse from which, as of the present draft, he would later plummet to his death. The beginning would foreshadow the end, which was a solid structure, but she'd gotten lost in the tree as a metaphor for his life and some nonsense about the rings before falling asleep on the couch last night, so she would revisit that today.

Pop-Tart yawned. Millie did too and then got up to brush her teeth.

"Breakfast?" she asked Pop-Tart, before shuffling to the kitchen.

Her heart jumped at the knock on the door. Patting down her hair and running through some of her better apology drafts, she opened the door, expecting Drake and finding his sister instead.

"Good morning. As captain of the *Eleanor* and the *Ginsburg*, I am here to invite you to the 48th Annual Fisherman's Festival," Jules said.

Millie laughed and gestured for her to come in, but she stayed put.

"I just got in and I smell like, well, dead fish."

Millie stepped outside.

"So, my eternally guilty brother met my boat this morning and mentioned that he had failed to invite you to Fish Fest. Super rude."

Millie hadn't grown up with siblings, but she'd had plenty of roommates at boarding school, so she understood some of the dynamics. There was a reason Drake hadn't invited her. *I'm a raving lunatic*, she wanted to say, but Jules obviously had no clue and Millie was fine keeping it that way.

"I would like you to come," she said so simply that Millie was thrown. Nothing sarcastic or manipulative to get her way. A straight-up, sincere invitation that could not be declined.

"Do I have to wear anything special?"

Jules clapped her hands together in small victory. "Nope. I mean you can wear a fish hat if you want, but my parents will have plenty extra. Bring yourself and"—she peered through the open door—"your adorable little cat if you want to walk in the pet parade."

Pop-Tart sauntered out of the bedroom and dropped onto her back at Millie's feet.

Jules laughed. "I think that's a no."

"She's not much of a joiner."

Drake's sister nodded; her expression might have conveyed: *I can't imagine where she gets that from.* But she said nothing.

"Do you have any pets?" Millie asked. Super awkward question, but she'd met Jules once for like a second.

"I have fish."

"Really?"

"No." She shook her head. Millie was struck by how much her mannerisms were like Drake's. The same tilt of her head, identical sarcasm, and even the weight in her eyes seemed familiar. Millie had always been intrigued by people who shared a childhood.

Aware that she was staring, she glanced back inside the cottage. "When is the festival?"

"Now. Well, not right this minute." Jules checked her watch. "In an hour."

She handed Millie a flyer. "Westside Park. There's a map on there if you don't know how to get there."

After thanking her for the invite and a few more minutes of Jules explaining that the festival opened salmon season and what a "blast" it would be, Millie closed the door and already wished she'd politely declined or had made up some excuse like she'd be working. If she'd been back in the city, no one would ever randomly knock on her door to be friendly. She had security and a doorman. Besides, what happened to barely tolerating tourists?

Millie went to the kitchen and only then realized she'd answered the door in her pajamas. That made two Branches who had seen her cats playing poker. At least Jules was polite enough not to mention it. Pouring coffee, she watched the sun speckle and dance along the surface of the glasslike water, cut only by the white wakes of the incoming boats. She did love the way sunlight played with things.

"Well, looks like I'm going to a festival today," she said to no one. Pop-Tart was now sprawled out on the kitchen windowsill.

"I know. Who would have thought?" Millie took her coffee into the bathroom.

Moments later, she'd brought to life Alistair's brother. A stocky guy who might be the one to push Alistair to his death. Maybe.

She jotted a few notes down and turned on the shower. Before hopping in, she returned to the notebook for two more notes and finally made it into the shower. In the words of Virginia Woolf, Millie "arranged whatever pieces came her way." She had notebooks and scraps of paper, apps on her phone, and even a couple of napkins with words, images, and whole chunks of dialogue. She tried to organize them every Sunday, so her best thoughts made it into her books, but for now, she was happy to write about something other than Alistair's dead body.

After scratching two more bits of dialogue, Millie wrung the extra water from her hair and pulled on a pair of jeans and a T-shirt that was too big, so she tied it at her waist. She put pomade in her mass of curls and hoped it behaved before grabbing the flyer Jules had left. Wooden boat-building competition, tents with food and crafts, and the Blessing of the Fleet. Curiosity piqued, Millie put on her shoes and knew Drake would be there.

"It's not like I've been avoiding him," she said out loud. She needed to stop talking to herself when she wasn't writing, especially in this town. First, she cried on their sidewalks and now she blurted out random thoughts. Someone could have her committed. On a shrug and some brief imaginings about what the process of committing a person was, she realized she still had time and threw herself onto the couch. She picked up the book Jade had given her at dinner. An advanced copy that was "totally worth breaking the no-romance rule."

Tucking the flyer into the back of the book, Millie decided instead of worrying about how she was going to apologize to Drake, she'd escape to New England. That way if things became too much, she could simply close the book. Not that she'd ever been able to close anything written by Kristan Higgins, but at least she had options.

~

The 48th Annual Bodega Bay Fishing Festival or Fish Fest to the locals had kicked off every fishing season, save a couple of years that were so abysmal there was nothing to kick off, for as far back as Drake could remember. He'd been at his father's side since he was seven and even helmed the boats for a few years. Later in the day, his sister would stand tall as Father Frank blessed her fleet. Jules was a pro, a better captain than Drake had ever been, not that he was sharing that with her. Ever. But it was true. She'd returned to Bodega Bay and taken up the slack faster than he'd have given her credit for back when she was famous for her in failed attempts to sneak out of the house.

This year was looking like one of their best seasons yet. They would hoot and holler, laugh and celebrate, but first they had to build a boat in four hours. One that would hopefully float, or at least not take on water two seconds after launch.

Shoving a hand through his hair after dropping the rest of their allotted wood under the BP Glass Works tent, Drake tried to focus on his town, his life, and the traditions that kept him solid. Millie was passing through. Kiss or no kiss, he needed to remember that. The fact that he couldn't get the feel of her mouth or the taste of her tongue out of his mind was doing nothing for his mood.

She'd freaked out seconds after that sweet moan slid from her lips. Completely freaked out, but technically she had shared. Granted, he would have preferred less yelling and more kissing, but that's not how the evening played out.

At first, the door slam seemed like a bad ending, but now that he'd had a few days to think about it, they had made progress. Freaking out was honest. It was better than holding all that crap inside. Drake could handle it. God knew he had doled out his fair share of outbursts in the first few months of his recovery.

Life was messy and feelings could get ugly. Tyler instilled that bit of wisdom one night when Drake's not-quite-healed leg gave out and his best friend found him on the floor by the kitchen. His parents weren't home so the two of them sat there on the floor, ate pork rinds, and hashed out some pretty ugly feelings.

If that's what Millie had done the other night it was fine, great even. It meant she trusted him enough to lay it out. That was a compliment, and he preferred her temper over the vacant stare in her eyes when he'd watched her collapse in the alley.

She had obviously been avoiding him since, but hope bloomed eternal that she'd put on that much-talked-about bra and show up at the festival. She could even yell at him again as long as she kissed him too.

Chapter Nineteen

*M*illie had been to some of the biggest writing conferences in the world. She'd been on book tours with lines outside the building, but somehow Fish Fest in Bodega Bay, with its makeshift tents and rainbow laughter, was awe-inspiring. She'd been to other countries, stood among crowds of cover models and enthusiastic readers, but all of that seemed temporary. Quick flashes of posters and color that eventually ended up balled in the trash once it was time to move onto the next signing, the next event, the next book. She was aware that Bodega Bay didn't rest in a perpetual state of festival, but it did seem that most things were permanent, maybe with minor adjustment to the volume based on the day.

She was never happier than at the beginning of a book. Two new people, their friends and family. Beginnings were joyful and full of choices yet made. There were no mistakes yet, no wasted words or hair-pulling rewrites. Every book she'd ever written, even the ones tucked away in her closet that would never have a cover, started with a rush and ended with her alone and crying. Not because the ending was sad, she always ended with love and promise, but because she had to say goodbye.

Books were permanent. She could always revisit the story. The polished version was permanent, but the journey was over and as a writer, her work was done. After all the long nights and struggle, she had to let them go. From that moment forward, she could return to their final draft, but only as a reader. Her work was done and with equal parts joy and pain, she cried every time.

In the years since her first signing bonus, through the realization her bills were on time, Millie had never laid down roots. It was possible she didn't know how. She was so used to observing, writing, and saying goodbye, she never sorted through the mess of her own first draft. The stability of Drake and the invitation in his eyes before she kissed him had felt grounded, much like the man. A surge of belonging followed by the ebbing fear that if she kept kissing him, touching him, wanting him, it would all be snatched away.

It was easier to believe that he was taking pity on her. Acknowledging what was happening between them, losing herself in his concern, the kiss, and his shoulder to lean on was not something Millie knew how to do. Not out from behind her laptop anyway. When she wrote her books, she decided the beats. She knew the dark period and how her characters would make it to the other side. Life wasn't that way. Dark periods came out of nowhere, chapter 4 or chapter 30, life didn't care about structure. Hate sometimes won and love, no matter how strong, often died.

None of these thoughts helped Millie come up with a proper apology as she found Westfield Park, but by the time she spotted Jules, she'd edited herself down to a few simple sentences.

Millie met Drake's niece, who promptly said that Millie reminded her of Merida from the movie *Brave*. A major compliment. Bella, who had gorgeous dark hair and a toothy smile like her mom, was astride what looked like a bike attached to a table saw. As she pedaled, the saw slowly chewed through the wooden boards Esteban pushed along the table.

Drake's T-shirt was wet and clinging to a chest Millie would admire even if her hands didn't now know how incredible it was to touch him. His left hand clamped him in place, supported the muscles in his shoulders as he hammered one piece of cut board to another. Jules sat painting other pieces but spotted Millie approaching and hopped to her feet.

"I would hug you for coming, but again, I am a mess," she said, holding her stained hands at her sides.

Millie leaned forward, hoping her crazy nerves were not obvious, and gave her a small hug anyway. If she were able to write herself a sister, she would write a woman exactly like bold and perpetually messy Jules Branch. Drake glanced up. His eyes were hidden behind sunglasses. When he returned to work without a word, she understood he was the kind of man who listened when a woman told him to leave her alone.

"So, this is the... wooden boat-building competition?" She glanced back at the banner in front of the cordoned-off area and took in their setup.

"The one and only. Four hours, no power tools, which explains Bella's pedal power there." Jules pointed to her daughter, clad in a mermaid T-shirt and a sparkly fish hat. "I'm sure you recognize the rest of your neighbors."

Hazel looked up from measuring larger pieces of wood, propped her sunglasses on her head, and waved, as did Esteban, who took over for Bella on the saw cycle.

"Nice to see you, Millie," he said. "No time to talk. We're down one man."

"Where the hell is—"

"Right here. Reporting for boat duty, Captain." Tyler stood next to Jules.

"We're already an hour in. Maybe you should give Drake a—"

Tyler held up his hands. "The guy has more strength in those one-and-a-half arms than the rest of us have in our entire body. He'll be fine for a few minutes. Besides, he doesn't look all that ready for a break." He looked over, and Millie wondered if Drake shared everything with his best friend.

"I don't know, Fancy Pants. You have some decent guns to contribute."

For a breath, Tyler seemed like a kid who'd been called on in class for the first time, but his expression vanished behind a glossy smile as he pulled his sunglasses from the neck of his shirt.

"Aw, thanks for noticing, Jules. Makes all that time at the gym so worth it."

She shrugged. "No problem. I had to squint to see them under that blinding shirt, but they're there."

Tyler ignored Jules. "Always a pleasure to see you again, Millie."

"You too, Tyler."

"Jules." He nodded. "The paint-explosion look is good on you."

"Thanks. Did you have trouble picking out your Fish Fest outfit? Is that why you're late?"

He shook his head. "Millie, this is a great shirt, right?"

"Oh, no. I thought us out-of-towners didn't have a say."

"You do now. The shirt?"

"It suits you. I like it."

Jules scoffed.

"See, it suits me." He looked over at Jules, who smiled. The instant before Tyler dropped his sunglasses over his eyes Millie thought she recognized what she considered the most tragic of romance tropes—unrequited love.

Tyler pulled his shirt from his shorts and unbuttoned the front. Jules was on her way back to painting but stopped when he slid out of his plaid and stepped in front of her. Millie's mouth went slack. Plot twist.

"I'm late because Sissy forgot to pick up the wreath for the Blessing of the Fleet," he said, close to her ear. "You're part of that fleet, right?"

Jules nodded, making a clear effort not to take in all the bare skin inches from her hands. If Millie were writing this scene, they would be in one another's arms already, but again... reality. So, she kept quiet and watched it play out.

"So, I kind of saved the day," Tyler said. "You're welcome, Captain." He draped the shirt over her shoulder. "Could you hold this for me since it's so offensive? I should get to work."

He walked off without a word and Millie had to take a sip from her water bottle to swallow her laugh. She wanted to shout, "Well played," but kept it to herself.

Jules, to her credit, recovered faster than most. Tossing his shirt on a chair, she rolled her eyes and picked up her paintbrush.

Drake had moved onto another piece of their boat and still hadn't said a word. She wanted to ask why they were no longer playing music and assure him if it was because of her, he needn't bother. She was great and maybe it was best that they were back to ignoring one another. She wanted to repeat his words: it was only a kiss. Right?

Annoyed by her never-ending thoughts and that she'd forgotten her own sunglasses to hide her wandering eyes, Millie turned her back on his stupid biceps and joined the crowd gathering by the ramp for the wooden boat race. After some scouting for a spot on the grass, she noticed an older woman wearing a great scarf and sitting on a blanket reading Lori Foster.

Unable to contain the glee of discovering another romance reader, Millie sat close in the hopes of striking up a conversation. She needed a little book talk.

~

Drake had always welcomed a challenge. Before his accident, he worked to outthink, outrun, and even out-earn anyone who got in his way. While his father's insistence that Drake take over the family fishing boats after college graduation was expected, he still pushed. He wanted to make his own way and relying solely on fishing, especially when he'd seen firsthand what fluxes in the industry did to the families he grew up around, was never part of his plan.

So, after graduation, he captained their two boats in the early mornings and took a job in San Francisco as an associate for a wealth-management firm. Five years later, Tyler bought the firm where they both started out and two others while Drake, driving his motorcycle home one night, his head full of ideas and wanting more, took a turn too fast and nearly lost everything.

Waking up in pain and more terrified than he'd ever been in his life, he was forced to start over. Dependent on his family for more months than he cared to remember, Drake had channeled everything he had left into recovery. He pushed through ten surgeries and defied every statistic and threshold his doctors laid out. Pain became his new normal as he once again fought for his independence.

Physical therapy led to strength training, which led to yoga. When he was plagued by nightmares, he meditated every morning and had a standing weekly acupuncture appointment until they were gone. When his body was strong and his head calmed, he started a business with Tyler and moved into his own place. Drake had gone to hell and come back stronger and humbled. "An unstoppable combination," his dad had said the night they showed his parents around BP Glass Works.

With all of that behind him, the few things on his sister's list should be an afterthought. He should be done and moving on to bigger and better things. Yet here he was hoping he could at least check off "getting on the boat" before the day was over. Jules would go out for the Blessing of the Fleet and he would be by her side, on that boat. He had no idea if being back on the water would trigger any "issues"—Christ, he hated that word— and a big festival was probably not the best time to find out, but he needed to get over some of this stuff if he was ever going to be okay without the music.

Speaking of music, he'd planned on casually saying hello to Millie when she met Jules at their booth, but when he looked up, he lost his nerve. It seemed like he was doing that a lot lately. Hell, if he needed dating practice, there were plenty of women, far less complicated. The problem was he'd kissed her. He'd played it off as her idea, her first move, but he'd be lying if he said he hadn't thought about it. A lot. And when she kissed him, he was right there with her for every minute.

Drake finished attaching the sail to their makeshift boat and left to grab a water before watching the race. He had decided to jump off the dock before the height of the season in case he made an ass of himself. Then hopefully he'd learn to tolerate the sound of grinding metal or celebrating Chase moving into a larger space sooner rather than later. That left dating.

Taking a long pull of water, he couldn't get the way her eyes lit with challenge and humor or the memory of her body snug against his out of his mind. Unlike the rest of his list, wanting Millie wasn't something he could jot down. She had to want him too and, well it seemed like she had a list of her own, so he'd left her to it.

But now, she looked so at home among his family and friends that he hadn't been able to quiet the pounding in his chest long enough to say something. Anything. Dating would have to wait.

BP Glass Works' wooden boat entry was finished with five minutes to spare. Esteban and Hazel volunteered to race since Tyler and Jules would most likely kill each other and she had to decorate her boats before the procession anyway. After helping their father-daughter team over to the ramp, Drake scanned the shore for a place to watch. There were hundreds of people, maybe thousands this year, so how he found Millie sitting on a blanket in a lively conversation with Auntie N, had to be fate. Right? Did he believe in fate?

Undecided, but drawn to her like a moth, he settled on the "What? Were we fighting?" denial strategy and walked toward them. His godmother, who hadn't noticed his approach, jumped when he sat down next to her and quickly slapped his shoulder for "scaring the bejesus" out of her.

Drake laughed, noticed Millie's surprise, and was again grateful for his sunglasses.

"I see you've finally met Millie," he said.

"Oh my God. You're—" Auntie N smacked him again. "You're such a little stinker."

"What? I assumed since you two were talking that you got over your... What do you call it?"

"Fangirling." She glanced at Millie, who was equally surprised that she was not just sitting next to any romance reader in the middle of a festival.

"I was trying to play it cool and it was working until you barged over here. We were talking romance and favorite tropes. That's an industry term," she said, her expression very secret-handshake.

"Is it now?"

Millie nodded and reached over to take Auntie N's hand in such earnest that Drake found he was back to staring at a woman who continued to surprise him. She'd expected the Millers' cottage to be a refuge and had ended up with an obnoxious neighbor. She was obviously dealing with her own issues but set aside mornings to help Hazel get into college, and now here she was entertaining his godmother's love of romance novels.

She'd sold millions of books and was not only routinely on the *New York Times* best-seller list, she'd written several articles on everything from the value of reading to a plea to save an inner-city library, according to Tyler's extensive Google search. If ever a woman had the credentials to be as pretentious as her glossy bio photos, it was Millie Hart. And yet here she was again, seemingly enthralled by the ordinary of Bodega Bay.

"It's even more of a pleasure to meet the woman who has dedicated her bookstore to romance," Millie said.

Both women squeezed hands and Auntie N beamed.

"Now I can gush. I have read every one of your books, sweetie. Some of them twice. You write great men." She fanned herself, and Millie laughed before thanking her graciously.

Ignoring that they had gone from kissing to days of silence turned out to be the right move. Hazel and Esteban raced BP Glass Works into a respectable third place in the Fish Fest Wooden Boat Race amid laughter and standing cheers. Before the Blessing of the Fleet, Millie asked him to join her while she explored the rest of the booths. Drake quickly got to his feet and recommended the oysters first.

"You write great men, huh?" He asked, brushing the grass off his jeans.

Millie nodded, seemingly nervous or distracted.

"Do you base them on anyone in particular?" He grinned at the stupidity of his question, but he didn't care so long as they didn't slip back into silence.

"Are you asking me if I model my characters after my ex or current lovers?"

"Yes."

"No."

Okay, well that went nowhere. He tried a more direct approach.

"You a big dater, Millie?" They stopped to buy some baked oysters. "Back home, I mean."

"I have dated." She ate two oysters in a row without hesitation. Drake didn't know why he was still surprised. Since the day she'd arrived, anytime he pegged her as one thing, she proved him wrong.

"Fascinating, but please stop talking. It's too much information."

She ate another oyster and side-eyed him. He could tell she was considering how much to give up. He could have declared he wanted her to share all of it right there in front of the entire town, but he was, as already established by pretty much everyone now, a little rusty, so he refrained.

"I have been on some dates. I'm not great at it."

Welcome to the club.

"Why not?"

"Well." She exhaled as they walked toward the kettle corn. "According to a lovely psychologist I went to in my twenties before I gave up figuring out my own love life, I have issues being vulnerable. God, I hate that word"–she scrunched her face—"issues."

Reading my mind again.

He nodded but said nothing and hoped she'd continue.

"There was some stuff in there about expectations, but I don't remember most of it." She shook her head and glanced at him. "Was that even your question?"

Her face flushed when he nodded some more. "Yes, I have dated and... a few years ago I almost moved in with a guy. So that's totally sharing, right?"

He wasn't sure if she was having this conversation with herself, but she'd stopped walking, so he backtracked and answered. "Living with someone is a big step. What happened?"

"A lot of things, but it all came down to yawning."

Drake tried to follow and failed.

"He never yawned when I yawned, ya know?"

"Yawning is important?"

"Super important. It shows empathy. People are supposed to yawn when others yawn or sometimes even at the mention of yawning."

They both yawned. And Drake smiled. It was so easy to be happy around her.

"See," she pointed out. "That's normal. If we were going to share the same apartment, we should have been yawning together. I yawned and he didn't. We split on good terms. Kind of. Does anyone ever truly split on good terms?"

"Has not been my experience."

"Speaking of your experiences, how about you?"

"I walked right into that one. I have... yawned with a couple of people in my life."

"It's good to yawn."

They had been to all the booths before she stopped again.

"I'm—"

"If we head over—"

Drake nodded. "You first."

"I'm sorry about the other day... night. The thing is," she continued, her expression that same mixture of sadness and joy, "I'm trying to be something I'm not... I think that's it. And so when I kissed you it—" She sighed. "I don't know what I'm doing. I really don't know what I'm doing around you."

Drake tried to remind himself she was leaving, but his heart didn't care.

"I should not have taken my crappy day out on you." She faced him. "You were only trying to help, and I appreciate it. I'm... my life is... my past is—."

He smiled. "You're editing again."

"Occupational hazard." She grinned.

He shrugged. "I'm kind of honored that you took your crap out on me. In fact, it might be a new step in our relationship."

"Our relationship, huh? Not the best start."

"I don't know. I think, having only read one romance novel—"

"So far."

"Right, so far. I think we're pretty standard. Small-town romance writer who occasionally wears a bra arrives. She's the worst neighbor and is so rude that the guy, our hero, backs off, but—"

She laughed, pulling the fish hat he'd bought her firmly into place, and Drake suddenly saw a life with her. He knew they were at a festival, an exception to everyday, but he wanted more time. Sunshine or rain, kissing or arguing. She somehow breathed more life into everything he already appreciated. Like an extra gather of glass or a color that changed the whole piece. He wanted her, and he knew from experience he'd never have a shot unless he showed up.

"But, what?" she said, tears of laughter glistening along her eyelashes. "Finish the story."

"But he can't stop thinking about her." He moved closer. "Or that kiss. He's..."

Her breath caught. "He's?"

"He's not sure what he's doing around her either, but he wants to keep doing it." Drake's eyes fell to her mouth and this time when she pulled him between two booths, he kissed her first.

Chapter Twenty

*L*ife Edit: Millie Hart *was* very good at dating and kissing the right man.

A key component to any relationship, real or fiction, was being able to apologize. She'd done that, and now she stood tucked away in Bodega Bay clutching at a man she would not in a million years be able to commit to paper. The first time she'd kissed him she worried that her damaged parts had led her to fall into the arms of a man, any man, to heal her own pain.

That wasn't it at all. She'd found Drake despite her damaged parts and no matter how much she shared, good and bad, he seemed to want more. There were only three people Millie had allowed into her heart. Her mother filled it with love and was taken away. Her father had mocked that full heart and broken it in two. It had taken her awhile, but she learned to share her heart in friendship, and Jade had protected her ever since.

She had no role models for romantic love after the age of twelve, so Millie turned to books. Romance taught her that it was okay to be quirky. That she was strong and capable of anything she dreamed possible. The women who came before her, who picked up where her mother had left off, taught her to find her fierce and her pleasure.

Most importantly, those writers showed her that settling was a fool's game. If she held strong, made her own life, and stayed true to her heart and her choice to be happy, someday she would find a partner who had done the same.

"Send out all the good energy and remember to be grateful when it is returned." Her mom used to tuck her in with those words when she was a little girl. When she was gone, dozens of other women filled her with the same dreams. And with that strength, she'd gone on to do the same for other women. It was a chain of hearts she'd always been so honored to be a part of, and now kissing a man who wanted both her happy and her sad, Millie was so sorry she'd been led astray by one cold Christmas Eve. That she had allowed her father to continue taking her good energy while sending nothing in return. Despite the messiness of family, she knew better. She'd been taught by the best.

A horn blew from the direction of the docks and her eyes flew open. Drake eased back, a smile teasing his well-kissed lips.

"Have you ever been on a fishing boat?"

She shook her head, still basking in the gloriousness of rediscovery. Drake kissed her again. This time her hands fell to his chest and the steady beat of his heart. She could count on this and stand shoulder to shoulder with him. Her own heart knew it.

~

Drake offered Millie a hand as she and a few other dozen people climbed aboard the *Ginsburg*. Once she was secure, he released her hand, but she didn't let go. As he stepped over painted steel and onto the deck, Millie held on. It wasn't a gesture most people would notice, but with the exception of his accident, he'd spent most of his life as the responsible one. He had two younger sisters to look after and parents who saw him as part of the family succession. Emotionally, he held them up and they did the same, but Drake didn't lean unless he physically could not stand on his own. Branches got up and got on with it.

Grasping her hand, allowing that support felt a bit like testing the legs of a chair before plopping down and kicking back. She'd been yelling at him that the feelings they clearly shared were a mistake. She'd back off, but now here she was helping him without even knowing how much he needed her at that moment. Or maybe she did know. She was the most observant person he'd ever met, so anything was possible.

His pulse quickened as the boat pulled away from the dock to a frenzy of horns and celebration. It was joyful and supposed to be fun, but it was also on his list. There was a reason Drake had avoided getting back on their fishing boats for six years. He was sure it had something to do with control or being in a situation he was no longer confident he could escape. He knew himself. He just didn't always know how to get over himself.

"So, how does this work?" she asked, her curiosity helping dismiss the fear creeping around his collar.

"All of the boats go out to the *Elena* where Father Frank will bless them," he said before giving her a little history of the industry in his familiar tour guide tone.

Millie listened, they both laughed a few guys already several beers into their celebration, and Drake found a steady breath.

"They do a fundraiser every year for the hospital. The fishing company that raises the most money gets to pick a boat from their fleet to be the blessing boat."

"Is everything in this town based on tradition or set in stone?"

"Pretty much."

"Have your family's boats ever won?"

"Three years running. Jules lost out to Mike this year by three hundred dollars. She claims he cheated and put the money in himself, but—"

"But nothing. He did cheat." Jules stood behind him and smiled when he faced her. He hadn't realized he was still holding Millie's hand, but he was and wasn't letting go despite his sister's gleeful expression.

"Welcome aboard," she said to Millie.

"Thank you. I've never been on a fishing boat."

"I will let my more-than-capable predecessor show you around."
She pulled on a knit cap and threw her scarf across her shoulder.
"Because I need to go be leader-like."

"Are you feeling festive?" he asked.

Jules scrunched her face. "Not particularly. How are you?" Jules
hesitated and met his gaze.

"More than capable. You said it yourself." Beads of sweat rimmed
his hairline, but Drake swallowed, kept breathing and reminded
himself that a fishing boat had not gone over or sunk in Bodega Bay
in his lifetime or his fathers. That was a long time.

"But I do not want to piss off the gods so I will get up there and
pray my ass off."

Drake and Millie both laughed as Jules walked toward the bow.
She glanced over her shoulder one more time as if to survey Millie in
case she needed backup. He shook his head and Jules moved on.

Alone again, Drake directed her to the stern for the best view of
the ceremony.

"Were you nervous on boats when you were the captain?"

Drake grinned. So much for putting one past her. "No. I've spent
my whole life, save the past six years, on these boats."

"Huh? First time since your accident."

"You're good."

She shrugged. "Part of the job. And, it makes sense. Control, I get
it."

Her eyes trailed over his body. It wasn't the first time he'd felt
examined by Millie, but there was nothing hesitant. She was full on
checking him out. She had a way of making a guy feel downright
fascinating.

"Why hasn't some loud-music-playing woman snatched you up,
Drake Branch?"

He shrugged. "Maybe it's the bum arm."

"I guarantee you that women are not even looking at the arm. I
mean, they are looking at both of them, but the part you lost is not a
factor."

"No?"

She shook her head. "There is so much... no one is missing it."

He laughed.

"Except maybe you."

"It can be a pain in the ass sometimes."

She touched his shoulder, fingers trailing gentle and cautious like she was still learning his body, before leaning up to kiss him. Small town be damned, he released her hand and wrapped an arm around her waist. All at once, Drake wasn't worried about drowning, at least not in the water.

After several oohs and ahhs, they went back to holding hands.

Drake watched with pride as his sister rode toward the blessing boat on the helm of the *Ginsburg* her crew of all men lined up behind her. The *Eleanor* was close behind. Both Branch Fishing boats were decked out in quilted cloth flags of red, salmon, and blue.

Their parents' boats used to be named the *Juliet* and the *Sistine*, but after Jules took over as captain and following several heated family dinner discussions where there wasn't enough beer to make Drake stay, they had agreed to let her rename the boats.

"How the hell am I supposed to helm a boat named after me? Like the guys don't already think this is a joke."

"Who thinks it's a joke?" their dad said in that tone that suggested even at sixty he was still ready to roll up his sleeves and kick ass.

Jules had won and named her boats after her two favorite women. She'd even managed to get their father to spring for a full repaint, which was a testament to either Jules's persuasive nature or her relentless hounding. Drake never figured out which finally tipped things in her favor.

She and her ten-man crew now wore the same knit caps they'd had for years. Sistine had knitted all of them a few years ago to celebrate their sister being the first female fishing boat captain in all of California. Jules wore pink and green, Bella's favorite colors. All the caps were different shades and flared at the top like fish tails.

Ten massive men, some of them with beards they had to tie in a bun when they were working, several with well-earned beer guts, and most of them tatted to the neck, all wore rainbow hats in deference and total respect to the woman who led them.

As it should be, Drake thought, swallowing the lump in his throat. Jules was a fair and phenomenal leader. She'd taught him so much and now he was proud to be out there on the boat to watch her represent their family and her fleet as Father Frank blessed them all. The ceremony was a mixture of humor and honest tradition. Bodega Bay was a town that counted on a thriving fishing season. Sure, tourism had taken up some of the slack during the "scraps of a season," as their dad put it, but fishing and crabbing were the town's industry. The thing that got them up early and achy to bed at night.

It was in their blood, every one of them, whether they were out on a boat or not. When the fishing went to crap, so did the town, and while Drake was now on the artsy tourist side, he wanted nothing more than for all these men and the one woman to have a blessed and thriving salmon season. He caught Millie out of the corner of his eye as she watched in fascination at the processions filled with joy as Father Frank finished speaking his last words into a megaphone.

She caught him staring at her.

"You've watched this since you were little?"

"Story goes my mom was seven months pregnant with me and dressed like a crab on John Finney's boat before we ever had boats or the Crab Shack."

"Incredible. What a wonderful way to grow up."

"It wasn't always festivals."

She looked back at him. "Of course not, but there's such laughter and freedom here. Look at everyone." She gestured to the crowd, most of whom were now singing a song Drake knew by heart.

Millie laughed and pulled her fish cap down over her ears, her own pride in participating written all over her wind-pinked cheeks and wild hair begging for escape. He squeezed her hand in silent gratitude he hoped she could feel. It had taken him six years to get back on the boat and support his sister, but this was a solid check off the list and Drake was happy he was able, with a little help, to "girl-up" just in time.

Chapter Twenty-One

*A*fter the festival, Millie drove back to the cottage, her mind like cotton candy, after what was the best day she'd ever had in her adult life, maybe ever. She dealt in fiction and was intimately familiar with exaggeration, yet the sunshine-warmed satisfaction in her chest was real. It wasn't a fleeting summer or anything that would go away with a good night's sleep.

She loved these people. Her heart was full of their stories, experiences she'd only ever explored in plotting sessions or pinned to inspiration boards. Bodega Bay was made up of men and women, families and friends, and even those pesky tourists who grabbed life and held onto happy as tight as she had known was possible her whole life.

Pulling into the narrow gravel driveway of the cottage that felt more like home than any place she'd ever lived, she knew Drake was right behind her. He would park his truck ten moss-covered and uneven pavers away from her and crawl into his Airstream. She would wake up to his music and if she ventured away from her writing, she would see him. If she walked into her cottage, locked the door, her night would wind down same as all the others and give way to another sunrise.

She grabbed her fish hat off the seat and closed the car door. The night nipped at her cheeks and as she had done since arriving in Bodega Bay, she looked to the sky. It was overcast with clouds that reminded her of cold winter huffs of breath. The stars peeked around the open spots, mischievous and scattered. A truck door slammed behind her and her heart thundered wild in her chest.

"Stargazing again, neighbor?"

Millie turned and hoped her expression said everything coursing through her body because she wasn't sure she could speak. Drake walked across their little divide.

"Are you okay?"

She was staring, but she didn't care. She was about to ask a man to her bed, so the gauge for her normal was good and broken.

"Millie."

God, she loved the way he said her name. The gravel of his voice. Standing in front of him, she realized she had no words and no idea how to seduce a man in the real world. She wanted him. Needed to feel every inch of his body and show him everything he'd given her, but she wasn't sure—

"I want you." Her voice was almost lost in the vastness of the night. Drake took the last step between them, tilting his head to meet her gaze, which had fallen to the floor.

"It took you awhile to edit that down."

She nodded and when his hand slid into her hair, Millie closed her eyes. Drake pulled her into his body, kissed her jaw, and trailed his lips to the base of her ear. With his mouth nestled into the curve of her neck, he took in a deep breath and when he let it out, her entire body shivered with need.

"I want you too." He kissed her neck and teased her lips before entwining his fingers with hers and walking her past the gnomes.

"Please tell me you have the keys?"

Millie laughed, grateful for the break before her body melted all over him. She let go of his hand and pulled the infamous keys from her back pocket. Attached to the silver ring was a small plastic gnome.

Drake raised a brow.

"I wanted to keep them with me always." She unlocked the door, tossed the keys on the table, and didn't bother turning on the lights. The moonlight reflected off the clouds, filling the cottage with a glow she felt in her heart as she kissed him and walked toward the bedroom.

Not sure where to start, she reached for his shirt and he stilled her hand. She met his eyes, hoping to all things holy that he wasn't about to tell her he couldn't be with her. That he had a girlfriend he had not mentioned, a wife hidden away somewhere, or that he was an alien sent to destroy Earth. She almost chuckled at the depths to which her mind went when she was filled with longing and a touch of fear.

Drake lifted her chin and kissed her again, this time more desperate and searching. She ran her hands along his chest and around to the massive plane of his back, her fingers at the edge of his T-shirt. He stepped back. There was nothing wrong between them. In fact, the heat threatened to swallow them both up before they ever got their clothes off, so what was the problem? She turned on the anchor-shaped light near the bed.

The expression on Drake's face was a mixture of lust and apprehension. What in the hell? Sensing her unease, he stepped closer but didn't touch her. Was she supposed to read his mind? Because she was going to need a narrator or at least access to internal thoughts. As he touched the side of her face, seemingly giving it another try, she begged for a quick POV change. She knew head-hopping was frowned upon in fiction, but maybe this once in the real world, she could know what the beautiful man who clearly wanted her too but was not taking his clothes off was thinking. Maybe it was—

"Condoms?" Millie blurted out before she could stop herself.

Drake laughed and sat down on the bed.

"Is that what this is? Because believe it or not, the Millers are stocked." She sat next to him.

"I bought them a television, so we can totally use the whole box."

Drake shifted to face her, a lingering laugh still at the edges of a more serious expression, and Millie had a sinking feeling this had nothing to do with protection. Not the kind that came in a box anyway.

~

Drake would gladly have jumped off a dock or even listened to an hour of Chase's grinding-metal torture if it meant he was not sitting on a bed with Millie like some nervous virgin. He wanted her more than he'd ever wanted anyone in his life. Ever. But every time she reached for his shirt or he thought about whether he was going to take his prosthesis off, his jaw locked and he pulled away. Sex wasn't conducive to lists or nightly routines, but the facts were he'd been rejected hard after his accident and had been with only one woman since. That time had been pleasantly buzzed sex and nothing more. He'd kept his shirt and his arm on, but this—Millie was different. He wasn't crawling out of bed an hour later and going home before the sun.

He wanted to show her how much he cared about her and stay as long as she'd have him. That kind of naked scared him almost as much as his ever-growing list.

Drake exhaled and met her still-smiling eyes. Christ, she was easy to love.

Here goes nothing.

He started and stopped again. "Shit." He closed his eyes.

"There is nothing you can't tell me. Well, except you're married or an alien."

For a moment neither of them said a word. Drake opened his eyes and hoped like hell he wasn't going to regret this.

"The men you write about." This sounded stupid already.

"What about them?"

"They're based on an ideal, right?"

"I... suppose. I like to think they're fully developed, but yes." She nodded. "They do often jump out of planes and usually have the best comebacks."

"They're full."

"I... is that a question? You didn't like the rest of the book and you're bringing that up now?"

Her brow scrunched and Drake wished to God his life was simple if only for one night. That he could hoist her into his arms and watch her fall apart around him, but nothing, especially lately, was simple.

"You... don't want to sleep with me because my book sucks? That makes no sense, but didn't you like when Brix—"

"Millie."

She cocked her head.

"I haven't finished the book yet."

She snorted. "Sorry, I... never mind. You were saying."

Silence. He should probably rip her clothes off and worry about everything else much later. That's what Brix would have done. Yeah, he was now looking to fictional characters for sex advice. *Perfect.*

"Okay." Drake stood. "Here goes. You write men who I'm assuming are the kinds of men you find attractive. Guys who are... Yeah, I don't know. Forget it. I dated a woman for about two years before my accident. After I healed... damn it. I'm sorry. This is not how I wanted this to go, but I can't—"

She stood and took his arm. Drake was reminded of the first time she touched his prosthesis without hesitation. She was still that woman, only now she wanted him in her bed and he was jacking the entire thing up.

"I'm... only saying that people say they're 'totally fine' with a guy who has been broken all over the road and sewn back together, but I know from past experience that when faced with the real thing, women—"

He lost his courage, lost his words at her expression.

"I'm not looking for that." He waved a hand at her. "Stop looking at me like that. I don't want sympathy. I want you to know what you're getting into."

She stepped into him and ran her hand up his prosthesis and to the skin of his upper arm, her eyes shifting from concern to heat in less than a breath.

He shook his head. "Why are we doing this? We should leave well enough alone. You don't want to be vulnerable and I'm—"

"We should definitely leave well enough alone." She went up on her toes and kissed his neck. "I need you to listen to me." Her voice was thick as she moved along the edge of his T-shirt.

Drake mocked a sigh because if he didn't find humor, she was going to burn him alive with her clothes on. "More talking?"

"You'll be okay." She found his eyes. "I have written all kinds of men, Drake Mortimer Branch. All of them, yes, lovely to look at, but broken on the inside. You—" Her eyes glistened. "I could never have imagined a man like you. I'm not that good of a writer. You are more—"

He looked away because again it was easy to say.

"You know what? Rule number one in writing a great story is show-don't-tell. I'm going with that." She pulled off her sweatshirt and smirked when his eyes went to her bra.

"Told you."

His grin fell when she unzipped her jeans and slid them off her legs. A few more clips and Millie was standing naked in front of him. She pulled the elastic from her hair, curls tumbling over her shoulders, and Drake clenched his fist and begged for breath. She ran a flat hand up his stomach and over to his prosthesis.

"May I?" Her hand hovered at the release near the back of his arm.

"How do you—"

She grinned.

"Seriously? What did you Google?"

She leaned in to kiss him, her gorgeous breasts pressing against a T-shirt he suddenly couldn't care less about.

"I'll tell you later," she whispered, her eyes still asking for permission to remove his arm.

Nodding, he closed his eyes. She pulled his prosthesis free, set it down somewhere, and removed the cover that protected his skin.

Drake opened his eyes. Millie kissed his shoulder, down his bicep, across to his chest, and down to his waistband. Eyes now on him and checking in every step of the way, she lifted the edge of his T-shirt before kissing her way up his chest, sliding the material over his shoulders and letting it drop to the floor.

Without a single word, she took his breath away. When she lifted his hand to her breast and whispered, "I need you," he lost his mind.

~

How in any world a man like Drake would question a woman wanting him was beyond Millie's comprehension. He wrapped his arm around her waist and lowered her to the bed, his mouth and body over her in a passion so powerful she could barely breathe. His body was bridled strength and so magnificent it reminded her of a marble statue in a museum. Chiseled, dented from years of stories, and a part that had given way during a struggle that might have pulled other men under. Warrior. Survivor.

Tossing a wrapper to the side, Drake settled over her body resting on his forearm and she breathed him in. Her heart was beating so fast she didn't know how it would ever return to its normal rhythm again.

"Are you okay?"

Millie reached for his face and took his mouth, hoping that was enough of an answer. She could feel his lips curve and when he moved into her, she arched hoping to get closer. His skin was raw silk, smooth and worsted, knotted in places she assumed were scars. Even inside her, he still wasn't close enough. She wanted all of him. All his joy and pride, every last one of his fears. The thought of everything they'd both been through to get where they were washed over her and she took his mouth with hers, warm and breathlessly willing.

"Please," she whispered at his ear, giving them both permission to let go. Drake released their kiss only to pull her nipple into his mouth one last time before closing his eyes in complete ecstasy. Millie bowed into the last crest and when her own eyelids fell closed in unbridled pleasure, she knew even with all the words in the world, some things defied description. They had to be felt, and she let go with her whole heart.

~

Drake woke to the next morning with a start until he realized it was Sunday. No boat to meet and not his day to take Bella. He dropped back onto the bed and realized he was alone. His hand reached out to touch the empty side where Millie had been, and every memory of her body and the places they'd taken one another flooded his senses. The house was quiet. Brewing coffee in the air and the tick of the clock next to him, but nothing more.

As he stood and found his clothes, he thought maybe she was writing or she didn't like sharing a bed. The bedroom door creaked as he pushed past it into the living room. Pop-Tart was in the middle of the floor sunning herself. After scratching her belly and running a hand over his face to acclimate to the sunshine, he noticed Millie was on the patio.

Wrapped in a robe and holding a cup of coffee in both hands, she was staring out at the bay, stunning and still undeniably complicated. Pouring himself some coffee, he walked onto the patio, kissed her on top of her head, and sat in the other chair. She smiled and continued looking at the water. Drake did his best not to project his past onto the present, but it had been his experience that quiet women rarely had good news.

"I've never done that before," she said in a soft husky voice that spurred all the best memories. He sipped his coffee and waited. He was getting good at listening too.

"I mean I've done"—she gestured with her head toward the bedroom—"that. I've done that, but I don't normally... Ugh, forget it." She focused back on the water. "I really should not speak."

"You've never had sex with a man outside of a relationship." Drake faced her.

She nodded. "Well, I did have sex with Chris Portman my sophomore year in college, but when I woke up, he was still free-bird naked sitting on the couch playing video games with his friends, so I was honestly grateful for the one-night—"

Drake knew he was staring, but she was unbelievable. How could a person seemingly share so much and so little at one time?

"Right, babbling again. Sorry."

"Don't be. Is that what you think this is? A one-night stand?"

"I have no idea and please don't think I told you that because I'm expecting anything because I'm not, at all. I'm leaving soon and you are staying here." She threw her head back and closed her eyes. "Dear God, someone save me from myself."

He laughed. "Let me see what I can do." As he took her hand, Millie opened her eyes. "I am going to take ten steps back to my place, shower, and reassemble my hardware." He squeezed her hand. "That should give you some time to sort through any lingering feelings you still have for Chris. I do not play video games, naked or clothed, if that helps my case."

She snorted a laugh and her shoulders relaxed. Drake was already addicted to watching her go from so wound up to easier on herself. He sure as hell hoped this wasn't a one-night stand because he was falling fast.

"You can shower here."

"I have a routine and a few things I need to take care of." He flexed his left shoulder.

She reached across and touched his face, letting her hand trail down his neck and his shoulder until she reached the end of his arm. "The light likes you, have I told you that yet?"

Drake shook his head.

"I might have watched you a few times from my window."

"Stalker. I knew it." He rose to leave.

"Drake?"

He turned back. "Yeah?"

Millie took a deep breath. "My favorite color is blue."

"Mine too."

"Thai food."

He smiled, warmed that the sharing was practically spilling out of her now. "Good choice."

"My mom died when I was twelve."

The moment was a bit like one of those audiobooks his mom listened to in the kitchen. Like someone else was telling Millie's story, narrating her pain. Drake held onto the back of the chair because he needed to be steady for this. He would never understand why she gave him that piece of herself in that moment, what he'd done to make her feel safe, but he had never been more grateful.

"I'm sorry," he said as softly as possible.

"She had ovarian cancer. In my childlike memory, she went to the doctor one day, cried while she was reading me a bedtime story, and then she was gone. I'm sure there were a thousand steps in between during the eight months before she died, but that's how it plays out in my head."

"Trauma is that way." Drake sat back down next to her.

She made to correct him and explain that she'd never thought of her mother dying as trauma. His accident was trauma, she'd said. Trauma was something. How she didn't see a young girl losing her mother in the space of months as catastrophic he didn't yet understand, but he wasn't going to argue. Not now, not when she was so wide open.

"My father did not do well. He—" She couldn't seem to find the words. He took her hand and willed any sadness from his expression. He knew what pity felt like. No one wanted pity.

"I don't talk about things because my real life is... it is not like yours."

"Millie. My life is full of—"

"It's not the same."

"Why not?"

"Because you're missing half your arm. I'm missing—" A tear spilled down her cheek, followed by another one, and the weight of her pain rang so deep he could feel it in his own chest. She wiped at her eyes.

Exhaling, she said, "When my mom died, my father sent me away to school. I don't have any of this." She let go of him to splay her arms along the bay.

"Okay."

She looked at him. "I'm not okay. I'm all these broken pieces. I don't know how to share that. Everything in your life is so different, so... whole."

He skimmed his knuckles along her jaw.

Millie took his hand back and kissed it. "Can't we stick with what's on Google? I'm super together on Google."

Drake smiled through the emotion in his throat. He wasn't sure when he'd come to care so much, but he was too far gone to turn back now. He wanted to give her whatever she needed to feel whole. Hell, he'd pick up every last piece and somehow put them back together if it meant drying her tears. One breath changed everything. When he was in his studio, he knew that, but witnessing it in real life was a different kind of magic.

"I'm not sure that's an option anymore."

She closed her eyes. "Why not?"

"Because despite everything I know about tourists and women from the city, one night isn't going to be enough, Millie."

She opened her eyes.

"You have met all of my good parts. Believe me, there are things—"

"I know about the music. Hazel told me about the music."

"That's why you gave up so easily." He sighed. "See, pity. Damn pity." He brought her hand to his lips again. "I'm working on the music, by the way."

"I miss it. Although, I wouldn't mind a good singer-songwriter playlist."

He laughed.

"See what you can do."

"Maybe Alistair is a struggling indie rocker who... falls off the stage. That's how he dies."

"You are proving quite the plot master." She laughed again but grew serious. "Thank you for yesterday and last night. Thank you for sharing your life with me. I'm sorry I was out here stewing in my thoughts instead of wearing your shirt and making you breakfast."

It was his turn to laugh. "Is that how you would have written our first morning?"

"That is exactly how I have written practically all morning scenes after incredible sex."

"Incredible is the right word." He leaned in when the heat returned to her eyes.

"No editing?" she whispered.

Drake shook his head, kissed her again, and stood. "I could make *you* breakfast or it's probably safer to take you to breakfast."

She stood and leaned on the gray wood railing. "I would like that."

"Which one? My overcooked eggs, or a much better breakfast at Matt's by the bluffs?"

They agreed on Matt's, and Drake left before he carried her back to bed.

Chapter Twenty-Two

"When did you get your arm?" she asked, completely unedited once they were several questions into two stacks of pancakes.

"Two years after the accident. My mom pushed the insurance company and broke them down until they gave me a Hanger Clinic prototype. After a few months, they fitted me for the final product." He held up his arm. "In exchange, I did all kinds of testing for them. There's an app and everything."

"Worst part of being a writer?" Drake asked, stealing a bite of her pancakes.

She sat back in the booth. "I'd say your interview skills have also greatly improved with me in your life."

Her in his life.

Drake knew he was smiling, and he also knew he loved her. Christ, falling for a tourist had to be way up there on the list of what not to do as a local in a small town. She was going to leave, he knew that, and while he could hold out hope that she'd weekend in Bodega or even spend her summers at the bay, it would never be enough. Small towns had a shelf life for most people. They were an acquired taste for the long term.

Drake knew Millie was having more fun than she'd planned. He knew she had feelings for him too, but he'd jumped headfirst into loving her. He should have sensed the danger when she'd first come barreling into his world.

"Worst part. Huh, kind of a tricky question. Most people ask me the best part and there are so many best parts." She took another bite. "Oh, I have one." She set her fork down. "Skyping. I never know where to look and when I do get it right, I come off as scared. And... I ramble weird things. It's awkward."

"Seriously? That's the worst part?"

She nodded, laughter in her expression. "Yes. Even worse than my after-incredible-sex awkwardness."

Before Drake could laugh, he realized who was in the booth directly down from them.

Unbelievable.

He ran a hand over his face and after bracing himself for impact, he took Millie's hand across the table.

"Admit to nothing," he whispered like they were in a secret hiding place. "Maybe... pretend you were talking about a book."

"What? Why?"

"Please, trust me." He released her hand and resumed eating. Millie was about to experience the downside of having sisters.

Jules stood at their booth smiling like she'd heard Millie share her brother's sex life. It was a distinct look. Millie was sure her face was as red as the leather booth they were sitting in, but she tried to be brave and waited for Drake to speak first.

"Were you like hunched down over there spying on us?"

Jules feigned shock. "No. I'm five-ten, big brother. I don't hunch."

"If you call me big brother one more time, I swear—Oh, give me a break."

Another woman who had to be Sistine because she looked like a Branch and a good-looking man with a massive arm tattoo stood next to Jules.

"Hi." The woman extended her hand, clearly giggling as she confirmed she was Drake's youngest sister, and then introduced her fiancé, Cade.

"You own the knitting store in Petaluma," Millie said, hoping to distract.

"I do." She slid in next to Drake and took a piece of his toast. "It's so great that my brother has told you about my shop."

She was going to mention that Cade ran the tap house, but her lack of siblings was obvious because Cade sat next to Sistine, smushing Drake into the side of the booth, and Jules slid in next to Millie.

"So," she said, leaning on her elbow like they were two best friends. "On a scale of one to ten, how incredible are we talking?"

"Do not answer that." Drake lunged toward Jules but could barely move. "None of you were invited to breakfast. This is like an ambush."

"Oh, let's not be dramatic," Sistine said, smearing jelly on the last piece of toast.

Drake glanced at Cade, who was shaking his head and trying not to laugh. "Small town. Rookie mistake."

"It was my fault. I... ramble."

"And we love that about you." Jules nodded to Sistine before holding up six fingers and a questioning glance. She was intent on driving her brother crazy and Millie could not help but play along. She lifted Jules's other four fingers to indicate Drake was so much more and the entire table, save Drake, pealed with laughter

"Do you not find it disturbing that you're so interested in my sex life?"

Jules shook her head. "Nope. If I had one of my own, I would be... self-interested, but since I'm forced to live vicariously through my two siblings, no. Not one bit of creepy. Clearly our sister is having great sex, so that leaves you."

"This is not normal. Cade, back me up here."

"I'm wondering why I'm great sex and you're incredible." He grinned at Sistine, who kissed him.

"Holy hell, you are all crazy."

Jules smiled. "That we are. But it's still great to know you are carrying on the Branch name, big—"

"Don't say it."

She shrugged. "Fine. Millie, you're fantastic." She held up her palm and Millie gave her a high-five. Jules leaned over and kissed her brother's cheek, as did Sistine before they all scooted back out of the booth. He shook his head, but the affection shone right through his annoyance.

"Nice to meet you," Cade said, shaking her hand.

"You too. By the way, I tried your beer at Fish Fest, and it was delicious. I love the names."

Cade told Millie a little about the brewery and took an interest in her writing while Drake and his sisters exchanged a few more jabs.

"You'll have to stop by and see us the next time you're heading into the city."

"I would like that. I'd love to see your shop too."

Sistine smiled, a more delicate version of Drake and Jules. "Do you knit?"

"I do. Not well, but I try."

"Drake can probably help you with technique. We all—"

"Okay, out."

After goodbyes and more laughter, they left.

Millie was still smiling. She couldn't stop. "Tell me that you knit."

"I do not knit." He took another sip of coffee before mumbling, "Anymore." He grinned and shook his head.

"Are you kidding me?"

"We all did. Auntie N taught us. Punishment if you ask me."

Millie held her hands to her mouth like she might catch the extra joy at the thought of Drake Branch making a scarf. *Of course, Nikki taught them to knit, because why not?*

~

Millie's mom used to take her to bookstores for reading circles and "just because." For as far back as she could remember, bookstores and libraries were extensions of their home. She knew exactly when all of that changed and recognized the irony of her father managing to suck the fun out of even the most beloved places. The man was a testament to the power of despair.

Swept Away was like a bookstore from Millie's childhood. A mishmash of everything that made them a haven for kids and adults alike. From the worn, comfy chairs to the amber lighting, it was a place to gather, sit out the rain, visit, and most importantly get lost in the wonder of romance. Millie loved it and the woman who turned her own pain at losing her husband so early into pure joy even more.

Drake sat on the floor surrounded by books, legs outstretched as he leaned back on one of the shelves.

"So, what's the key to a good romance cover?" he asked Nikki who was next to him rearranging. He and Millie had intended to stop in for a minute after breakfast and had ended up staying for lunch.

"That is a hot-button debate," Nikki said, flipping over some of the books in her hand. "I suppose its primary job is to tell the reader about the story, so" — she held up a book by Tessa Dare — "this one is obviously historical and classic. That longing pose, determined look, gorgeous man, and that dress." Nikki held *Do You Want to Start a Scandal?* over her heart like it was a dear friend before putting it back on the shelf.

Millie loved covers, especially romance covers. The contemporary shirtless men were always fun, but Millie enjoyed covers that teased or were grand and sweeping. The ones that invited the reader to climb into a far-off castle or a mountain town.

"Got it. Is this one Beauty and the Beast, the fairytale?" He held up *When Beauty Tamed the Beast.*

Auntie N and Millie shook their heads at the same time and said, "So much better."

"Eloisa James has five retellings of classic fairytales, but that's my favorite," Millie said. "A perfect example of a cover and the title showing you what's inside."

"Okay, here's one that...looks interesting. Thoughts?" He held up *Asking for Trouble.*

"I have a lot of thoughts about Brent Mason from that book," Nikki said, fanning herself. "He's the hot man holding Hayden up against the wall." She nodded. "Accurate cover."

Drake laughed. "Millie, thoughts?"

"It's a very... very good book."

"Very good?" He met her eyes, pure mischief. "Should I add this to my reading list?"

She nodded and returned to the shelf she was helping restock before she blushed.

Nikki pulled another book from her side, "Ooh, remember this one." She held up *Fool Me Twice*.

"Gorgeous cover," Millie said. "That orange dress."

"And she's a redhead," Nikki added before sliding Meredith Duran's book back onto the shelf.

"Seems like we have a lot of dresses and naked men," Drake said.

"Both are..."

"Important," both women said amid nodding and laughter.

Millie was sure this was not the first time Drake indulged his aunt's love of romance or reorganizing her shelves, but perhaps this was the most in-depth. He seemed to be enjoying himself.

She ran her hand along the shelf she'd finished, still amazed at an entire bookstore dedicated to a genre she'd spent her professional life justifying to her father and even some of her acquaintances. Small towns normally had less than a shelf for romance books in an effort to cover most tourist needs. The courage to give an entire shop over to romance both thrilled and made her feel special all at once.

"Favorite cover?" Drake asked.

"Too many to choose." Millie dusted another shelf and lifted a stack from the floor. "And it's hard for me because I know the stories inside, so even if the cover's not great, I don't care."

"Auntie N?"

"Oh, it changes every month." She scanned the shelves but then pointed to a framed Loretta Chase cover. "For the longest time *Lord of Scoundrels* was my favorite cover just because it's one of my all-time favorite books. But covers only... let's see." She pulled a book from a corner shelf. "Up until last week, it was this one." She held up *A Princess in Theory*. "Because again... that dress." She went to a display near the front. "But now." She held up *Devil's Daughter*. "This one is my favorite because... that dress," she exclaimed, clutching both Alyssa Cole and Lisa Kleypas to her chest before returning them back to their spots.

Millie looked at Drake whose mouth was now hanging open and smiled. "Like I said, too many to choose."

"Unbelievable."

"It's a healthy obsession."

Customers wandered in during the hours they spent at Swept Away furthering Drake's romance education and relishing another chance to talk all things love. Tourists took suggestions from Nikki, sidestepped her piles, and were happy to accept her offers of cookies and extra bookmarks. Auntie N was a treasure and everyone, including the man presently surrounded by her latest remodel, seemed to know it.

Drake cleared his throat a few minutes after the last customer left. "And this one must be about... firemen?" His brow furrowed before holding up *Hot Head*.

Millie smiled and Nikki snatched the book away from him. "What's that doing over there? It's signed and another one of my all-time favorites." She walked behind the register and propped the book on a shelf with others. "Griff and Dante's story is a classic, right Millie?"

She nodded. "It's hot too."

Nikki fanned herself again before adding, "Such broken, but sweet men."

"Men?"

Millie nodded. "Romance has all the love," she said.

"Hey, here's one with a dock but I can't see their faces. I'm guessing that's on purpose?"

"Tara and Ford," Millie and Nikki sighed in tandem.

Drake laughed when Millie grabbed the book from him. "I loved every single Lucky Harbor couple."

"Me too. And then there are these." Nikki held up several of Millie's books.

Drake stood and took the stack from her.

"That's only a few. She's written so many great stories."

"How many?" Drake asked.

"I think this new one is... thirteen, maybe?"

Millie nodded, instinctively switching hats from reader to writer, before accepting they were one and the same.

"Do you like your covers?" Drake asked.

"Some of them."

He held up a book as he came to stand in front of her.

"Not that one. Ugh." She snatched the book from him.

"Seems like a decent cover to me."

"You wouldn't think so if you'd read the book." She pointed to the picture. "My hero's hair is brown, not blond. It's mentioned in the story and throughout the entire story. And they never get anywhere near a hot air balloon."

"Ever?"

She shook her head and set the book face down on a table.

"That's false advertising, isn't it?"

"The publisher liked the *feel* of this picture. That's what they said."

"Well, you did say the feel was important."

Millie scoffed. "Feel had nothing to do with this decision. I think the intern searching iStock found her own love story in the millions of pictures and plastered it on my book for all eternity."

"I think I just found my favorite." He held up *Wicked Bite*.

"Shapeshifter, huh?"

"I have no idea what that means, but this picture is intriguing. Wait, the guy shifts from bear to human?" He turned to the back copy. "Yeah, this is my kind of book. Do they have—"

She nodded.

"While he's a bear?"

She nodded again. He stepped closer.

"Wow."

"Yeah, it's pretty wow," Nikki called from the register.

Drake and Millie laughed.

"Small town," she whispered.

"What would your cover look like, Millie?"

"You saw them?"

He shook his head and set her books down. "If you were that intern, what picture would you choose?" He was close enough to kiss her. Millie put a hand to his chest and was absorbed in the steady thud of his heart until she realized they were standing in the front window of the store like two brought-to-life characters from any number of covers. The bell on the door jingled again and Drake, not needing any more gossip for the day, stepped back.

Millie grinned, bowed her head, and returned to restocking. She rarely considered her own love story, let alone its cover, but however it turned out, incredible sex, a stack of pancakes, and an afternoon in a bookstore with a man who looked at her the way Drake looked at her would surely make it on the inspiration board.

Chapter Twenty-Three

Alistair was alive. Millie woke to the harmonizing of boy bands the following Monday and knew in her creative soul that her hero deserved a good life. She'd fallen asleep looking over her notes, all her notes, in the pages in her leather-bound journal for her yet untitled literary novel. Not for the first time, she questioned why she'd set the book in London. She'd only been to London once and it was a miserable trip. Running her hand over a picture of an overcast sky, she reflected on how it had inspired her to write the lines *Alistair didn't know why he bothered with an overcoat anymore. He would forever be drenched in his past so long as he stayed in this city.*

It was a good line, maybe a little wordy, but the idea behind the line, the burden of a past, was a solid motivator to make a better life. She was certainly the writer to pen that story.

Millie turned the page to the collage of pictures she collected for Alistair's past. Some happy, most painful, she was suddenly filled with emotions she felt ready to tackle. Like her journey with this story had not only been for Alistair, but for her too. She'd lost her mother in sixth grade and while she knew that was tragic, she'd had her for twelve years of her life.

Somehow, she'd always managed to focus on those years, the years *with* her instead of the years without. Despite her father's best efforts, until recently she'd been happy. Her dad chose the dark side of that moment that changed them forever. Millie chose the light, wanted the sun, so what if Alistair did too? That's what she'd wondered last night. She'd turned the whole story on its end and decided a joyful journey had the same, if not more value.

She was back. Millie hopped out of bed and pushed back the last bits of her father's voice declaring—*One good roll in the hay and you've abandoned all literary focus. No wonder you write fluff.*

He was wrong. She knew that now. Not about the excellent "roll in the hay," but about everything else. She'd never been defined by things missing, ignored, or forgotten. She'd always tried to fill her life with her mother's brief but vibrant love. That was up until she'd walked by her father's shop last Christmas Eve. She would never know why last year affected her differently than any other, but it had. Maybe she needed to turn her life upside down to let go of him for good. Or maybe letting go led her to her future.

Whatever it was, that night had made her believe if she worked harder, reached farther, she could be in that window instead of standing outside. She'd been foolish, she knew that now. She was never going to write anything other than what she loved to write.

Millie enjoyed being alive. She liked festivals and riding bikes. She wanted more face painting and great sex. All those things made life worth living. They reminded her of the joy her mom left behind and allowed her to refocus on that joy. So, why the hell shouldn't Alistair have those things too?

She had plans for Alistair and hadn't looked back all morning. Millie reworked her outline so Alistair was alive at the beginning of the book. Alive and struggling with his job as an antique stamp curator at the Smithsonian. Someone was... blackmailing him or needed his expertise?

"Yes, I like that," she said, standing in the kitchen moving images around under seashell magnets. Alistair was alive, and Millie was mad inspired for the first time since arriving in Bodega Bay.

As hard as she'd tried at the beginning of every book to outline a plot, the story never came to her that way. It trickled in as a snapshot or even a dialogue exchange and branched from there. She was inspired to write one of her first books, *Catch Me*, after overhearing a conversation at a clothing store. Early on in her career, she'd envied writers who had the whole story, but envy never made anyone happy or successful. She knew that so she learned, as she'd told Drake, to collect her bits and pieces until she had a story.

Through the eighties, nineties, and that morning's excellent singer-songwriter playlist, Millie worked effortlessly for the first time in a long time. She found a stopping place so she could get ready or she was going to be late for the first unofficial stop on her book tour.

~

Swept Away lit up the evening sky like a beacon ushering readers to safe passage. Millie parked in the adjacent lot, stopping to admire BP Glass Works studio first. The front window of the bookstore was decorated with her latest release. The deep aqua of her heroine's scrubs and the clever twist of her stethoscope into a heart had Millie again thankful for her publisher's art department.

Drake's studio window was filled with swirls of glass. Blues and orange, gorgeous pieces he'd made from his vision of the world. Millie had signed thousands of books at this point in her career and would sign thousands more in the coming months after she left Bodega Bay, but being invited to Nikki's shop had been an honor. She knew her romance, appreciated all the shades of love, and for that Millie would always treasure her.

Pushing the idea of ever leaving Bodega Bay behind, Millie took one last deep breath and walked toward the front door. She stopped to take in the picture of herself that Nikki had put in the front window. It wasn't her author photo. It was a recent shot of her here. Maybe at the Fisherman's Festival? She was laughing, and something in her eyes said she was looking at Drake when Nikki took the picture. It was not a traditional author headshot. Millie looked sun-soaked and... in love. She knew that look. She'd described it for readers time after time, but staring back at herself so obviously in love stirred her chest with equal parts joy and fear. Before she had a chance to overthink it, the door flew open.

"Millie," Nikki exclaimed. "Everyone, Millie Hart is here." Nikki began clapping, as did the crowd, before she'd even made her way to the podium. The love was so overwhelming she thought she might cry.

"Thank you, Nikki. Thanks to all of you for taking time to visit with me this evening."

Nikki explained to the crowd sitting, some standing, that there was coffee near the register and that Millie would be reading a couple of passages first and then answering questions.

"About this book or any of your other books. Is that right, Millie?" Nikki asked.

"I... sure. That sounds great."

"Okay, well without further delay, I give you our local author at least for another month or two: Millie Heart and her fantastic latest release *Revive Me*." The group clapped again. She'd never received such enthusiastic applause, and the only child in her loved every minute.

After reading the first chapter and a few random bits Jade and some of the beta readers highlighted as favorites, Millie answered questions. Her writing processes. Why she set her latest series in Louisiana, if she was planning to set one of her stories in Bodega Bay, and whether she might stay in Bodega Bay forever. Millie laughed and thought of Drake.

"Rumor has it you and our glassblower are an item," a woman said near the front.

Millie was sure she blushed, as if she'd been caught spinning impossible stories.

"Joyce, that's none of our business," Nikki said. "Unless Millie wants to share." She waggled her perfectly penciled brows.

Millie managed a smile. "I'm guessing you ladies are always looking for the small-town romance angle, am I right?"

They nodded.

"Drake and I are... friends." She coughed on the last word and needed to take a sip of the water Nikki had put on the podium. By the time she looked up to apologize, they were all buzzing like bees. The dangerous swarming kind.

"Dead giveaway."

"Did you see her avert her eyes and cough?"

"She couldn't even get the word friends out."

"Definitely an item."

"Aw, can you imagine those babies. Gorgeous, curly mops and blue eyes."

Wow, that escalated quickly. Millie cleared her throat.

"We are friends. See, I said it perfectly that time."

Nikki put a hand on her shoulder. "It's too late, honey. They're off like a wildfire. You'll need to let the rumor burn itself out." She patted her hand. "Unless it's not a rumor. You can tell your Auntie Nikki. I promise not to tell a soul." She crossed her heart right over her bumblebee brooch.

Millie smiled and closed her copy of the book. It seemed question-and-answer time was over. She leaned in like she might have a juicy bit of gossip and whispered, "Thank you, Nikki."

Nikki laughed. "Oh, aren't you a clever girl." She swatted her shoulder. "You're sticking around for cookies and cake, aren't you? Please don't let us scare you off."

When Millie had signed almost every book in the shop and had way too many cookies, she sat in one of the big chairs near the front as Nikki ushered the last of the guests out the door. Turning the shop sign, she leaned against the locked door and sighed.

"That went well, right?"

Millie nodded and stood to collect the remaining cups and napkins.

"I'm sure it's not like your big city signings, but it was fun."

"It was better than any big city signing." She tossed a handful in the trash.

"Oh, stop that. You don't clean up, you're the star."

Millie laughed as Nikki brought her back to the chair and sat with her.

"What are the big city signings like? I mean, I went to a big reader event in San Francisco once. Got Julia Quinn's signature right there." She pointed. "And Priscilla Oliveras signed a copy of her very first book before she became a big deal." Nikki pointed to a copy of *His Perfect Partner* propped behind the register.

Millie knew that one well; she'd read it twice.

"Both of them were lovely women. Like you." She kicked off her clogs and rested her stockinged feet on the table in front of them. "What's it like being the author at one of those?"

"It's big and sometimes intimidating. Larger posters, long lines. Tons of people, but they're all happy to meet you and talk about books. Signings are exhausting, but also exhilarating."

"I'll bet." She offered Millie one of the two remaining cookies.

"When did you start reading romance, Nikki?"

"When my husband died. I was young, but a late bloomer by most standards." She laughed. "How 'bout you?"

"I was in high school. My friend let me borrow a Nora Roberts book. I don't remember if it was *Inner Harbor* or *Chesapeake Blue*."

"Ooh, I love all the Quinn brothers. Her latest is fantastic too. Dark, but that woman can write everything, you know?"

Millie nodded in agreement and finished her cookie.

Nikki sighed and lay her head back on the chair. "Thank you so much for bringing some magic to my store, Millie. I can't tell you what it means to us to have you in our town even for this short time."

"It's my pleasure. Truly." Their eyes met and Millie realized her mom was frozen as a young woman. Watching Nikki, she wondered what her mother might have looked like as an older woman. If she'd lived outside of the worn photographs and outdated hairstyles. How would her mom style her hair now? Would she go gray?

For a second, Millie understood that she'd never know her mom on that level, woman to woman. The ache for what they both lost was so overwhelming she had to stand up.

"I should probably get going."

"Oh, absolutely. I don't want to keep you from your next project. Have you written the kissy parts yet?"

"I am... getting started on the kissy parts."

Nikki squealed a little and Millie was right back in the happy present.

"Why did you start reading romance at the saddest time in your life?" She asked before she realized she was speaking.

Nikki didn't miss a beat. "Because it saved me from the darkness. I loved a man and lost him, but I loved him." She took Millie's hands. "That's the important part."

Millie nodded and felt less alone. Grabbing her bag, she promised to visit again soon.

"You can't stay too cooped up. You know? Fresh air is good, especially since you're just getting to the kissy parts. Unless there's real kissing you'd like to talk about."

"Goodnight, Nikki."

Millie drove back to the cottage more certain than ever that Alistair needed a great love. She wanted new kissy parts for Nikki. More swooning and sighing after she shared favorite parts with gathered readers. She wanted all of it.

Her father would have to continue in his disappointment and her books would never sit on his stark white shelves. That was okay because love was her life's work. Nikki and romance readers all around the world were her people, and there was no way she'd ever turn her back on them again.

~

"How was it?"

She spun at her front door, eyes wild and face flushed. "It went fantastic, that's how it was. And you know what?" She fumbled to get her bag to stay on her shoulder, almost tripped over the gnome pushing a wheelbarrow, and ended up a few inches in front of him. Under the stars. Smiling brilliantly, her big blue eyes dancing and happy to see him. Earlier Drake had thought he might like living in the city. That's how gone he was. How was he supposed to ever let her go?

"I"—she pushed her hair out of her face—"was going to say hi to Pop and then come over to see you." She was out of breath.

So was he, and he had not moved an inch. "I'm right here."

"Yes, you are." She set a hand gently on his chest. "Nikki is wonderful."

"She is."

"And she and the group had lots of great questions."

"That you answered."

"Most of them. I kept some things to myself." She went up on her toes and kissed him, soft and fleeting. He held her face and took a bit more before she eased back. The stars shown in her eyes. He'd read that a time or two, but never really knew what it felt like, looked like, until that moment.

"I love you." Her voice was soft, but so full and sure that it nearly knocked him over.

"No editing." He took her face, held her and drank her in the way she'd done to him dozens of times.

Her heart was full, he could almost see it overflowing, and he wanted to give her all of that in return. Three words didn't seem like enough, but he said them anyway, his voice shaking and so serious he almost didn't recognize it. Then he kissed her all the way up the stairs to his Airstream until they stumbled inside and into bed.

~

Sometime in the middle of the night, she woke up to Drake touching her so gently she'd thought she was dreaming.

"I can't stop touching you."

A smile melted across her lips when she opened her eyes to find him facing her.

"I like your bed." Her eyes traveled around the cozy enclosure.

"It likes you."

"I've never been in a trailer before."

He smiled, warm and so sexy she'd seriously consider losing sleep just to watch him too. She reached out to touch the side of his face.

"Can you ask Tyler how many tourists decide to stay?" She couldn't stop her voice from quivering. She didn't want to leave but wasn't yet sure how to stay. All her love stories ended shortly after the I-love-you part. The details were off-page for a reason.

Drake inhaled and turned her until her back was nestled into his front. Right as Millie thought he'd turned her away from him because he had no answers, he kissed her neck and whispered, "We'll figure it out."

Millie felt her eyes well and she smiled because she knew she hadn't been wrong for all these years. It was possible to love with her whole heart and have that love returned.

"Bella leaves on Sunday to visit her dad. So, we are having a big dinner." He kissed her neck again. "I would like you to come."

"At your parents?" She cleared her throat.

Drake nuzzled confirmation at her ear. Millie turned in his arms again to face him, unable to be without his face. "I would love to." She kissed him and fell asleep with a deep sense of something she now recognized. Belonging.

Chapter Twenty-Four

The Branch home was tucked behind the Crab Shack, which was closed for the night. Laughter and conversation spilled from the peaked roof and windswept trees as she approached and pushed aside the ever-present, if less intense, feelings that she didn't belong. Armed with cookies she'd baked after a crazy successful day of writing and a bottle of wine Nikki had mentioned was a Branch family favorite, she made her way up the path toward people who, in a few short months, had changed her life's narrative.

Bodega Bay had not existed for her before that night she arrived to battle the gnomes. Drake was a stranger back then. Festivals, joy, and affection she'd been starving for her whole life were now added to her handful of happy memories. Millie wondered how many more pages there would be for her and Drake. She wanted to believe they would have volumes together, but even in the newfound glow of loving someone, she still sensed the darkness of the past at her shoulder.

Not that her past was all that ominous. People came from far worse than a stoic father, but there were also people who knew only the deep-rooted bonds of family. The joy of fighting and making up, get-togethers when it was hard to squeeze in a word, holidays of honest joy and deep gratitude. Loving and alive people were not so rare, it turned out.

Millie had wanted for so much for long. She'd spent senseless years on the cold side of the window, and now here she was at the front door of something new.

Adjusting her offerings so she could ring the doorbell, she tried not to run through her opening lines or edit at all. She never answered Drake's question about her self-edit, but the truth was the need for the "right" answer or the "most concise" thing to add came after her father threw her into the world alone. Up until that point, Millie had memories of rambling stories and missteps in phrase. It was a testament to Bodega Bay and Drake that she'd rambled more since arriving than she had in years. Every great writer knew not to edit while the story was flowing. She also knew the importance of moving the story along, so after another deep breath, Millie rang the doorbell.

The porch was painted bright white and lined with flowerbeds. A rainbow of blooms, vibrant even under the dim light of the porch. Not a dead leaf or weed in sight. Everywhere she looked were signs of care and people who knew the value of their space.

Jules opened the door, and the shock on her face made Millie smile.

"Oh, yes! The party just arrived," she said, setting her beer down on the entry table and taking Millie's plate of cookies and the bottle of wine.

"She brought sugar *and* wine!"

Bella came peeling around the corner of what Millie assumed was the kitchen and wrapped her arms around Millie's waist before squeezing. Millie squeezed back.

"I'm so glad you're here. Did you know that Harry's wand is made from a phoenix feather?"

"She and Drake are re-reading the entire series." Jules rolled her eyes and disappeared back around the corner.

Millie laughed and confirmed she remembered that detail of the story.

"I missed that the first time. It's so cool. He's reborn when he goes to Hogwarts."

"Bella, how old are you?"

"Ten."

"I'm not at all surprised you missed that the first go-round."

She shrugged. "Yeah, I can't be responsible for my five-year-old mistakes."

Millie smiled, and Bella took her hand as Drake came around the corner.

"You're here."

"I am." How was it she loved him more every time?

Jules called Bella and, on a huff, she ran off to what Millie could now see was the backyard.

"You look incredible." He leaned forward and kissed her, soft and quickly before glancing over his shoulder to check they were still alone. After what Drake called "the breakfast ambush," she could hardly blame him. Siblings, it turned out, showed up at unexpected moments.

"You can have my beer," Jules yelled from outside. "I just opened it and you'll need it if you're hanging out with this crew."

Drake kissed her again, longer this time, before pulling her close. "You ready for this?"

Millie nodded before reaching back and grabbing the glass Jules left behind. She took a sip. "I'm happy to be here."

His expression deepened and Millie hoped her eyes were saying everything she had not found words for yet.

"And you baked," he said, clearing his throat and shaking them both free of the undeniable need.

"I did, and let me tell you, the Millers' oven is right up there with their bicycle."

Drake laughed and guided her toward the kitchen. His hand barely at her back was the simplest of gestures, and yet Millie felt supported in a way she'd rarely known and never with a man. Just shy of the kitchen entrance, she pulled him aside toward the hall until his back was against the wall and she kissed him like they were alone. Deep and free in a way she now knew that kind of support allowed. "You look pretty incredible too."

She inhaled to say more, but her self-edit was back. Telling a man she loved him under the quiet of a night sky was one thing. Saying it again with his entire family in the next room would take some practice. His expression faltered for a minute like he'd overheard her thoughts and wanted to relieve the weight of everything she was feeling, everything *they* were feeling.

"I love you, Millie Hart," he whispered at her ear. "Now take another sip of that beer and tell me how you feel about charades because after dinner things are going to get pretty intense."

Millie whispered her love back to him as Drake led her toward the patio. "It's a game, right?"

Drake cast her a glance. At her wide eyes, he laughed.

She made things up for a living. Acting them out might be a different story.

~

"Auntie, are you and Uncle Cade going to have a baby?" Bella brought a bowl of chips into the living room while Drake and Millie set up the game.

"I'm not." Sistine eyed Jules, who shrugged and went back into the kitchen. "Not right this minute or for a while. Why?"

"I'm the only grandchild and the pressure is a little much, you know?" Bella crunched a chip. "And Mom and Dad named me Bella Bartlett. Kids like to make fun of that."

"How would having a cousin change your name?"

"I was going to ask if you could name your baby something super weird to help me out."

Cade and Sistine laughed before pulling Bella onto the couch between the two of them.

"Tell you what," Cade said. "If and when we have a baby, we'll do our best to pick a name as beautiful as yours."

Sistine smiled.

And as everyone gathered for another rousing and guaranteed rowdy game of Branch-style charades, his little sister pulled her man in by the shirt and kissed him.

Bella was not impressed. "My name means beautiful—was that supposed to be like a joke about beautiful?" She rolled her eyes and stomped off to the kitchen.

Sistine looked to Jules.

"Why are you looking at me? Are you thinking I understand her because I'm her mother?"

"You two were both ten-year-old girls. Don't you remember what that was like?" Their dad sat on the couch next to Millie, who seemed right at home in the jumble of their lives. He knew she was an only child and wondered what she was thinking. She seemed engrossed as always, observing and probably taking mental notes. There was a whole lot to observe.

"I was not that ten," Jules said. "That sulking, eye-rolling ten going on thirty, I was definitely not."

Their dad scoffed like a man completely unafraid of daughters, young and older.

"What?" Jules grabbed a handful of chips. "Ma, back me up here. I was a dream daughter. Wasn't I?"

"You were a wonderful daughter." Their mom took her seat in the best chair in the living room as they all waited for the "but." Muriel Branch was famous for her sweet lead-ins followed by an honest revelation.

"But."

Everyone sighed and Jules shook her head, plopping down next to their dad.

"But," Muriel started again once they'd settled down, "you did have moments when things were not fair or you felt awkward."

"No way. There's no way I was more awkward than Sistine."

"Hey."

"What? You were odd. I love you and now striped socks work on you, but remember your pigtail phase?"

"Drake, help." Sistine turned to him with pleading eyes.

"Sistine was totally weirder, right?" Jules said before he could answer.

Drake knew how this would play out if he tried to lie, so he gave in and nodded. "She was weirder."

"But," they all said in concert.

Drake smiled. "But, you're the weirdest now."

"Am not."

"You really are," Sistine said.

"Because I fish?" Jules flailed her long arms.

"No." Drake took some chips, crunched, and smiled. "Because you're weird."

Jules huffed. "I'm done having this conversation." She straightened. "Let's play because I might be weird, but I'm going to kick your asses." She scanned the room.

"Even the people on your team?" their mom said, often having the last word.

"Mom." She grabbed their dad's hand and held it up. "You see this?" She nodded. "New favorite."

They all laughed. "Millie, ignore them. I'm super cool."

Millie smiled like Switzerland, lovely and neutral. Smart play in a room full of Branches.

~

Hours later, all the Branches, even the ones by marriage and love had accepted defeat at the hands of Team Jules and Bella. They had all bowed their heads and acknowledged both as their "true and rightful queens" by the time chocolate cake was served.

Lying awake now, satiated and so in love with the woman tucked into his shoulder, that he wanted every day for the rest of his life to end the exact same way. Listening to her stories, laughing his ass off at the quirky things she came up with, and slowly getting her naked before sinking into her over and over again until neither of them could hold on for another second.

Somewhere in the back of his mind he remembered a teacher once assigning: Describe your perfect day. He grinned. Not the answer he would have come up with back then, but damn if Millie wasn't a testament to the thrill of the unexpected.

The perfect day had started with his family, they were in the much less X-rated version. It was good to see Sistine and Cade, who drove back to Petaluma after bowing to the queens. It had been a good day and a better night.

It was that simple, so why was he still awake and back to counting the bolts in his ceiling? Why was he filled with this sense that one man, especially a man who'd raised hell the way he had, could be given so much?

"I was an asshole." He hadn't meant to say that out loud.

Millie shifted and came to rest her chin on his chest. Her warm, naked body pressed to his, as though they had been molded together from the same furnace.

"You're awake," he confirmed the obvious.

"I was wondering when some of whatever was churning in your head would make it out." She kissed his chest, her hair everywhere and crowning thoroughly-kissed skin. "Go on."

"My hometown was too small. My parents weren't doing enough. We were in a dying industry. Just your basic asshole."

"Or young."

"Young and stupid. God, when I'm around my parents like we were tonight, I wish I could go back and grab that guy. I was so caught up in wanting more."

"Ambitious."

He leaned up to look at her. "Are you playing that many-ways-to-say-the-same-thing game you did with Hazel?"

She nodded. Her lips curled into a smile he could feel on his skin. "You can't trust hindsight. Good and bad, we have to leave it behind. Believe me, I've tried."

Moonlight slipped soft through the window casting everything from the white of his sheets to the curve of her hip in magic.

"It's weird how the good fades but the bad sticks around."

"It is." She ran her fingers along a scar on his stomach.

"Can you remember any of the good from back then? You weren't all asshole. I know that much."

"Most of it was good. Until I felt trapped by responsibility and wanted out."

"I can't imagine that. This town is so much a part of you, aside from your dismal tour guide skills."

He laughed. "You didn't know me back then."

"No. I didn't," she said, moving up his body and kissing every bit of him as she went. By the time she sat straddled across him, passion so thick and wanting in her eyes that it stole his breath for the hundredth time, Drake forgot all about the past. All he wanted when she took him into her warmth was that moment, their now. Millie Hart was his very best day.

Chapter Twenty-Five

*D*rake startled awake at the rap on his door the next morning. Millie, who had been curled into his body, rolled over like she was used to ignoring not only her alarm, but a hurricane. For the first time in forever, he had no idea what day it was or even the time. He had a list, surely there was a list of things to do somewhere waiting for him while he was tangled in the warm body of... he leaned over to kiss her shoulder. The draw to ignore whoever was at the door and stay in bed all day was further confirmation he was stupid in love, but Drake pulled on his jeans and knew in the pit of his stomach that it wasn't Sunday. And if it wasn't Sunday, then he was —

He pulled open the door to find Tyler, in a full suit and as surprised as Drake was that he was still asleep.

"Why are you here? Crap, what time —" He ran a hand over his face. "Are you? Is that your council meeting suit?"

"Morning, sleepyhead. It's so cute that you know my clothes. Yeah, the meeting just got out."

Drake's head was spinning like in one of those movies where the guy wakes up and realizes he's in a different life or repeating puberty. He looked back for his phone.

"What in the hell time is it?"

Millie, who was up and dressed in record time, handed him his phone.

"It's nine," Tyler said in his calm-during-a-crisis tone. "Morning, Millie."

"Morning." She patted down her hair.

Drake's heart was racing as he practically fell down the steps of the Airstream.

"It's not what it looks like. I know." Tyler stepped aside as Millie followed Drake.

"No." She took a doughnut from the box he was holding. "This time, it's exactly what it looks like," she said, turning to face Drake and obviously seeing the dread.

He kissed her before she could tell him everything was all right. "Sorry. I'll see you later." And then he took off running because despite the blue sky and billowing clouds overhead, everything was not all right.

~

She could have followed him, but there were some family things everyone faced alone. Case in point, her father had called again. He had not left a message either time, not because he didn't know how, but because it was beneath him to speak into a recorder. Once again, Millie wondered how one person could change so much.

By ten o'clock, Hazel had left the cottage with a big grin and rough draft of her third and final essay and Millie had introduced Alistair to the woman he would fall for by the end of the book, once they figured out who killed her family. Like she'd said to Drake, romance left room for everyone. Turned out death gave Millie instant conflict. She'd never been great at conflict.

She spent most of the day writing.

~

He didn't even need to look at the docks to know both boats were docked, and Jules was gone so he kept running.

Bella was already on summer break. No band practice. He'd finished the pitcher that needed international shipping. Drake ran down a list of what he knew for sure before finally swinging open the door to his parents' place and following the sound of laughter into the kitchen.

"Where's the fire, son?"

"I... I'm sorry." He'd meant to say it more to clarify, but he was out of breath. He went to rest his hands on his knees to catch a breath and realized he'd left his arm at home.

Shit!

Jules jumped to her feet. "What is wrong? Oh my God. Is it the dreams again? Are you okay? I was kind of worried when you weren't there this morning, but I assumed you were sleeping in with Millie. Did something happen?"

"Jules, give him a minute." His dad stood and rested his hand on Drake's shoulder.

Drake swallowed and tried to keep the tears behind his eyes, but it was too late. A drop hit the tile of his parents' kitchen floor and he closed his eyes wishing that would transport him back to his bed instead of standing in front of his family vulnerable and so obviously broken.

"Drake? Cut it out." Jules always had a way of snapping him to, even in the worst situations.

Sniffing back emotion, he straightened and patted his dad back.

"Sorry about that. I—" *Yeah, I what?* "I thought... something had. Eh, forget it. All good. Everything is good."

"Could you both leave us for a minute?" Drake glanced up to find his mom and Jules dumbstruck. "I need a few words with my son."

His mom nodded, and she and Jules left the kitchen. His father hadn't looked stern in a very long time.

"Do you remember when you were in high school and the cops called?" He pulled at the front of his Crab Shack apron and sat down. His dad's movements were always so precise. Even as a kid, he was a little in awe of it. He moved like he had marks, like a movie star on set.

"Which time?" Drake asked. Grateful for the change of subject, he took a seat.

His father smiled through his salt-and-pepper mustache. "The time you stole that tourist's dinghy and filled it with ice."

Drake nodded. "One of our tamer Saturday night plans. We were such shits. Nice of the guy not to press charges, although I'm not sure what the charges would have been."

"What I'm sure you didn't know at the time was that the guy, the tourist who owned the obnoxious boat, came to the house. He wanted a thousand dollars to clean up his dinghy and for his wife's emotional distress."

Drake swallowed and faced his dad.

"He said he knew people and he'd get you on breaking and entering. That you'd do time. On and on."

"Jesus, Dad. I didn't know."

"You didn't need to know. You were fifteen, messing around, and you got caught."

"Did you tell the guy to screw off?"

"Did you go to jail?"

Drake shook his head. "You paid him?"

"I negotiated it down to seven-fifty and then, yeah, I paid him."

"You negotiated?" His brow furrowed, but his dad smiled.

"The thing is, when you have children, you're responsible for all of it. You don't get the vacation pictures and the sports trophies without the rest. I guess some parents do, but that's not how we work. You were growing up, you see?"

Drake looked away. He knew his dad had had a wild childhood too, but nothing compared to Drake. As their grandparents liked to say, "Drake bent the Branches until they almost broke." A reputation he used to flaunt before it nearly killed him.

"I need you to stop depositing money into that account."

He looked up. The instinct of being caught was almost involuntary. "Mom," he said.

"She should have told me. You should have told me."

"Dad, I'm not a kid anymore. I wasn't a kid when I had my accident. There's no reason I can't pay the two of you back for my bills, my arm. I'm not some war hero or even a victim. I ran my bike off the road because I was everywhere but where I belonged."

His father stood, eyes glistening, and Drake, after everything he'd been through, Drake thought he might die right there.

"I'm grateful you're alive. Don't you see by paying for it yourself, you're robbing me of being your dad. I was so happy that I still had my son I would have sold everything, done anything to help you. I don't want your money. I invested in that arm and oh"—he wiped a tear—"look what I have now. Look what we all have."

Drake tried to keep it together, and his dad took hold of his face.

"My sweet boy all grown into the man I knew he would be. Never one doubt in my mind."

Drake blinked back his own tears. "Hell of a windy road getting here."

His father shook his head. "Doesn't matter. Worth every phone call, every dollar for that fancy arm."

He let Drake go and collected himself. "You're done paying for this now. Six years of guilt or whatever you're carrying around, it stops now."

Drake laughed. "Oh, because you say so."

"Damn right. I'm the dad and you, no matter how many handstands you manage out there on the dock, are the kid." He stood to leave and turned one more time at the door.

"You're the gift, Drake. Being your father is that gift."

"You too, Dad."

He snorted and swiped at his eyes one more time. "Now, to quote your sister and your mother, 'Get back to that woman and move the hell on.'"

"Since when do we listen to them?"

"Since forever. Where the hell would we be without the Branch women, eh?"

Drake turned left before either of them had a chance to respond. Jules followed him out. No surprise there.

"Drake," she called after him.

He stopped. There was no point in trying to outrun her.

"I'm sorry I missed you this morning. I fell asleep. That's all I wanted to say." And the tears were back.

Son. Of. A. Bitch.

"I'm glad. You needed rest. Did you think I thought you'd be there every morning forever? It's good that you missed the boats."

"Why is that good? Meeting your boat is the least I can do."

"For what?"

"Stop, Jules. For saddling you with this." His hands, well one of them anyway, splayed as he gestured to the whole of their family business.

"You didn't saddle me with anything. I no longer allow that in my life." She took his shoulders. "I'm here. Bella and I are here because we want to be here."

Drake paused, giving her a minute to self-correct.

"Fine, Bella is here because I dragged her here, but it's been six years. She loves it here as much as I do. Why are you still thinking this is your fault? Look around. Our life is so much better."

"Yeah? You're exhausted all the time."

"Said the kettle."

"I'm exhausted because I still have a list of things I'm avoiding. You're—"

"You've started an entirely new business. You're working too. Life is hard. Haven't Mom and Dad always told us that? Is it only hard for you? I love what I do. I love that I'm part of the family business."

"But you had a life. You got married and moved away. You—"

"Caught my husband boning my best friend in our laundry room. Boning? Do people still use that word?"

"I'm not sure people have ever used that word." He laughed despite the weight of their conversation.

Jules shrugged. "It's totally appropriate. That's what they were doing. Grunting like a—"

"Okay."

"Sorry. Anyway, my life was a mess before the boning. Being called home saved me, saved Bella. We're—" She teared up and smacked his shoulder. "Shit, don't you know that? Quit being so stupid."

He pulled her under his arm and her head rested on his chest.

"Speaking of boning," she said.

"And we're done here." Drake let her go and walked back toward his place.

"So, does that mean I'm not getting doughnuts anymore?" she called after him. "Just as well. I'm kind of into these overnight oats Mom started making. Gotta watch the waistline, you know."

Drake shook his head. She kept going.

"You never know when this fishy woman might meet someone who wants to—" Jules's laugh rang out over the bay.

Drake turned to see his sister in hysterics. "You see what I did there? Bone. Fisherwoman."

He shook his head. "You're nuts."

"True, but I'm your nut. Quit being so stupid, okay?"

"I'll try."

She blew him a kiss. He blew her one back and turned before he made more of an ass out of himself.

Drake grabbed a T-shirt from his trailer and walked toward Millie but stopped at the path the separated them and glanced at the dock while everything he'd known only months ago swirled around him like a storm coming in from the ocean. He should go to her, climb back into bed and love her all over again, but his eyes found the rental car. She was going to leave, tourists always left, and he needed to get some bearing, something to hold on to, or he was going to be face down on a different kind of road this time. He suddenly needed his own life, his work, so he turned and walked toward the studio.

Chapter Twenty-Six

The number Millie had saved in her phone as "Penelope- Dad's Assistant" flashed on the screen at seven o'clock the following Monday morning. Still in bed, Millie's heart raced as she scrambled and finally answered.

"What's wrong, Penelope?"

"Mildred. Could you stop by my shop sometime today?"

All at once relieved and disappointed the man was still alive, Millie closed her eyes and took a deep breath.

"I'm in Bodega Bay," she said slowly. "I will be back in the city in—"

"This can't wait. I need your"—he cleared his throat—"professional opinion."

Seriously? Millie mouthed to Pop-Tart, who was looking at her like she'd been neglected and needed some attention.

"Um, okay. Can't I give that to you over the phone? I'm kind of busy looking for a man and making a pan of brownies right now."

Silence. Millie thought it was a pretty good tie-back, but again her skills were lost on him.

"I would prefer in person. You could drive into the city today. It's not that far."

She loved how despite the pure venom that came from practically every one of their encounters since she was twelve, the man still assumed she was on hold for him. Part of that was her own fault, she was the "enabler," as she'd learned from the articles Jade sent her after Millie had declared her truth. They were informative and as with so many things in her life, she grew curious. Knowledge was power, especially when dealing with family. Of course, knowledge was one thing and practice was another.

She stood from the couch. "Fine. I'll be there by lunch."

She was still working on putting things into practice.

"See you then." He hung up before she could respond. She wanted to yell, "What the hell is wrong with you?" But there was no point, she already knew.

A two-hour round-trip drive would do her well, she rationalized, but at least she knew she was rationalizing.

"Progress," she said, and then turned on the music before she smacked herself upside the head.

After narrowly squeezing through before Highway Patrol blocked off the PCH to tend to a multi-car accident, and the joy of finding an open parking spot less than two blocks from Hartfield's Books, Millie grabbed a cream puff and a coffee. She knew it pissed her father off when she arrived with a take-out cup. He hated sugar too. She smiled. She might still be an enabler, but... small victories.

$\sim$

"Let's go." Jules loaded Bella's suitcase into the back of his truck and bit into a granola bar. "We need to be at the airport an hour early and you drive like Grandma Branch, so let's get a move on."

"Grandma Branch rode a bicycle. She didn't even have a license." He held the door open and Bella climbed into the backseat.

Jules raised her brows. "Exactly."

Drake laughed despite the joke being on him. He was used to teasing.

They reached Point Reyes Station before the traffic came to a dead stop. It was the PCH, so backup was expected, but this wasn't normal traffic. Drake saw the sirens ahead as the line of cars began to move. He could see Jules looking at him out of the corner of his eye, so he turned up whatever Bella was playing as "DJ of the Drive." There were cops and flares, they were closing Highway 1 and diverting traffic at Olema.

Jules touched his arm as they got to the turn.

"This is not on the list," she said softly. "Just turn around and we can..."

He glanced at her. "Can what? We're not turning around. I got on the boat, Jules. I'm fine. This was bound to happen—"

"But you—"

He followed the sharp gesture of the officer in the middle of the road and turned onto Sir Francis Drake Boulevard with the rest of the traffic. This was his road. Named after him, he used to tell people when he was a kid, and his road of choice in his commute to and from San Francisco years ago. It was windy and green. Christ, how he used to get off on the fact that he was named after a pirate. All swagger and arrogance as he pushed away the small town that had raised him.

He could still remember what it felt like to want more, the unmitigated need for better. A beautiful and bright girlfriend in her first year of law school at Berkeley. Drake was in line to take over the fishing boats for his father after he graduated from Berkeley, but instead, he'd taken an internship at the same wealth-management firm as Tyler. Tyler had already moved to the city and Drake was going to join him as soon as he could shake his small-town responsibilities. He'd thought of his family exactly like that back then. Something he needed to shake. The memories were still embarrassing all these years later.

Instead of taking the 101 or even The PCH straight into San Francisco back in the day, he left every morning after bringing in the boats, turned onto Sir Francis Drake Boulevard, and opened up his motorcycle along the uneven twists and turns of a road many agreed was the worst road in Marin County.

For months he left all his angst about what he didn't have, what he wasn't able to do, on the asphalt of the back road he was now on with his sister and his niece. Until the night he'd laid his bike down and nearly lost everything. Drake had not felt that same invincibility nor had he been on his namesake road since the night he was rushed off in an ambulance.

Rarely thought about his bike or that night much anymore. He drove a truck now and stuck to the roads everyone else took, except for today. Today he needed to get his sister and niece to the airport. He glanced at Bella in the backseat, oblivious to the worry on her mom's face.

"Hey, you're going to want to keep your eyes peeled back there, Beauty. This is a gorgeous road and it's named after your favorite uncle."

"Honestly? You have your own road?" She sat up, craning to look out the window.

"I do."

"Lucky."

He nodded and patted Jules's hand. On a slow exhale as the traffic moved, Drake held tight to the wheel and prepared to move past another hurdle.

~

"Mildred. I see you've brought your own beverage."

She sipped, feeling surprisingly badass. "I'd like to be back in Bodega by three," she lied. "So, what is it you need?"

Millie rarely projected her father's chill back on him, but she already missed her happy and was not in the mood to placate.

He closed his book and adjusted his glasses, walking up next to her.

"Well, thank you for making time for me."

She noticed he was limping. Of course he was limping. The one time she decided to give as good as she got. "What happened? Why are you limping?"

"Broke my ankle." He held up his pant leg to reveal a boot.

"And you didn't call me. You didn't have someone call me?"

"Oh, don't be dramatic. I slipped off the back step while I was putting boxes out to recycle. It was a fluke and I'm on the mend. Now, I have some regular customers and the occasional visitor who have asked why I don't carry romance novels."

Millie almost choked on her sip but kept it together.

"I normally ignore them, but yesterday I had a group of young women come in and accuse me of being sexist."

Her eyes widened and her father turned to face her.

"I have never been sexist a day in my life. I have hundreds of female authors in my store."

"Did you tell them that?"

"I did, and I shooed them out of my store."

"You shooed them?"

"Oh, you know what I mean. I moved them along. But they went on social media and claimed I was rude and a slew of other nonsense." He shook his head. "My point is, I don't want my business to suffer, so I need you to cultivate a small and tasteful selection of romance novels for my very back shelf. I will have Penelope, my assistant, keep that shelf updated, but since you seem to travel in romance circles, I thought you might help with the initial purchase."

Penelope had been her father's assistant and bookkeeper for fifteen years, and he still insisted on attaching her title at every mention. Millie wondered if he did that all the time or assumed since his daughter "traveled in romance circles," she wasn't bright enough to remember the woman who managed to put up with him.

"And you called me. Had me drive all the way down here so you could again, in a round-about way this time, remind me how distasteful, but suddenly necessary my career is?"

"No. Well, I am, was disappointed when you chose that genre, but the last time you dropped by unannounced, you mentioned you were finally correcting course and writing a real book. 'Good for her,' that's what I said to Penelope, my assistant. Didn't I?" he asked, and the sainted woman nodded. "But right now, I need you to help me fill a small shelf before those... women barge back into my store."

"Alistair is alive," she said, like a secret reminding her heart not to break.

"Pardon?"

She met her father's eyes, the color of her own, but icy. Like the difference between the calm Caribbean and shark-infested waters. Most of her life she'd felt bad for her dad, sad that he couldn't see the world as she saw it. That he'd wasted years not knowing her, but in that moment, she was angry. She was tired of being yet another silly woman he "shooed" or moved along.

"There are several best-seller lists that Penelope can reference online. You can order your bottom shelf from there." Millie crumpled up her cup and tossed it behind the counter.

"What? Why would I refer to some publication when my daughter is in the industry?"

"You make me sound like a hooker."

He said nothing.

"I'm not helping you." Her eyes welled, but she held them wide to keep her tears inside. "Those women were right. I'm not sure if you're as horrible as they said, but I no longer know you, so maybe. But they were right that you're rude. You're rude to me, your only daughter. I've seen you treat strangers well, but only the ones you deem worthy."

She walked toward the door because if she didn't leave soon, years of tears she'd kept locked tight would wash them both away.

"Now you're high and mighty?" He scoffed and narrowed his eyes. "Why in God's name did you ever start writing such rubbish? I sent you to the finest schools. You were given every opportunity and you wasted it."

She'd meant to take the high road as she always had, but something like survival stirred in her chest, and she turned on him. This time she didn't wait for an invitation, she stepped right into his space.

"Are you asking me why I write stories about people finding love, making things work and riding off into whatever version of the sunset they choose?" One step more and she was inches from him. Closer to the man than she'd been in forever. "Is that what you're asking?" she said, her voice a whispered dare.

He sneered now but took a step back. "I suppose. I'll try that angle instead of cursing God. Yes, Mildred. I'm asking why you write such unsubstantial nonsense."

"Because I've spent more of my life unloved than loved," she shouted. "Because when I write my stories, it's like I'm recycling the tiny fragments my mom left behind. Weaving them into something new and wonderful to share with the millions of readers who love my books." This time when she stepped into him, he took two steps back and she relished the shock on his face. "Because contrary to you and everyone else in your obtuse, deprecating crowd, I am not oblivious to the ugly realities of the world."

"I see. So, you knowingly push a counterfeit human experience."

Millie almost laughed. It had been awhile since she'd gone a round of ten-point words with her father. "You are cruel. Do you know that?"

He said nothing but stared at her like she'd sprouted a horn in the center of her head. She felt like a unicorn most of the time, so she allowed it.

"I'm not sure what happened to you, Dad, other than Mom dying." She shook her head, intent on leaving without another word, but she turned back. "You're the one who seems out of touch. People lose the one they love all the time. It's tragic, but rarely..." She faced him again. "Rarely do they make an orphan of their child in the process."

He held up a hand and made to leave her feeling ridiculous again. Millie grabbed his arm. "This isn't about my writing, is it? It has never been as simple as a difference in taste."

He looked at where she had ahold of him and met her eyes. In that moment he looked pale and weak. She let him go. "I write love with full knowledge of the ugly, in defiance of it and you hate that." Her eyes welled, but she swallowed back her pain. "You hate me."

"Don't be ridiculous."

A tear fell on her cheek. "I have tried to find you in the darkness." She swiped at her eyes. "I thought maybe if I wrote myself there you would see me, love me." She stood with her hand on the all-too-heavy white door and realized she'd always been equipped to write sad metaphors for Alistair's life. Her father was surrounded by them.

A couple crossed the street, obviously on their way into the chic neighborhood bookstore.

"Mildred, if you're going go, then go, but I will not have you making a scene in my shop."

She chuckled, once again aware of the thin line between joy and pain. In that instant, she realized her father wasn't the formidable man she'd spent so much time chasing after. He was a scared, pathetic man.

"Don't call me again." The breath backed up in her chest at the finality of her decision. "Leave me alone." She knew with the final push of the door that her story would be changed forever, for the better.

"I'm your father, now come away from the door. We can discuss this after I—"

Millie shook her head and let an entering couple walk through the door she was now holding open. Her father greeted them but remained quiet as they disappeared into the perfect order of his store, that look of disappointment at her defiance so familiar, so tolerated by her for so many years that she thought she might be sick right there all over his pristine shelves.

"Never again," she said, barely realizing she was speaking. "I'm saving myself."

Millie walked out, and this time, she didn't look back. She was no longer that lonely child watching his life from the outside. She'd thrown open all the doors, especially the one in the back, letting in the glorious bay breeze.

Alistair had escaped death for a while now. His life was coming together nicely with a bit of mystery, that Millie had been surprised to find she enjoyed. But his story was still missing that one ingredient that all her stories had, that magic. She smiled, walked toward her car, and wiped one final time at her damp face. As soon as she got back to Bodega, she would give Mr. Alistair Holt a grand and passionate love.

Millie plopped down into her rental car on a free and easy breath that allowed a joyful memory she'd nearly forgotten. A year before her mom's diagnosis, the three of them had rented a beach house. They had stopped for lobsters and ice cream on the way. Millie bought two packs of bubble gum that afternoon. When they arrived, the first thing her mom did was turn on the music—"anything but jazz," she used to say—and open the windows and doors.

"Millie, my sweet, always remember to air things out and make room for the new," she'd said, allowing the ocean air in with complete abandon while her giggling daughter followed close behind.

Millie had her memories. She would write them down so she would remember always and keep them with the pictures of her mom. That would have to be enough, she thought as she left her father in the rearview. "You would have been proud of me today, Mom," she said to the empty car as she turned onto a back scenic road. She rolled down her windows, put on Alistair's newly-created playlist, before realizing she was letting go and holding on at the same time.

Chapter Twenty-Seven

They made it to the airport and Drake gave himself one hell of a check mark. Granted, he had not done it alone, but parking his truck and grabbing the luggage, he still felt damn powerful. Bella, who'd brought *The Half-Blood Prince* with her, had read aloud a few minutes after they'd turned off the familiarity of the Pacific Coast Highway and onto Sir Francis Drake Boulevard.

It had helped, having them there. It was his responsibility to make and keep himself well. He'd burdened the people he loved enough, but as he stood back and watched his sister check and double check everything, Drake knew Bella's voice and the magic of a story was the reason they had made it all the way. And when they got to the turn in the road where he'd made the arrogant mistake to outdo all his others six years ago, Jules closed her eyes, but Bella kept on reading.

Instead of the pain and scraping metal or the cold fear of dying, Drake clung to the sound of his niece's voice. The first time they'd read Harry Potter, she was all chubby fingers and wide eyes. They had read themselves out of broken bones and ugly divorce and into the world of Hogwarts. They'd rescued one another back then without even knowing it, and now here she was a grown girl, reading him through one more thing he had been avoiding. He'd been sweating like a fool around every bend, hand white-knuckled on the wheel and his Iron Man arm aching to high heaven, but joy won out and he drove on.

Jules tugged up the handle of Bella's bedazzled suitcase, tied the equally bedazzled sweatshirt around her daughter's waist, and let out an exhale that would make any yogi proud before Drake handed her the coffee he'd been keeping safe from her travel whirl. His sister often whirled, and never more so than when she was taking her precious daughter to spend time with the man who had "trampled her heart," according to their mother.

They walked toward the elevators as Jules sipped her coffee and balanced on this invisible edge of competent mom and complete breakdown. She had navigated that edge for as long as Drake had bothered to pay attention, which was about five years now. He'd been too wrapped up in his attitude when she first got married and too wrapped up in his recovery when she'd come home to save him and their family. But now, now he paid attention and did his best to help when he could even though he had no idea how she did what she did day in and day out, every morning breakfast and every nighttime tuck-in.

Drake had done the work of running his family's fishing boats. He knew the stress and the aches. He hadn't even been able to keep a houseplant alive during those days, let alone a child. And Bella was so much more than just alive. She was content and joyful in a way Drake had not seen since, well, since meeting Millie. She had that kind of joy, which was a super feat considering what he now knew about her past.

Strong and joyful women. Drake had been surrounded by them all his life. His mom managed to survive his high school years with a dry sense of humor and a vise grip on his ear that could bring him to his knees. Both Jules and Sistine invited, more like demanded, he participate in tea parties and WWF matches where Jules was always his opponent and Sistine called the matches from their parents' king-size bed. He'd let them down once, jeopardized everything his parents had worked for in the name of nothing ever being enough, but that was then, and this was now. He lived in the now, and as the elevator dinged, he was taking two of his favorite strong and joyful women toward the airport security checkpoint.

"Do you have your stickers?" Jules asked.

Bella patted her backpack.

"Your Woob?"

She patted it again.

"Okay, I will give your inhaler to Daddy when we land," she said as they walked along the glossy corridor speckled with gray and black.

"Did you pack your red, white, and blue?" Drake asked, hoping if he asked some of the questions, his sister might chill out a notch.

Bella looked up at him, smiled that crooked smile, and rolled her eyes.

"Just checking. You know, where you're going, is kind of run down, so I want to make sure you have patriotic glitter too."

Bella laughed and swatted him. "Dad and Pepper are fancy and you know it, Iron Man." She glanced at her mother, checking for a reaction. Was it possible at the age of ten to already know the damage of divorce?

"But... I have all my colors and shiny stuff. Mommy packed it all special," she said in a louder voice that tore Drake's heart. Before his eyes welled at the thought of being away from Bella for two weeks, he scooped her up under his arm and took over wheeling her bag while she squirmed and giggled. Jules, still running through mental lists and refastening her ponytail as the line moved forward, shushed them both, and Drake set Bella back down.

"Okay, well those stern-looking people in uniforms will not let me get on the plane without a ticket," he said, squatting to his niece's eye level. "Kiss me now on this cheek and the other one because it will have to tide me over until you come home."

She wrapped her arms around his neck and surveyed him in that way only Bella did.

"Mommy says the pretty lady with the red hair is your lovey-heart."

Jules closed her eyes and mouthed sorry.

"Does she now? Huh, well Millie is special, but lovey-heart is a big step, and I have my hands full with all of you guys."

His sister cleared her throat.

"Sorry. I have my hands full with all of you... people?" He looked for clarification, and Jules sighed.

"True." Bella nodded and put her finger to her mouth like she was thinking. "If she becomes your lovey-heart while I'm gone, you know, just in case..."

"I'm all ears."

"Make sure she knows that she has to live with you. You can't move away like Aunt Sissy."

"Okay." Jules grabbed her backpack. "Kiss Iron Man and let's get going."

She kissed both cheeks and his nose before letting him go. Then she held out her pinkie. Drake smiled and wrapped his pinkie around hers and said softly, "Promise."

Bella moved in front of her mom in line and struck up a conversation with the two older people ahead of them.

Jules let out another breath. "Sorry about that. She's—"

"Your daughter?"

That got half a smile.

"Well, yeah."

He had a hard time reconciling his ballsy sister when they were back home with the woman standing in front of him. He supposed they were all stronger in Bodega Bay, but every July when she had to drop Bella off with Ass Hat, Drake worried about her.

He worried when she was out on the boats too, but this was a different kind. Jules knew her way around a boat. It was instinct bred into her, into all of them, like walking or riding a bike. But no one knew their way around heartbreak until it happened. Granted, she'd been divorced for a while, but she still had to raise a child with the guy.

"I'll be back tomorrow morning." She held out her empty coffee cup seemingly in search of a trash.

"I'll be here." Drake took the cup from her.

"You excited about that Fourth of July parade?"

"Oh, absolutely. It's keeping me up at night."

"Speaking of that, how's your—"

"Eh, line's moving."

Jules shook her head and waved as she caught up with Bella. Before they went through to the maze of plastic bins and body checks, they both looked back and blew kisses. Drake held up his pinkie and Bella did the same.

As he drove out of the city, he should have taken the 101. It was open and so was the PCH. He had a clear shot home and nothing to prove. Driving Sir Francis Drake Boulevard wasn't even on his list. No one would ever expect him to revisit that night alone and it could easily be avoided, but the knowledge that an accident, any part of an accident over six years ago still had any hold on him, was unsettling. The thought that Millie was his lovey-heart and deserved a guy who had his life together all fed the need to push it.

Sitting at the light, Drake should have taken the smooth way home, shelved his ego, and accepted that he was human. He could have taken Millie out to dinner, sat on the dock, and made love to her until the sun came up the next morning. And if she left for home because she needed more than he could give or he needed to keep his promise to Bella, that was fine. He had limitations, they both did, and there were no guarantees other than the fact that his life was full just as it was. But he turned left anyway, convinced he could handle anything on his own without Harry Potter. He was Iron Man, wasn't he?

It takes some people a little longer to learn certain lessons.

Once again, his dad was right. Ten minutes in and miles before even the worst part, panic didn't give a crap if he was Iron Man or anyone else. It gripped him by the neck until no breathing exercise in the world could save him, and he pulled over and put his truck in park on the gravel shoulder of the road.

~

Millie stood at the window of Drake's truck and tried to remember everything she'd ever been taught, for real and for the benefit of readers, about panic. Sweat soaked, hand locked to the wheel and eyes usually so alive and mischievous, were now vacant.

He was in a full panic attack and while she knew how to pull herself from a spiral, helping someone else was a very different story. When she tapped on the window, he closed his eyes but still didn't move. His breathing was steady, which kept Millie from going with the break-window-climb-in-after-him option. Returning to the rental car, she grabbed her purse and clicked the lock. A few cars had passed by, but this part of the road was a scenic pull-off, so she felt comfortable they were safe.

Drake's engine was still running, she noted as she approached the truck again. He seemed to be in park, so she walked around to the passenger side. Finding that side locked too, she noticed the small open window over his shoulder and climbed into the bed of the truck. She would not be able to climb in through the window, but at least he'd be able to hear her when she said whatever the heck it was she was going to say. He was still frozen as she sat near the window. Her back to him, she closed her eyes and called on calm.

There was no music, not a sound from the truck save a blinker he'd left on and the whip of another car passing on the nearby road.

"That's great," she said, gently at the window. "Keep breathing." Scrambling for what to do, Millie remembered that afternoon in the alley and the strength he'd shown to a virtual stranger. This was a little more complicated because she loved this man senseless.

"My father wasn't always mean." She glanced over her shoulder. Still nothing so she kept sharing. "I have these great memories of the three of us. Sometimes... we went to the park." Millie tucked her hair behind her ears. She had no idea where this was going, but stream of consciousness was a thing with a lot of writers. She'd wanted to try it out and, well no time like the present.

"They used to swing me by my arms. Oh, this one time"—she pulled her legs in and shifted to the side so she could see him without facing him— "they were swinging me and this woman complained they were going to 'pull my arms from the sockets' my dad laughed and told the woman they had no idea whose kid I was." Millie smiled at the memory. "That they'd just found me over near the pond and I wouldn't leave them alone. Can you imagine?"

Drake's eyes were still closed.

"The woman huffed and stormed off. We had a picnic in the park that day. My dad picked flowers for my mom. They were in love and the love they both felt for me was like the sunshine that day. Warm and everywhere."

"What?" He cleared his throat. "What happened?"

"He got lost in the grief. Twisted in loss. I realized that a while ago. That he was mean because he was in pain. Like a lion with a thorn or... Professor Snape. You know the guy from—"

"Harry Potter. I know." His eyes were still closed.

"I tried to save him, but eventually he didn't want to be saved. It took over."

"And you think that's what this is? My pain is taking over?"

"No. I was going for a whole good vs. evil theme and that was the first story that came to mind." She turned to face the window.

Drake opened his eyes. She willed herself not to look away at the trailing tear at the edge of his jawline. She wasn't a child anymore and if she focused on her own pain at seeing him like this, she would never be able to help him.

"You know, I've never driven a truck. I remember this one time, another happier family story, my parents took me to a farm for pumpkins. I have no idea where they found a farm, but it was truly a farm."

His eyes were still open, hand still clutching the wheel. "Now you talk."

"I know, right? Anyway, that was a hayride and I got to ride on the back of a tractor, but I'd like to give driving a truck a shot. What do you say?"

Nothing. Millie swallowed and tried again.

"Please unlock the door and scoot over so I—"

"I," he croaked before clearing his throat again. "I need to do this." He still hadn't looked at her, only stared straight ahead.

"Not today, you don't."

He seemed ready to argue, and Millie knew she needed to give him exactly what he'd given her that day in town. She needed to help without making him feel small.

"Drake Mortimer, if you solve all your issues before I have a chance to catch up, I will be so mad. Please unlock that door and give me the satisfaction of knowing that driving is not your strong suit."

Releasing his grip on the wheel, he crossed over his chest and hit the button to unlock the door. Millie wiped at her eyes and jumped down from the back of the truck. Another first. She'd never been in the bed of a truck or about to drive one, but it was clear by now there wasn't much she wouldn't try for this man.

Opening the driver's side door, she met Drake's eyes when he finally looked at her. There were bits of him trying to make their way back, she could see in his eyes even though his face was too pale. His hair was damp at his forehead with moisture that matched the patch at the center of his T-shirt. She let out a slow breath.

"How did you know I was here?"

"Your license plate reads 'We Blow,' and it's a company truck. Your logo is right here." She patted the open door.

"Tyler's idea."

"Pulling over?"

He shook his head. "The truck. The logo."

"It's a great idea. Draws attention."

"Why are you here?"

"I was driving back to you. Thought I'd take the scenic route. Scoot over."

"I can't."

"Sure you can. I'll drive and—"

He touched her hand, his fingers cold and shaky. "Millie, I can't scoot over because this isn't a bench seat."

"Oh, right. Real life is so not like fiction. I would totally write your truck with a bench seat."

The corner of his mouth twitched before he took a couple of deep breaths. She felt like she'd won some terrific prize already and she wasn't even behind the wheel yet.

"Okay." She held his expression. "You're going to get out and slowly walk over to the other side. Got it?" She hoped she sounded as sure of herself as he had that day the Miller's basket broke.

Drake followed her instructions, still dazed. She wanted to reach out, hold onto him or ask if he needed help, but she knew better.

No pity.

Letting out another deep exhale, he ran his hand along the hood of the truck, rounded to the other side, and climbed in.

"What are you going to do with your car?" he asked, voice more solid this time.

"It's a rental. We'll come back for it later."

Resigned, fear still in every crease of his face, Drake rested his head back and closed his eyes, as if he'd thought of everything that could go wrong and decided to let go, trust her to get them home safely. She had never felt so relieved or so honored at the same time.

On her own fortifying breath, Millie adjusted the seat, then the mirrors, and drove them home.

Chapter Twenty-Eight

"I have this list," Drake said before he even realized he was awake. His chest loosened, allowing him to take a deeper breath, but he still couldn't open his eyes. He was so tired. Tired of being all right, of getting up and getting on with it. The idea that after all these years his accident still had the power to do that to him registered as weak and dependent. No amount of rationalizing was going to change the fact that he was still broken with or without a playlist.

"That does not surprise me. I've noticed your notebooks."

He looked over at Millie driving his truck with expected competence. It was possible the woman wrote about all these other lives because her zest for everything, like her hair, could not be contained. She was so strong. Sunshine fighting her way through no matter how many clouds.

"I thought I knew what I was doing. Thought I'd cleared all the hurdles."

"I know. Turns out we both did." She quickly glanced at him and then back to the road. "I think it might take a lifetime. What is the list?"

"Things I've been avoiding since my accident."

"Like the sound of metal?"

"It started with that, actually it started with you." He closed his eyes again. "I was doing a great job lying to myself and letting everyone else play along until you showed up and called me out." His lips curved at the memory of that first day.

"Well... someone had to call you out on your taste in music." Her voice cracked. He could tell she was nervous, and he hated that he'd put her in this situation.

"Jules told me it was a Band-Aid, that the music wasn't a fix. She also told me I was being rude."

"So, she was on my side from the very beginning."

Drake nodded.

"That doesn't matter now. I like your music."

"She told me in addition to the music that I had not been on the boats since the accident, had not jumped off the dock, and had not dated."

She scoffed. "Looks like you showed her."

"I still need to jump off the dock."

"I'm sure you'll take care of that one soon," she said.

He heard the blinker and knew they were back on the PCH. Big inhale, bigger exhale, and back in his sandbox. Safe from any number of other things that might bring him to his knees. The list was never-ending. He had survived, but he had not won.

"Are you okay?"

He opened his eyes, swallowed, and lied. "I'm good. Thank you for saving my ass. Can you imagine the flack I'd have to deal with if Tyler had to come and get me?"

He tried to laugh but it came out shallow and fake. Millie pulled into the lot behind the studio, turned off the truck, and faced him, concern so deep in her expression it registered painful.

"Is that the road where you had your accident?"

"It is. Ironic that it's my name, right?"

"You don't need to do this, Drake. I don't need the you who laughs it off or is the town hero."

"No? You didn't come here to hook up with the town hero?" He felt something ugly bubble in his chest. Something that told him she was just waiting for his life, the one she'd perceived as so perfect when she arrived, to show cracks.

"I definitely do not want the town hero," she said on a chuckle, still unable to see the ugly behind his eyes.

Drake got out of the truck without another word. He needed distance, room, before he said things he didn't mean. Things that would make him feel better, get rid of some of his anger, but hurt her.

"Christ." He ran his hand through his hair and kept walking, pulled open the door to the studio, and turned on her. "I've got work to do."

Millie stopped so fast it was as though she'd hit a wall. "Oh. Right. Okay, I will leave you to it." She leaned in to kiss him and although he wanted to kiss her with everything he was, tell her he would get over this and throw open the doors of his little town and let her right in, he didn't write romance novels. In those stories, the hero dodged the bullet, saved the day. There were no stories for heroes afraid of a road, afraid of a little noise, and scared to jump off a dock.

No one wanted to read that story, so he didn't kiss her. He pulled away and said, "When do you leave?"

"Don't do this."

"Do what?" He was still standing in the doorway. "Your time is up. Alistair is alive and it's time for you to go. I'm not doing anything."

"I'm going to the city next week, but I'll be back. You know this. We've talked about all of our plans."

He shook his head. The foul thing grew larger and was now in his chest, making it hard to breathe. "I don't know a goddamn thing anymore."

"What are you talking about?" She pushed past him into the empty studio and turned on the lights like she belonged and wasn't going anywhere. "This is absurd. It was a road, a trigger. Everyone has things that set them off. You are no different. Do not push me away. I have come too far to be with you. I love you."

Drake laughed. He loved her too, never wanted her to leave. But the idea that she was another part of the charade, which assured him that he was great when he was a mess, grabbed hold and would not let go.

"Don't." He met her unwavering expression with indifference. "Don't love me" he said, leaning against the counter to keep from falling over. "This was a mistake. You were right all those months ago."

She shook her head and reached for him.

"I'm not fighting with you."

That should have been enough to scare her away. Pain and disappointment were powerful repellents, but she just stepped in front of him.

"How far we've come, right?" she said. "That first day when I burst in here a complete mess and you thought you had me all figured out. A little bit of sarcasm and I'd be on my way." She was inches from him. "Annoying little tourist."

Drake swallowed and held his ground.

"I...am in love with you. Do you hear me? That counts, Drake. That changes everything." Her voice shook right along with her hands and Drake knew he was a bastard, but he also knew if he could get her to leave, she would be better off. She'd have her great romance with some guy who was as strong as she was, a whole man who wasn't going to crawl under the table at a loud noise.

She would go back to her world and leave him to his glass. Then he could return to the life he knew before she showed him more. It didn't matter if he jumped off the fucking dock or played his music too loud. No one cared before she arrived, and no one would care once she left. It was a win-win, as Tyler always said.

"We all have things. Can't you—"

"Go home, Millie."

Gloves off.

She nodded. "Was it easier when I was the only one broken? When you were picking me up, driving me home? Let me ask you something, when you were wiping my tears and showing me around this place,"—she spread her arms wide—"did you think I was some pathetic, broken soul?"

"You know the answer to that question. I never once made you—"

"You're right. You didn't. You picked me up and showed me I was stronger than I knew."

"I never said that either."

"You didn't have to." She wiped a tear. "It was there every time you looked at me." She stepped into him until they were chest to chest. "Don't you see the same thing when I look at you, Drake? You are not broken. You are—"

"Enough." He slid past her and behind the counter that separated them all those months ago. "It has been fun and I am... glad you saw all of those things in me, but I—"

Son of a bitch.

He swiped his eyes with the back of his hand. "*I* don't see those things in me. Why can't you understand that? I'm not you." He cleared his throat. "I have work to do. Have a safe trip home."

Drake stood facing the furnace, unable to look into those limitless eyes for one more second. Glassblowing had rules, a set of steps that all but guaranteed results every time. He would fall back into those steps and find his way again. He'd done it before. He would do it again.

"I was wrong. Kissing you was never a mistake. Loving you has been the best thing," her voice cracked, and he closed his eyes, as if that ever worked. "It has been the best thing that has ever happened to me. But, this, what you're doing now, *is* a mistake." The entire studio filled with blaring music. She must have hit the remote. Drake opened his eyes but didn't dare look over his shoulder.

George Michael. There they were, full circle.

When he heard the studio door slide closed, he sunk back onto a workbench, fully aware that the moment of impact was just around the corner. Another wreck of his own doing. She would leave, and his heart would undoubtedly stop beating for good this time. Drake flipped the page in his notebook. Until then, he'd work.

~

She should have left. The tow truck she'd asked Karen to call had safely delivered her rental car an hour ago. She should have packed up her things and gone back where she belonged, but she wasn't so sure where that was anymore. That's why instead of shoving everything into the trunk and rambling all her heartache to Pop-Tart while they drove south on the freeway, Millie was outside Swept Away Books.

Nikki and another woman in bright yellow clogs were standing near the window holding the latest Sonali Dev, with the magnificent red and gold lettering on the cover. They were laughing and the woman opened to one of the pages, read something, and put her hand to her chest in that swoon every romance reader, young and old, knew on sight. Millie understood the swoon and wondered if the woman had cried at the same parts she had while reading the gorgeous story.

Romance seemed to be the only adult genre left that allowed for the broad strokes and windswept bluffs of childhood books. They were intriguing, the good ones anyway, and beckoned the reader to join the author in a story of not mere reality, but also what could be. Romance was the winding road or the hot rush. It was the story for which every kind of "we" was imaginable and celebrated.

So, with her own very real and broken heart, it made sense that she was outside a bookstore dedicated to romance novels. They called to her, saved her for so many years. Then she'd gone to college and everything, everyone became so serious she'd often wondered if she had opened the wrong door or missed the orientation on being an adult.

Reading became about ostentatious literary terms, and she'd lost count how many times her creative writing professors told her she was being ambiguous. She began reading books she should read rather than stories she wanted to read. It wasn't like these literary terms were anything new. She'd read all the classics. She could pick out allusions. She'd simply never understood why her teachers couldn't call them references to make things easier all around.

By her second year at Berkeley, it was clear that terms and layers in literature and writing were meant to weed people out. To create an elite group of writers, of whom she would never be one. Of course, that didn't keep her from trying. She worked and reworked her assignments into the wee hours of the next days until she'd forgotten why she loved reading or writing at all.

Her father had never wanted to know the details of her college life; he only ever wanted to know her grades, and even though he hadn't bothered to show up for the ceremony when she graduated top of her class, he kept a picture behind the desk near Penelope of her diploma. Not her holding her diploma, only her credentials. Yet another sign she should have seen.

After graduation, her father had gone his way and free from the constraints of university, she found romance again.

"Hi," Nikki said in that soft tone people who recognized far-off thoughts used.

Millie blinked, smiled, and stepped through the door being held open. "Sorry. I... had a super crappy day and I thought I'd stop by to—"

"Hang out with your people?"

"Yes, exactly," she managed around the lump in her throat.

The woman Millie now called her friend clapped ring-clad hands together like a genie and grabbed a purple cardigan off the back of a chair behind the register. "Well, feel free to browse. We are open as long as you need us. Or... we're about to discuss Roni Loren's new one. Do you want to sit in?"

"We?"

"Just a small group of older gals and a bottle of Prosecco."

"Who are you calling old?" one of the women yelled from the back and made her way toward them. "Holy Toledo, you're Millie Hart. I missed your reading because my—"

Nikki shook her head and held up a finger to shush her friend. "She doesn't want to be Millie Hart right now."

"But she is."

"So? We're going to pretend she's not for tonight."

"Like when we pretended the sweater Meghan crocheted didn't look like an electric spiderweb had attached itself to her boobs?"

Nikki nodded. "Yes, exactly like that." She grinned at Millie as the woman returned to her seat.

"How did you know I didn't want to be Millie Hart tonight?"

She shrugged. "Jules is around your age. I recognize the look. Love can be rough."

Millie was stunned. Maybe Auntie N was a genie.

"Let's get this show on the road," another woman called out.

"Oh, hush." She returned to Millie. "Have you read Roni Loren's latest?"

"Is there anyone left who hasn't?"

Nikki laughed and Millie thought she looked a bit like a genie too, sweet and magical and sent to make Bodega Bay a better place.

"Like to join us?"

"I think I would."

Nikki smacked her hands together again and quickly ran to the front of the store to flip her sign and lock the door.

"Now I need to warn you"—she looped her arm through Millie's on their way back—"Doris takes her teeth out and sets them on the table right in front of her like it's the most normal thing," she whispered. "Something about the Prosecco and the bubbles messing with her dentures." She giggled. "Don't let it freak you out."

Millie patted her arm. "Thanks for the warning."

～

An hour and a half later, Millie's sides hurt from all the laughter. In the time it took to drink a Dixie cup of wine, the "older" women of Bodega Bay rated their favorite Roni Loren scenes, which led to a discussion about their own favorite "get-it-on positions." A smile still on her face, Millie drove back to the cottage. She'd spent the evening with incredible women discussing a sexy book that made them all happy. A story that made them cry, then laugh, then think about their own lives and loves.

Doris had lost her husband but told the group he was her best friend like the hero in the book. The woman in the clogs was Clara. She and her wife were still "making passionate love" when their granddogs weren't over, of course. Meghan lost her sister to cancer recently and shared that the book was the last one they'd read together. Seven women nearly twice Millie's age giggling and free with their feelings.

She sighed as she stood outside Candy Land, taking in the bay she would leave behind in the morning. It was getting warmer and there were more people. Drake had said there would be. Millie looked over at his Airstream. Lights out, not a sound, exactly as it had been that first night. She couldn't make him trust her with his heart. Convince him that they were stronger in their love then they would ever be apart. Unlike Alistair, she couldn't rewrite his future any more than she could undo the pain either of them had endured in the past.

Maybe he needed space to work through things. She understood needing to be alone. Maybe time would heal things and their paths would cross again. Or maybe she was only meant to have him for a little while.

However their story played out, she wasn't the same person she'd been that first night she arrived in Bodega Bay and for that she would be eternally grateful to all of them.

Millie turned her face to the stars. Still there, all of them as bright as ever and just as out of reach. She wasn't sure she believed in heaven, but the stars over Bodega Bay seemed like the perfect place for her mom if there was such a thing.

Chapter Twenty-Nine

*D*rake couldn't sleep in his bed or the studio, so at around midnight, he settled for the only place he had not made love to Millie, the new leather couch in the gallery. He fell off to sleep thinking he should have set an alarm, but he had left his phone in the studio.

"Kind of a dick move saying you're some kind of lone wolf, ya know?"

Drake sat up, squinting into the sunlight, and found Tyler. "What are you talking about? Is that coffee?"

His friend grabbed both cups and sat down next to him on the couch before sharing the caffeine. "I had plans for this couch, and they did not include you drooling on it."

"Why are you here?"

"Because Jules called me at seven o'clock this morning. Seems someone forgot to pick her up at the airport and she couldn't get ahold of you."

"Shit." Drake slumped back into the couch. He was too far gone to worry if he was letting anyone down.

"Don't you want to know what happened?" Tyler removed the lid from his cup.

"You saved the day?"

"Not exactly." He sipped his coffee. "After I enjoyed what is probably the only time I will ever hear Jules's voice in my ear that early in the morning."

"Probably?"

"A guy can dream. Anyway, after our… moment, I told her I would find you. Then I sent a driver to pick her up."

Drake snorted. "You sent a driver to pick up my sister at the airport? Like black Town Car, suit and tie, driver?"

Tyler grinned and took another sip before slowly nodding.

Drake held up his fist and his friend met it with his own. "Balls, Pace. Big balls."

"I know. I keep trying to tell people."

Drake ran a hand over his face. "How did you know I was here?"

"Called Auntie N, she told me about Millie and that you're all high and mighty that you're a lone wolf who fixed yourself. We'll save that discussion for later. By the time I got to the Millers' place, she was packed up and gone. I figured you weren't sleeping anywhere you'd slept with her before, so,"—he held up the hand not holding coffee—"voilà. New couch."

"Is this your first cup of caffeine?"

"Third."

"That explains it. Okay, well you found me. I worked until late last night. And I know there are a ton of orders to work on today, but I need a minute."

"Esteban and Hazel are on those orders already."

Drake waited for Tyler to circle back around.

Never one to disappoint, he said, "Remember what you said when we tried to make those glass wind chimes our first year in business. The ones that kept breaking?" Tyler stood.

"No."

"Colossal mistake. That's what you said. I remember because we were practically rolling on the floor of the studio laughing at the accuracy of colossal and how much money we'd wasted."

"Okay."

"That's what this is, my friend. A colossal mistake."

"The gallery?"

"Oh, no." He spread his arms. "This is another one of our brilliant ideas, but you letting Millie leave was a colossal mistake."

"That's your opinion." Drake drank his coffee.

"Nope. I haven't done the town poll yet, but I'm guessing it's the consensus. She loves you. Do you have any idea how rare that is?"

"That someone would love me?"

"No, smartass, that you found someone to love. That you have... a person. I thought you weren't taking things for granted anymore."

He swallowed the last sip and tossed the cup. "I'm not taking anything for granted. Millie was here for nearly four months. We had fun and now it's time to get back to our lives."

"Right. She's just some tourist and off she goes. Makes sense." Tyler smacked Drake's shoulder. "Cut it out. Why are you doing this? You're not made to be alone, none of us are."

"Did you read that somewhere?"

He shook his head and tossed his own cup. "It's just life, our town. We pick each other up all the time, it's what people do. You helped Millie, she helped you. This is kind of simple, which is why I'm surprised you messed it up."

"I have to focus on fixing my own issues." He couldn't believe he was using that stupid word.

"Oh, for fuck's-sake, will you let the list go?"

Drake met his eyes. Stupidly surprised that Tyler knew about the list.

"Damn small towns," they both said together.

"You will be working on things forever, Drake. You had stuff to work on before your accident. We all do. When did you get this idea that if you can crack your own eggs or drive some road alone that you're done?"

"You sound like Millie."

"Yeah, well smart minds."

Neither one of them spoke for a while.

"Colossal?"

Tyler nodded. "Afraid so."

Drake reached behind the couch for his prosthesis. "I need to get to work."

"Yeah, you do. Do you want me to take you to your truck? Or you could call her first, I brought your phone." He held up the phone.

Drake pushed on his arm, not caring about the maintenance at the moment. His whole body ached, so one arm made no difference. "No. I meant the studio. I need to get to work."

"Oh, come on. You're not going to fix this? Fight for her?"

Drake furrowed his brow. "You watch too many movies. Look at me." He held up his left arm. "In the real world, who am I fighting?"

"So you're just giving up?"

He shook his head. "I agree I screwed up, but if I'm going to fix it, I need to use what I have. That's what Brix did in *Rescue Me*."

Tyler laughed. "And I watch too many movies?"

"Shut up. I need the studio."

Tyler drove him to BP Glass Works where it all began, and Drake got started on his biggest project to date.

Chapter Thirty

She had been home two weeks and still felt like her apartment was cold and her life, similar to how the lipstick she had pulled from the bottom of her bag months ago, was no longer her shade. Pop-Tart felt it too, restless for that sunny spot they'd left behind in Bodega Bay.

Millie arrived at Jade's office by eleven. They would lunch before she left for the Chicago stop on her book tour. Jade was on the phone when Millie knocked on the door and was ushered in. Her friend, now in super-agent mode, gestured to a box on the round table in the corner of her office where she normally kept fresh flowers.

The box was big, and Millie immediately recognized the BP Glass Works stamp on the brown wrapping and the attached note.

Hands trembling, she loosened the card from the envelope and read:
Millie –
Enclosed please find your pieces.

When she dropped the card and started tearing at the box, Jade hung up and grabbed the note off the floor. Hunting through the packing materials, Millie pulled out a vase and Jade gasped. It seemed to be a million colors. Millie set it carefully on the table and ran her hands over the smooth curves. It was unbelievably beautiful.

Her pieces. She brought a hand to her chest.

"Do you want to finish reading the card?"

Millie nodded, never taking her eyes of the glass. "Please."

"Oh, me. Okay." Jade cleared her throat. "The base is our first failed project, but also our first incredible kiss."

Millie met her friend's eyes, emotion swirling around them as she continued. "I added every blue I could find since it's our favorite color, but I will never be able to find the blue of your"—Jade blinked back tears—"the blue of your eyes so I didn't bother. The silver is Pop-Tart, the pink represents your bubble gum. The dark green is for Jade who never lets you give up on your love stories. Holy crap, this man." She wiped her eyes. "Last is yellow for"—Jade met Millie's eyes again. "I don't know that I can get through this last part."

"Come on. What's the yellow?"

She could barely get the words out. "Yellow is for your mom, who will always be your sunshine no matter how many times you try to kill poor Alistair."

They both laughed through the tears and Millie took the note and finished out loud.

"I know I messed up, but I wanted you to have this, wanted you to know that you are not just pieces. You have a foundation, a solid and amazing life that you made yourself, Millie Hart. I'm honored you let me share the best months of my life with you. I will leave the music on and I will love you forever. Drake."

Millie picked up the vase and held it in her arms, loving it and the man who made it for her more than she thought possible.

"Jade?"

Her dearest friend in the world wiped her eyes and held out her hands. "Go. I'll keep your pieces safe and I'll reschedule Chicago. Go."

"Are you sure?" Reluctant to part with it, Millie handed over the vase. She wanted it safe, wanted it on their mantel someday. There would be a mantel and lots of somedays, she knew it in her soul.

"Of course I'm sure. This is what I do. I'm the protector of the HEA. Drake put it in writing, remember?" Jade carefully set the vase on the table, kissed Millie on both cheeks, and handed over her car keys.

~

The following morning Esteban chose hair bands in honor of his daughter who was home packing for Berkeley.

They'd barely begun a set of six glass mugs when the door to the studio slid open and stayed open. At the glare, Drake turned to give someone shit for interrupting their work but stopped short when he saw Millie standing in the halo of sunshine.

Esteban muted the music and extended his hand to take the blowpipe. Drake handed it over and tossed his safety goggles on the bench.

Millie, totally familiar and clearly no longer willing to wait behind the counter for him, marched toward the back of the studio in the same pajamas she'd worn that first day. The breath nearly knocked out of him; Drake couldn't help but smile.

"Can we help you?" Tyler asked, standing from his desk.

Millie beamed as she nodded and then hugged Tyler before rolling her shoulders back to meet Drake's eyes.

"I received a package."

He looked around like he'd been transported back in time. "Where? How are you here?"

"She's staying with us." Jules walked in and stood behind the counter. When his mouth gaped open, his sister shrugged, "What? Small town."

"Is everyone in on this?" His heart was pounding as he took a step closer to Millie.

"Funny you should ask." Tyler pointed toward the door as Drake's parents joined them, followed by Sistine and Cade.

"Wait, don't do anything yet." Hazel barreled into the studio, out of breath.

Millie's eyes warmed.

"Okay, go."

"Congratulations," she said to Hazel.

"Thank you. We can talk about that later, after you..." She waved her hand toward Drake.

"Right." Millie faced him and when he met those eyes he'd missed more than he would ever be able to explain, the room and everyone in it, melted away.

"You can't just send a woman something like that and expect her to get on with her life. Don't you read romance?"

"I've read a couple."

"Great so you know how this has to end."

He nodded and stepped closer.

"You gathered my pieces." Her eyes glistened now as she touched his chest. "Incredible imagery."

"Yeah? Did you write it down?"

She shook her head. "I don't need to. I will never forget it for as long as I live." She went up on her toes and kissed him. "I love you so much, Drake Mortimer Branch. I'm bursting with it." Drake wrapped an arm around her, once again grateful for a second chance.

"So,"—she patted his chest—"about that list of yours."

"What are you up to, neighbor? Chase is moving into his new space next week, so the music is checked off." He exhaled. "Couldn't quite tackle that one, but I'm helping him move."

"We'll always have a list, Drake."

"We?"

She nodded. "I'm here for serious business, and you're not scaring me off again."

"Is that so?"

She smiled. "You know, I have never been swimming in a bay."

"No?" Esteban said, swiping at his eyes with the back of his hand. "It's perfect this time of year."

"If I remember correctly there's a great dock over near that adorable little cottage with all the gnomes," she said. "Although I did notice there are some new renters." She glanced at Jules.

"Damn tourists," they all said together.

Millie gestured to Drake and leaned in to whisper. "You should probably leave the hardware behind for this, Iron Man."

Drake closed his eyes for a beat and then looked around the studio. Why he'd bothered with pretense around any of these people was beyond him now. They'd all seen him at his worst, and he them. They had never expected him to be perfect. Maybe he'd felt like he had used up all his humanness on one big screw-up. He wasn't sure and now, as he released his arm from the prosthesis none of it mattered.

Bella, who'd only arrived home last night and was still in her PJs, had joined them too. Drake realized his entire family now stood in solidarity with the woman he loved. Again, he was lucky.

"I'll take good care of it," his niece said, reaching for his arm. She smiled, morning still creased on her beautiful face and what he'd thought was impossible happened, he loved Bella even more.

Millie grabbed his hand. "Ready?"

"That depends, where are you taking me?"

"You know."

"Jumping off a dock is not for amateurs. You should probably—"

She pulled him toward the door, "Ugh, you talk too much. Let's do this so we can start working on my list."

"You have a list?"

"I tried to tell you, but you were too busy playing your scare-off-the-tourist game." They walked toward the dock, a procession of nosy family and friends in their wake.

"I'm sorry." He stopped and held her face. "I said that in the note, right?"

She nodded and unable to wait any longer, he kissed her. Long, deep, and in front of the world. He'd fumble around and make a fool of himself forever as long as she stayed right by his side.

"You get your man, Millie," Nikki called from somewhere behind them. Drake wondered when she had arrived, but quickly didn't care as he and Millie took off their shoes and the warmth of wood beneath his feet welcomed him back once again.

"Should you have brought towels for this?" His mom said, like it was any other summer day.

Drake shook his head, holding Millie's hand and ignoring every urge he had to reconsider, stay safe. When they approached the middle of the dock, Millie glanced over. They would be each other's best day, every day. He knew it deep in his heart.

"Don't let go," she said, squeezing his hand.

"I won't." Drake backed them up a few steps and, on his count, they charged to the end of the dock, catching air like two people with enough love to handle anything that came their way.

Epilogue

Millie finished her book tour, returning to the bay on any available break. Drake had even joined her on her rescheduled Chicago stop. They'd been to the city a couple of times for dinner with Jade and gotten up to Berkeley to see Hazel. Their first few months together had been busy and full of new firsts they were learning to appreciate. Millie was working on the final draft of *Take Me,* Alistair and Sasha's story, as fall ushered the crowds away and brought new colors to Bodega Bay.

The sun was setting again. Blue and green with bits of rust as they sat on a blanket outside the Airstream. Drake had fallen asleep in her lap reading about another senator who was pissing him off, but this guy's bodyguard was about to risk her life in the name of love, so it would work out in the end. Millie had already read that one, but she kept the spoilers to herself.

Brushing the hair from Drake's peaceful face, she realized this was the cover of her love story. Blankets, fading suntans, and even a shiny trailer. Books and this town would always be her happy place. She wanted everything a life with Drake had in store, from the glossy cover to the very last page.

~

Thank you for reading *Blow – A Love Story*! I hope Millie and Drake's story was worth the wait. I loved moving The Love Stories to Bodega Bay and look forward to staying there for a while. If you enjoyed the book, please consider leaving a review at the book retailer of your choice, as well as Goodreads, to help other readers find this story.

Please make sure you're on my newsletter mailing list at: tracyewens.com to keep up with the latest news about my books.

Thank you, wonderful readers, for the tremendous support. I appreciate each and every one of you! Keep reading for a look at *Tap – A Love Story*, which is Sistine and Cade's story.

All the best,
Tracy

~

Chapter One

Cade McNaughton was in the zone. A few hours into a dance he had envied since he'd first stepped behind a bar a few weeks after his eighteenth birthday. Back then, watching people with far more experience balance hard work, casual chatter, and craft was powerful.

Now here he was, behind his own slab of polished wood. It had been scary when he and his brothers first decided to go big or go home, but almost two years later, the Tap House ran as smoothly as every other part of Foghorn Brewery.

Cade had made that happen. He passed glasses amid the mix of beer, food, and perfume. Tina waited at the end of the bar for him to pour the last drink of her order and then she was gone.

Smiling for no damn reason, he wiped his hands on the towel he kept tucked in the back pocket of his jeans and continued listening to Brandon, the owner of Petaluma Body Shop on the outskirts of old town, share his most recent bad-date story.

"She brought her mom?" Cade asked as he brought up a new crate of glasses.

Brandon nodded, shoving a wad of Foghorn's loaded fries in his mouth. "Swear to Christ. Some shit about wanting to make sure I wasn't a murderer."

"So, how was the date after the mom checked you out and left?" Brandon met his eyes and shoved more fries into his mouth.

"She... didn't leave?"

Pointing at him in a "bingo" move, the guy he barely knew in high school shook his head and washed down his fries with a gulp of Naked Neck. Bad choice—the garlic in the loaded fries called for a light beer, but Brandon never ordered anything else.

"Man, that's... You've got me. That's bad." Cade cashed out a couple who mentioned they were short on time before their movie and noticed the phone number scrawled at the bottom of the receipt as he cleared the spot next to Brandon. Call Me, it said above a San Francisco area code. The handwriting alone promised a good time. Tossing the dishes in the bin below the bar, Cade returned to get the receipt.

"Oh, come on." Brandon snatched the slip of paper. "Jade wants you to call her. Did you even talk to her?"

Cade shook his head and was gone taking orders before returning to Brandon while he poured beer. "She was sitting right next to you. Why didn't you get her number?"

"I tried."

Cade winced and gestured to the paper still on the bar. "Well, there it is. Give her a jingle. You could remind her that you were the quarterback in high school."

"Dude, we're over thirty. No one gives a shit about that anymore."

Cade wanted to tell him no one gave a shit about that an hour after they graduated, but Brandon was having a rough night, rough month. While Cade enjoyed playing around, he didn't kick people when they were down.

"How is it that you're wearing a T-shirt that says My Blood Type is IPA, and your hair is all jacked up, but women love you?"

Cade lifted a brow, sliding another glass of beer under the tap.

"Well, maybe not love, but they want you. Damn, I should have never messed things up with Kelly. Do you think she'll take me back?"

"Isn't she engaged?"

Brandon pushed his plate away. "True. Another one bites the dust. Well"—he brushed the front of his flannel shirt—"I need to do something. Maybe I'll get back to the gym and work on my ass." He huffed and took out his wallet to pay the bill.

"What does your ass have to do with going on a reasonable date?"

Brandon finished the last of his beer and stood. "You honestly don't have Instagram, do you?" He shook his head again as if Cade were some obscure freak of nature. He tossed a tip on the bar and was gone.

Several poured beers later, they had closed out happy hour, but the bar was still packed. With all orders in, the kitchen was slammed, so Cade did what he did best: he entertained.

"Give me a word, any word," he said, arms splayed wide.

"Gluteus Maximus."

"That's two words, and we all know what that means, ladies. I'm looking for a challenge here."

"The word of the night is definitely fine with a capital... F," another woman said, her gaze locked on Cade as if he should start running.

What the hell? Everyone normally loved this game. Cade glanced toward the kitchen. The crowd wasn't restless yet, but he must be slipping because they played Give Me a Word all the time. Someone shouted out a word, Cade gave the definition and used it in a sentence. Sort of like a spelling bee if the participants were buzzed and eating burgers.

"Oh no, fine is not the right word. How about delicious?" another woman purred and high-fived the woman next to her, who had long braided hair that reminded Cade of the movie *Avatar*.

"Ladies, you're losing me," he said as some of the food arrived and he lined up five drink order tickets. Practically every face at the bar was in his or her phone, and Cade once again cursed social media. What was wrong with old school socializing? He flipped glasses and started pouring.

"Is that my pale ale?" Tina asked.

Cade nodded.

"She wants a slice of orange." Tina rolled her eyes. She lost her patience when she was tired. Cade knew that about his favorite server now that they'd worked together for over a year.

"I'd offer you a break, but we haven't been this busy on a Thursday since, well, ever." He set four beers on her tray. "The crowd seems a little off tonight, and why the hell is everyone looking at their phones? Why come out, you know?"

"It's your body."

"Aw, Tina, are you checking me out? What's Pamela going to say when you get off work? She doesn't seem like she's up for sharing you."

"No." Her expression was unflinching as she added napkins and hoisted the tray. "I am not interested in your goods, but practically everyone else in the bar is. It's all over Instagram." Managing unbelievable balance, Tina pulled her phone from her back pocket without spilling a drop. After a few taps, she handed it to Cade and was gone. At the bell from the kitchen and Javier's growl, Cade set Tina's phone behind the bar and delivered orders. When he returned and flipped the phone over, Tina's screen saver was on.

"What's your password," he asked after setting three more beers and sending her off again. After typing in the numbers she called out, the image filled the screen.

A white bed in a room he recognized. A man lay on his stomach, arms overhead, holding a pillow in a tangle of duvet. The guy was naked save an edge of sheet barely covering his ass-ets. Soft light, definitely early morning, for an instant his tired mind ticked off the details as if it were an inventory order before finally screaming— *That's you, idiot.*

Cade touched the screen to make the image bigger, but the bell dinged again, and he went back to work. By the time he returned, Tina was holding her hand out for her phone.

"Not the best time to have a Jack and the Beanstalk tattoo, eh?"

Cade glanced at his arm, strangely embarrassed, and handed back her phone. "Who posted that? Where? How does everyone know about it?"

"I'm assuming it's someone you know... intimately." She laughed and when Cade didn't, she stopped. "The poster tagged Foghorn. Most customers follow us, so now they've all—"

"Seen my ass."

"Well, most of your ass."

Cade set a pitcher of beer and three glasses on Tina's tray.

She patted him on the shoulder and picked up her order.

"Wait a minute. Tagged, meaning that picture is on—"

"Cade." Patrick's voice, pissed and familiar, rang out over the crowd.

"Shit."

Tina winced and was gone.

"Get it down," his brother and co-owner of Foghorn said, stepping behind the bar, phone in hand.

"Where did you even come from? I thought you were at home... nesting." Cade slid past his older brother to grab two rolled sets of silverware and set them in front of a couple absolutely on their first date. Cade normally enjoyed watching people get to know one another, but not tonight.

"I was at home and now I'm here. Get it down."

Heat that had nothing to do with the kitchen or the fact that he'd been going nonstop for the last five hours bloomed across Cade's chest. He dropped off two orders and would have given anything to avoid returning to the other end of the bar. God, he hated it when Trick was on a rant.

"Could you give me a minute? I found out about it ten minutes ago. I don't know who posted it. Maybe it's not even me."

Four women said at once, "It's you."

"Where would someone get a picture of my—"

"Lauren," Aspen said, waddling toward him.

"Wow, both of you. Do you two have a Cade-Fucked-Up alarm that goes off in your house?"

"You remember Crazy-Eyes-But-Who's-Looking-Above-the-Neck Lauren?"

"That's not nice." Cade wiped the bar in front of Aspen and pushed Trick toward his pregnant wife. Aspen, Foghorn's business manager, married Patrick last year. She wasn't always happy to work with Cade, but he knew deep down, way deep especially now, she loved him.

"I'm about to birth a human and your ex has tagged our business to screw with you because that seems to be what your exes like to do. I don't care what you do in your private life, but I don't have time to be nice. We are running a business here, Cade. You get that, right?"

Cade looked at his brother. There was no way he would ever tell his sister-in-law to back the hell up, but Trick had no intention of saving him.

"Right. I see how it is." He tossed another set of dirty dishes into the bin.

Did she just ask him if he got that? Of course he did. He got everything. Even though he didn't wear his stress on his sleeve, it didn't mean he wasn't a completely responsible third of their brewery. It was an unfortunate picture and he'd ask Lauren to take it down, or at least get rid of the tag, but it's not like he'd posted it himself. And what the hell did Aspen mean by "that seems to be what your exes do?"

What the hell? He'd been on top of everything less than an hour ago and now, after one picture, he was relegated to an irresponsible exhibitionist who dates crazies.

"I'll take care of it," Cade said.

Patrick stepped behind the bar and followed him. "No, that's not—"

Cade spun with anger he hadn't felt in years. They were chest to chest. "Back the hell up," he said softly without a hint of his usual jest. "I didn't post the picture. Someone else did and I'm embarrassed enough. If you were acting like my brother instead of my damn leader, you would understand that."

Patrick didn't back down, but he took in a breath and his expression softened.

"I will get it taken down."

"Tonight."

"I will text her once you get out of my face, and if that doesn't work, after working this ten-hour shift, I'll call her."

They stood for a beat, orders piling up, and then broke apart.

Patrick and Aspen left and once Cade caught up and pushed away the resentment, he texted Lauren.

Cade: Lauren, take it down.
Lauren: Hey, babe. Take what down?

Cade kneaded the back of his neck with one hand. There were so many reasons he and Lauren hadn't worked out.

Cade: You tagged the brewery. I need you to take it down or at least remove the tag.
Lauren: Why? I'll bet your buns are good for business.
Cade: We're not running that kind of business.
Lauren: Sure you are. I'll bet the bar is packed. You think those women, and I'll bet several men, are there for your beer?
Cade: I do.
Lauren: You always were too humble for your own good, babe.
Cade: Please.
Lauren: Fine.

Cade let out a steady breath and almost smiled before his phone vibrated again.

Lauren: If we can get together.

He should have known better than to think it would be that easy. Before he could ask where and when she'd replied.

My place. ASAP.

Cade slipped his phone into his pocket, and instantly, what used to be fun and flirty felt stupid and dirty. He knew what "get together" meant in Lauren's language. She'd ended their relationship a year ago, but he'd do what was needed to clean up this mess.

"Cadre," Tina said when she returned to the bar, the crowd finally easing up.

"What?"

"You asked for a word. I'm giving you one. Cadre."

"A unit of trained people. She had a cadre of servers at her disposal," he said, barely aware of his own voice.

"You're a smart guy, Cade."

"Yeah? Could you post that on Instagram?"

She laughed, and Max slid behind the bar and fastened his apron. They'd hired a relief bartender a few months ago. Cade could finally have some time off after a two-year stretch at full speed while they were bringing up the Tap House.

Following a fist bump and a quick bar rundown where Cade told Max who was drinking what, Cade was untying his apron and calling it a night. When he walked out into the early night air, the sky was dark and the stars were crisp as if he could reach up and touch them. The sky used to fascinate him as a kid. He could point out all the major constellations. He threw his leg over his bike and pulled on his helmet. Tina was right—he was smart. When had his body become more important than what was on his mind? The roar of his bike shook him free. Now was not the time for introspection. He needed his game face and at least three shots of espresso if he was going to deal with Lauren.

Pulling onto Main toward *Grind It*, the only coffee shop open after six, he tried to forget the look on Trick's face. Tried to forget how it screamed disappointment.

Sistine Branch hoped the lipstick she found toward the back of her bathroom drawer that morning hadn't smeared onto her front teeth. Sweet Lord, convincing four women that Knitterly was the best place for Stitches was exhausting. The annual knitting and crochet expo was based out of Los Angeles, but they held the event in a new city every year.

Sistine had gone once when it was in San Diego and it was incredibly well run. Now she knew why. These women were practically running a white glove over every inch of her place. And the smiling—someone save her from the smiling. But, if she landed this, sore cheeks would be more than worth it. Stitches meant national exposure and, more importantly, come July, over a thousand knitters would descend on Petaluma and her shop. This was big and since Sistine had barely scraped together her loan payment this month, she needed big.

"So, like I said," Deidra, the woman who smelled like gardenias and seemed to be the one in charge, poured more tea while the other three women continued to "meander." Great word, Sistine decided and remembered now was not the time for collecting words.

"The committee doesn't normally choose a shop your size, but this year, we are all about organic fibers and returning to the roots of our craft, you know?"

More smiling and nodding as Deidra stirred in some sugar.

"Historic downtown Petaluma seems like the perfect fit," Sistine said, trying not to sound schmaltzy.

Deidra tapped the spoon against her teacup and pointed it at Sistine. "Exactly what we were thinking. We want to highlight some of the smaller shops like yours, and this building is so lovely."

They both took in Knitterly's dark wood floors and crown molding, a huge chunk of which Sistine had hot glued to the wall moments before they arrived, and Sistine felt like she was watching the same scene replayed on a loop. How many times did they need to look around, review her policies, ask her about her insurance?

As many times as it takes. Can you pass up ten thousand dollars, Ms. Cup-a-Noodles-for-Most-Meals?

Ten thousand dollars. That was the holding deposit, and she would make so much more on top of that in shop sales. This one expo alone could save her shop, get her in the black and over the two-year hump that swallowed most small businesses.

"So if, and I'm feeling it's more of a *when*, but *if* we choose to hold the expo here, are you certain you can handle the capacity? Two years ago, we partnered with this great place in downtown Boulder. The shop was adorable, but the event was a mess. I'm sure you understand, I can't let that happen again."

"I completely understand." Sistine offered Deidra a cookie from the box she'd picked up at Sift that morning. Deidra smiled and indulged. Cookies were universal. "The fact that I own the building gives me flexibility I doubt other venues will have. The back patio expansion will be finished next month, and we're adding additional meeting spots out front."

"I love that idea. It will be gorgeous in July and that water, tea, lemonade station in front was a brilliant idea." She popped the last bit of cookie in her mouth and set her teacup on the work table.

"And, don't forget my connections with the town. One of my best friends runs the bakery. Another manages Foghorn Brewery."

"We had lunch there. I love that place."

"Right? It's fantastic. We could host a dinner or get-together in that space too."

"Could you get us a discount?"

"I could work something out."

Deidra clapped her hands together and Sistine wanted to join her. This was going better than she imagined, so she finished strong.

"And I know people in fire and medical. All of historic downtown will be ready for your expo."

"Fantastic. Can we get a look at those construction drawings of the back patio one more time?"

"Absolutely." Sistine opened her laptop and wiped her hand on her skirt, hoping to hide her nerves. She tapped the touch pad, but instead of her screen filling with the artist renderings of a remodel she was barely able to afford, there was a pop and the screen went black.

"Uh-oh. Looks like it's time for you to plug in. We've exhausted your poor laptop." Deidra giggled and reached for another cookie.

Sistine's laptop was plugged in. It wasn't her battery. Glancing toward the front of the store, she noticed the lights she hung around the front window were out.

"Hun, what's your Wi-Fi password again? It seems to have dropped me." The woman with the pink bow on her sweater approached them. Carrie? Candy? Damn it, Sistine couldn't remember.

Hoping her voice wasn't shaking, she gave out the password. It wasn't going to work, but it would buy some time. Looking to the branches that hung from the ceiling of her shop, Sistine now knew what was wrong. The sun had not started to set, so the four women who currently held her financial fate in their manicured hands had not figured it out yet, but something had blown the electricity in her entire shop.

Sistine leaned a hip on the counter and continued staring at the dark screen of her laptop hoping for an idea, something to explain why even though her beloved 1929 building had its creaks and quirks, it could handle the expo. She'd grown up surrounded by small business. She watched her parents struggle and knew more than anyone that perception was everything. Even though she knew she could handle this expo and that it would be a huge success, if these women didn't believe that was possible, it was over.

"Deidra, I think the electricity is off."

All four women looked to Sistine. "Huh, I don't know what happened. Maybe the guys doing the remodel hit something," she lied.

"Well, that's not good." The women glanced at one another.

"All of this will be finished well before the expo. That's good, right?"

Sistine smiled. Again. She guessed the lipstick was gone at this point.

After a moment of awkward where Sistine wasn't sure what else she could add, the committee grabbed their purses and moved toward the door. She wanted to grab Deidra by the front of her expensive blouse and say, "I can do this. I swear if you give me this chance, you will not be disappointed." But she'd majored in marketing with an emphasis on branding, and nowhere in her best practices did it say go batshit desperate if you want people to do business with you. So, hiding her desperation behind her last thread of pride, she walked them out and pretended not to notice Deidra avoided eye contact as she said, "We'll be in touch."

Cross-legged in one of the overstuffed chairs in her front room, Sistine tried to focus on the beauty of the sky as day began giving way to night. Cobalt, she thought. It was definitely a cobalt sky, but the remaining sunlight added flecks of bluebell.

Bluebell or lunar. Which one was lighter again? She glanced at what she'd termed her Wall of Yarn in her shop and confirmed the sky was flecked with bluebell. She left messages with both the contractor handling her back patio and an electrician Aspen recommended. Maybe it was nothing, a blown fuse. She hugged her legs tighter into her chest. Who was she kidding? She was raised in an old home in Bodega Bay. She knew all about fuses. This wasn't a fuse. She didn't know how to explain it, but she'd spent practically every moment over the past two years in this old building. Something was wrong.

Darkness settled on her shop and she tried not to take it as an omen. Instead, she made her way to her apartment in the back of the shop and grabbed her wallet and her laptop. The coffee shop near the river was open until ten on Thursdays. She needed to pull up her spreadsheets, look at her numbers. Somehow, she would come up with a plan if the expo fell through, if the entire building needed to be rewired.

"Have a plan B, C, and D," her dad told her from the time she was little.

Sistine had forty dollars cash in her wallet. There was no sense sweating over something unknown, a bill she didn't yet have. She'd get some tea and one of those microwaved sandwiches. Maybe she'd splurge for a tea latte.

Maybe she'd call Melissa back and — No. She needed to stay in the present. She wasn't that desperate. Not yet.

OTHER LOVE STORIES BY TRACY EWENS

Premiere
Candidate
Taste
Reserved
Stirred
Vacancy
Playbook
Exposure
Brew
Smooth
Tap

Acknowledgements

I would like to thank:

Erin Tolbert for consistently reassuring me that today is not the day to give up.

Every romance writer and reader for keeping love alive in a world that is, at time, difficult to love.

My family for reminding me what is real.

Every. Single. Reader.

Tracy Ewens is a recovered theatre major who writes smart contemporary romance from a beautiful piece of Arizona desert. When not working on her next book, she drinks copious amounts of tea, prefers an exit row seat, and reads well past her bedtime.

www.tracyewens.com

60127948R00189

Made in the USA
Middletown, DE
14 August 2019